I0619593

# Fragile Scripts

## Daughters of the Duchess, Volume 3

Gemma St. Claire

Published by Frances Brown, 2025.

FRAGILE SCRIPTS

**First edition. August 5, 2025.**

Copyright © 2025 Gemma St. Claire.

ISBN: 979-8992789041

Written by Gemma St. Claire.

# Author's Note

There existed a bizarre psychiatric syndrome in Europe in the late Middle Ages.

*Glass delusion* afflicted mostly nobles who believed all, or part of their bodies were made of glass. Some forms had the victim believing he was trapped within a glass bottle. Another characteristic of Glass Men was their fear of sunlight.

The most well documented case of this mental illness was that of the French king, Henry VI. He not only refused to allow other people to touch him, but had special, reinforced clothing made for protection. Another sufferer spent his life with a pillow strapped to his backside, fearing that if he sat down without it, his arse would shatter. Some believed their heads and hearts consisted entirely of clear, very fragile glass.

Don't we all feel a little that way sometimes?

Although psychologists and physicians of the age were never able to pinpoint the direct cause for glass delusion, one theory was that it affected those in positions of wealth and power due to an innate fear of destruction by loss of either.

The Glass Man, although he may seem a stretch of the author's imagination, really did exist.

Gill Speak, "An odd kind of melancholy: reflections on the glass delusion in Europe (1440-1680)," *History of Psychiatry*, i (1990), 191-206.

# A Glossary of Medieval Terms

Here are some terms used in this book that the reader may not recognize.

Bailey: The open area between the castle buildings and the outer walls, also called the courtyard.

Battlement: A walkway around the upper edge of the curtain wall used by archers to protect from invasion.

Chemise: A lightweight, loose-fitting undergarment that acts as a slip under a dress (kirtle).

Club Foot: A birth defect where the Achilles' tendon is unnaturally shortened, resulting in a severely twisted ankle. In the Middle Ages, a babe born this way was labeled a...

Creple: A cripple.

Curtain Wall: The outer walls of the castle grounds, very tall and thick, made of stone.

Dais: A raised platform within the Great Hall, where meals were taken. The dais was where the royalty sat, along with honored guests and the Captain of the Guard.

Illuminated Manuscript: Hand painted decorations adorning the edges of medieval prayer books.

Keep: A fortified tower, either round (like a silo) or square, within the castle's curtain walls. This was the safest place in the castle, where the royalty slept, and was considered the last refuge if the castle were attacked.

Kirtle: An overdress, worn over the chemise (slip). Also called a cotte or cotehardie.

Leine: An old Gaelic word for shirt or chemise.

Ostler: The individual responsible for the care and training of the court's horses, and often the dogs and hunting birds (raptors) as well.

Portcullis: A heavy, vertically closing gate protecting the entrance to the castle grounds.

Roundlet: A medieval cap with a padded roll around the rim.

Scriptorium: Medieval writing room where manuscripts were inscribed and decorated.

Solar: These was the historical equivalent of a private living room, office, or den.

Quire: A sheet of parchment on which manuscripts, and their illuminations, were inscribed.

# Prologue

The candle on her worktable flickered, and Lijsbet looked up. An errant draft, or the quiet closing of a door not meant to be heard? The hour grew late as she worked, waited. She was sure he would come.

No footsteps forthcoming. She sighed. 'Twas only the silent breath of a studio whose ornate stained-glass windows allowed night's whispers to seep in around the leadings.

With a clutching in her heart, she faced the reality: fewer and fewer nights now, he came. Still, she worked into the darkness each night, hopeful. In her heart, Lijsbet knew it was over. He had been gone now for many moons, gone to his other workshop in Brussels, without a word. Even before he left, she'd noticed the waning. The spark missing in eyes that once danced for her.

Fewer and fewer late-night visits to the scriptorium, when he'd admire her work before whisking her off to his bedchamber.

A long time ago now, it seemed. Even her work had fallen out of favor with the Master. In the past months, it seemed nothing she did pleased him.

*Too much gold—these leaves cost the workshop too much.*

*Your beasts do not jump off the page, Lijsbet. They are flat, lifeless.*

*The tangle of vines is too thick . . . too many leaves, not enough flowers.*

His promises she knew now had always been empty ones. He'd never had any intention to make an honest woman of her. To marry her and make her his wife. Why had she waited so long? Why had she wasted so much of her young life clinging to an impossible dream?

'Twas only a matter of time, she knew, before her sponsorship in the workshop of the great Master, Rogier de la Pasture would end. Where would she go? How would she support herself?

Duke Philip's offer was her only option, she realized with despair. She had hoped . . . well, it did not matter her hopes for a future. She now knew better.

Pride girded her from answering the missives she'd received, three years in a row. Lijsbet did not want to fall back on her lineage. It was not her true father, after all, who had extended the invitation to Coudenburg. 'Twas his wife.

Isabella, Duchess of Burgundy.

Pride as well as suspicion had kept her from responding to Isabella's letters these past years. Why? Why would the duchess, a woman who knew Lijsbet was the result her husband's indiscretion, offer her shelter? A job, a future?

When the letter arrived yet again just days ago, Lijsbet knew 'twas time to make a choice. She would be a fool to ignore the duchess' offer.

When she heard the church bells chime Matins, she knew he would not be coming for her. Not tonight, not ever again. 'Twas over, truly. Swiping a tear from her cheek, she began cleaning the tools of her trade—feather quills, ink pots, the individual clam shells holding the pigments. Carefully, she set aside the still-wet parchment quire to dry.

When she was through, she opened the drawer under her worktable and pulled from it the letter she'd inked weeks earlier, but never sent. Tomorrow, she would speak to the master's courier about sending a messenger to Philip's court.

Tomorrow, she would begin planning for her departure. She would be headed eastward, toward Coudenburg Castle.

*March, 1449*

*Tournai*

*Most Gracious Lady Duchess Isabella,*

*My prayer is this letter finds you well. Please do not take as insult the fact I have not answered your letters these three years past. My situation in Tournai showed promise for my future.*

*Sadly, I must report this is no longer the case. I remain, an artisan skilled in my craft but still a woman, alone. I fear the master will soon have no longer need of my services. Although my work has been highly praised, by both the master and his patrons, there is little call here for miniatures in Tournai at this time.*

*I humbly request, Your Grace, that you find it in your heart to offer me patronage as you have so generously offered. I am aware Duke Philip has established an art collection there at Coudenburg Palace. He has expressed to the master his need for a manuscript illuminator. I am capable of book production from the creation of a quire to the binding. I am also experienced in the preservation and repair of damaged or ancient works.*

*Anxiously looking forward to your reply, Lady Isabella, I vow if you find it in your heart to accept my service, you will not be disappointed in my loyalty, nor in the quality of my work.*

*May Jesu for his great mercy save you. Written in Tournai, Wednesday, the xviii of March. By your humble servant, Lijsbet Lambert.*

# Chapter One

*July, 1449*
   *Coudenburg Palace, Brussels*
   *Earl Davion Price*

Lord Davion Price, Earl of Pembroke, strode beside the great duke of Burgundy, Philip the Good, along the halls of Coudenburg Palace. Having just arrived in this part of the world from England, the earl kept his words to a minimum. A foreigner in a strange land, Price knew he could learn more with his ears than his tongue. With Philip as his tour guide, his silence was not an issue.

If there was anything the Duke of Burgundy was good at, it was conversation.

"So you see, Lord Price, Coudenburg has plenty of room to house a generously sized library, along with vast chambers to display what I hope will be the most impressive collection of texts and artwork in all of Burgundy." Philip, a tall, thin man with sharp features, was dressed in his customary black from head to toe. This caused Davion to wonder: black to downplay his status as royalty? Or something more sinister? Darker?

He shook off the thought. Philip had not earned reputation as a kind and generous ruler. Yet not a soft man by any means, the duke took what he wanted as far as lands.

As well as women, from what the earl had heard rumored. That, of course, was none of his affair.

"What is it you would be expecting of me in this position of *curator*? I am not familiar with the term, your grace," Davion asked quietly, hands folded behind his back and eyes trained on the stone tiles beneath his feet.

Philip stopped walking and turned to face him. "I have been told you are well educated in the arts, my lord. My wish is to expand my collection from the few paintings and manuscripts I now hold. In addition to seeking out and securing additional works from the great masters of our day, I have need of an overseer. For the scribes and illuminators." Philip perched his hands on his narrow hips. "My lady, the duchess, has a fondness for the tiny texts... those miniscule prayer books... the ones proper ladies always seem to have hanging at their sides."

"Books of Hours," Davion offered.

"Yes. Isabella already has several. Why she needs more, I have no idea. Something about devoting each to a particular saint, or some such notion." Philip shook his head, his mouth twisting into a wry smile. "I indulge her, it's true. After all, who is to explain the fancies of a woman?"

Davion allowed a faint smile to play about his lips, but was hesitant to reveal his true feelings on the matter. Women, after all, had their place. The duchess held a higher ranking, but he knew little about the fairer sex in general. He'd spent the majority of his life, and his passion, on his studies, pursuing his love of art.

"Which begs me to enlighten you, Davion, about our newest illuminator. Very talented, extremely creative, if not ominously elusive. She is, as well, a woman."

Moments later, Davion followed Philip into the scriptorium. The chamber was expansive, with at least a dozen raised writing platforms, and walls lined with benches well stocked with the tools of the trade. Rolls of parchment leaned against one wall, waiting to be measured and cut. An elaborate shelving system on the wall held pots of dried powder—color for the paints, along with stacks of clam shells for the mixing. An earthenware pitcher held dozens of feather quills of various types and sizes.

But the windows... large windows nearly covered one wall of the room. Brilliant light streamed in over everything, the worktables, the pigments pots, the folios left to dry on the long table. The earl squinted and shielded his eyes.

"The windows..." he began, "Are you not afraid the bright light will fade the pigments?"

Philip glanced at him. "I did not consider that. An excellent observation, Lord Price. I shall have heavy drapes designed for the windows immediately. We cannot take too many precautions when protecting our artwork."

The earl nodded his approval. "Mayhap more torches can be hung. Candles on every workstation. The artisans will still need light by which to work."

The scriptorium was moderately sized compared to those Davion had seen in monasteries. A total of six workstations were lined up into two rows of three. Only two were occupied, one by a man the earl took for a monk. At the other, he realized, was the woman about whom Philip had just spoken.

She did not appear to realize their presence, so engrossed was she. Although seated on a tall chair and bent over her work, her back remained ramrod straight, regal. A very slender woman, one might not recognize her sex from this angle, if not for the bejeweled, padded roll containing her hair.

*What color, Davion wondered, was that hidden mane?*

Shaking his head to clear the unwelcome thought from his mind, Davion stepped closer as Philip approached the woman and spoke softly before laying a hand on her shoulder.

Jolting only slightly as she turned to face him, her dark lashes fluttered rapidly, as if she had awakened from a dream. He saw it now, the shiny bands of mahogany hair swept back from her face before disappearing beneath the headdress. Creamy, slightly rounded mounds visible above an embroidered, square neckline proclaimed her gender. Her eyes, a warm, golden color not quite just-plain-brown, flashed between him and the duke.

No expression, he noticed, other than surprise. No fear, no good humor, nor arrogance. Passive, frozen.

Davion wondered absently if this mirrored the state of her heart.

"Lady Lambert, may I present the court's new curator. This is Lord Davion Price, Earl of Pembroke. He shall be your overseer."

After only the slightest hesitation, the woman scrambled to her feet. Before she bowed to one knee before him, Davion immediately realized this illuminator was nearly as tall as he. Older too, he ventured, judging by the tiny glints of silver in her hair catching the light.

Aged from years, or from hard times? He wondered but did not really care. Why should he?

Philip wandered off to speak with the only other one working in the scriptorium at the moment, a stout monk clothed in brown robes. For the moment, Davion felt at a loss as to how to proceed.

Reaching one hand forward to help her up, he said, "I am pleased to make your acquaintance, Lady Lambert. Philip speaks highly of your skills." He paused, lifting one eyebrow as she raised her eyes to meet his. "A rare trait in a woman. Where did you receive your tutorage?"

Her rapid blinking puzzled him. Surprise or indignance? Embarrassment, perhaps?

"My training was in the workshop of Rogier de la Pasture, Master of Tournai."

Again, her tone was flat, emotionless. Certainly not indignance. 'Twas as though all spirit had been removed from the woman, leaving behind only an empty shell, as empty as those stacked on the shelves behind her. One aged, perhaps, by both years *and* ill fortune. Tiny lines fanned from the corners of those golden eyes. More bracketed a mouth seemingly set in stone.

*How much older than he? Again, why should he care?*

Mayhap 'twas her scent that attracted him, a distinctive, earthy smell from the ground pigments she worked with, and the fresh, raw egg used to bind them. Of course, she would carry the aroma of her trade. As a serious student of the arts, the earl found this quite appealing.

Her hand in his, he noticed, was far from that of a woman who did not know work. Bright colors stained her fingertips. Lapis lazuli, or azurite mayhap, marred her blush-stained cheekbone with a speck of blue. He yearned to wet his thumb and wipe it away.

*Why?*

Davion realized a very long moment had passed with their hands still joined. A warmth flowed between them, an invisible current that discouraged him from releasing her. She was still gazing into his eyes, questioning.

He cleared his throat and drew back. "I am anxious to see your work, Lady Lambert, and look forward to working with you."

*Lijsbet*

"An Englishman? No disrespect intended, Lady Duchess, but... an Englishman? Why did the duke select a curator from England?"

Lijsbet tried to temper the ire simmering in the pit of her stomach ever since she heard the news about her new overseer. She hadn't been in the service of the duke long enough to even get her bearings, or to learn her way around the scriptorium, to familiarize herself with the ways of the other scribes and monks employed there.

And now this.

She and the duchess sat in Isabella's solar, facing each other in the elaborately embroidered chairs before the windows overlooking the bailey. 'Twas a divine morning on this midsummer day. The duchess busied herself with her sewing, taking advantage of the beams of bright sunlight streaming in. A pewter pitcher and goblet stood on the small table to Isabella's right.

The coziness of the scene did nothing to alleviate Lijsbet's discomfort.

After a long, silent moment, the duchess looked up. She squinted at Lijsbet, though from displeasure or eye strain, she could not tell. She dearly hoped it was the latter.

"Why does this concern you so, Lijsbet? We have been at peace with the English since Henry VI's reign. His ambassadors prefer negotiations to warfare."

*Eye strain*, Lijsbet decided. The duchess, now in her fifty-second year, was beginning to show signs of her age. She married Philip later in life, Lijsbet remembered, accepting the duke's offer already in her thirtieth year. An older mother as well, Isabella gave birth to her only surviving son, Charles, when she was thirty-six.

*Mayhap life is not over for me yet*, Lijsbet thought. *I'm only just twenty-eight winters.*

Lijsbet fidgeted with her hands in her lap, hesitant to share her true feelings with the duchess. She did not know her well, after all. Knowing *of* someone is not the same as knowing them as a person.

Resuming her needlework, Isabella glanced up between stitches. A ghost of a smile lit up her face.

"I almost married an Englishman, you know. My cousin, Henry V, offered me the alliance when I was only eighteen winters old." She paused, gazing out of the window and sighing. "The negotiations fell through. I lost my mother that year as well." Her eyes pinned Lijsbet sharply. "The match 'twas not meant to be."

Lijsbet sat forward, speaking in hushed tones. There were servants about in the chamber. She had not been at the castle long enough to know in whose presence she could speak freely.

"Is not Duke Philip concerned this earl may be a spy?" she asked.

A chuckle jostled Isabella's shoulders. "Nay. Philip is much wiser than to bring someone into the court without thoroughly investigating his ties, as well as his loyalties. Lord Price's father is very supportive of the English king's way of thinking. In fact, so much so that some of his own countrymen are showing some dissent on the matter."

Lijsbet thought about the tall, distinguished man she'd met in the scriptorium. Everything about him seemed... precise. His perfectly tailored tunic dared not wear a single crease. His hair, black as a raven's wing, was cut short and molded to his head with exacting obedience. Not a very big man, but he was streamlined, carrying himself with regal poise.

His eyes, though—she found these the most unsettling. So blue, so intense on hers. 'Twas as though he could see right through her skin, to her very soul.

Lijsbet decided: she must not let down her guard around this man.

She sat back, again folding her hands in her lap. "He is a very handsome man. He seemed kind enough, but also very young."

"That is true. I believe Philip said he is turning twenty-one this summer. His education already is extensive. Well versed in art, his passion for the trade will enlighten him more than his years, I am sure." Isabella set her embroidery aside and reached to pour some wine into the goblet beside her. "He is unmarried, I hear. No betrothal that we know of." Her gaze flashed once to Lijsbet.

Shocked by this declaration, Lijsbet's mouth opened to respond, but she knew not what to say. What an inappropriate observation. Was the duchess suggesting—"

"As you said," Isabella continued, flipping one hand in the air, "he is an Englishman. No reason for me to assume you might be interested in getting to know him better than artisan to overseer."

Lijsbet tried to ignore the quirk at the corner of the duchess' lips. If she thought there was any chance of a liaison between her and this... this *earl*... well, 'twas impossible. Even if she was willing. Even if he was interested.

After all, she was Flemish, and he was an Englishman. Add to this the fact that Lijsbet was seven years older than the earl.

He probably thought of her as a used-up spinster. Which, in fact, she was.

Wasn't she?

After sipping from her goblet, Isabella levelled her gaze on Lijsbet. "We need to speak about the texts I wish you to design for me. I have several in mind. One, which I would like you to begin immediately, will be to honor the memory of my son's late wife, Catherine. She died so young. My son was barely a man before he was widowed." She made the sign of the cross. "I should like a Book of Hours dedicated to Saint Catherine of Alexandria. She, too, died an *adolescere*."

Worries over her new master evaporating, Lisjbet rose, feeling color rise into her cheeks as the pulse thrummed in her veins. *Her first royal assignment in the Burgundian court.* The excitement bubbling in her chest made her, too, feel like a youngster.

"I shall begin the research and the sketches right away, Your Grace. As the illuminations begin to take shape, I will bring them to you, for your approval." Bowing before the duchess, she asked, "May I now take my leave, Lady Isabella? I am quite anxious to begin."

Isabella held up one finger. "Before you begin, Lady Lambert, realize you must obtain permission from your overseer. He will control what you work on, when, and for what expanse of time. Even for projects I commission. Philip made it quite clear when the earl came to Coudenburg. Lord Davion will rule, both in the library and in the scriptorium."

As she made her way down the halls to her quarters, Lijsbet clenched and unclenched her fists. How dare this man—this *Englishman*—step in and take control of her life? She'd left the duchess' solar feeling as though she may explode at any moment. As she slipped into her chamber and closed the door, she could feel the heat radiating off her cheeks. She leaned back on the door and covered her face with her hands.

No, she would not shed tears. These were a sign of weakness. One must never—especially a woman—reveal any weakness. She forced her next breath through a clenched throat, into a chest clamped tight in rebellion. Shudders shook her entire body as she forced the air out.

A stark realization hit her then, as damaging and painful as a mace to the head.

*I am no better off than I have been for the past seven years.*

Her life, her work, her every breath, would continue to be controlled by a man. Just as it had been in de la Pasture's workshop. The difference in Tournai was she had given her heart to the Master. She had surrendered control willingly.

Now, she had no choice.

She came to court believing 'twould be a fresh start for her, for a life gone astray, led blindly down a dead-end path of the heart. She had been invited by the duchess. She was technically a vassal to the duke.

Yet in truth, ownership of Lady Lijsbet Lambert had simply changed hands. Until now, she'd been a treasured possession of the Master of Tournai—until suddenly, she was no longer. Lord Davion Price, Earl of Pembroke now ruled her world.

And he was an Englishman.

# Chapter Two

*Lijsbet*

Lijsbet's morning began much as it had since she arrived at Coudenburg three moons past. A fine chamber, she'd been assigned, along with a handmaiden of her very own. How lucky was she? A no one, merely a bastard daughter of the duke, Lijsbet had never expected to be treated with such dignity.

Surely, she felt as though she did not deserve this kind of treatment.

Yet each morning, her lady-in-waiting, Cecile arrived shortly after sunrise with a bucket of warm water, scented soaps, and linens with which she could refresh herself. Cecile helped her to dress, in clothing mostly provided—again—by the duke. The duchess, in reality. Isabella had, it seemed, taken Lijsbet under her wing as a sort of stepdaughter since the day she arrived.

A gracious duchess, to be sure. One generous beyond measure. Beyond comprehension. Lijsbet so wanted to make Isabella proud, designing for her the finest Book of Hours she had ever seen. The artist could not wait to begin the project.

Once she could obtain her overseer's permission.

*Surely,* she thought as she made her way down to the Great Hall, *surely the duchess had spoken with Earl Price concerning her wishes for a new manuscript.*

*Hadn't she?*

Lijsbet's answer came at table that very morning. The duchess sat alone on the dais, as she often did, with Philip off pursuing some negotiation—or other, more personal matter, as was the case most of the time. Lijsbet took her seat at the table on the common level, beneath where the duchess dined.

She was taking her first sip of sweet mead from the pewter goblet when the esteemed earl arrived to break his fast.

The *English* earl.

Undaunted by custom or convention, Davion Price strode into the hall and climbed up onto the dais without hesitation. Isabella cast him an appraising glance, one thin eyebrow lifting. Yet she said nothing. After all, in Philip's presence, the earl had always sat at the high table, along with Admiral La Laing, the duke's right hand in the management of Coudenburg Castle.

Why should the duke's absence change matters?

"Good morrow, Your Most Royal Duchess," Davion began, lifting the duchess' fingers to his lips as he lowered on one knee. " 'Tis a fine morning, no?"

His accent echoed foreign against the decidedly musical lilt of the French or Dutch spoken by all others in court. He had obviously learned enough of the other languages to get by, but did not speak them well. *Like a child just learning to communicate*, Lijsbet thought. She stifled a snort behind the rim of her cup.

"I am well, dear Davion. How is the reorganization of the library proceeding?" Isabella asked. She paused to take the platter of dried fruits from the girl serving the tables. "I am not sure when Philip intends to return, but I know when he does, he will be anxious to evaluate your progress."

*Ah, what a wise woman*. Lijsbet's respect for the duchess could not keep from expanding. Here was a woman who knew how to walk the line of maintaining her place, as a woman, yet at the same time, wise enough to weave her words, driving directly to the point of the matter. Keeping people on task.

Lijsbet had heard of the duchess' talents as a negotiator. She was quickly discovering why the woman held such power in a court dominated by men.

Davion took a seat beside the Admiral, and Lijsbet noted he did so with slow and deliberate care. Was he sore from some physical exertion? Had he sustained an injury? For a moment, she thought she had imagined it, but . . . no, the man moved as though he was afraid he would break.

The earl finally settled in his chair, blinked and hesitated in his reply. The duchess' question had surprised him, it was plain to see. He took the extra few moments to fill his goblet from the pitcher on the table before answering.

"There is much to be done, still," he began. "Most of the texts and artworks Philip brought to the library had been simply placed there, without much in the way of organization." He sipped, then set down his cup, finally raising his eyes to meet hers.

Luminous, blue eyes. Almost unnaturally blue, Lijsbet thought. She shook away the thought.

Isabella dabbed her mouth with a linen napkin. "I hope you are able to attain some semblance of order there soon, Davion, as I have other projects I wish you to oversee in the scriptorium." Her gaze flashed once to Lijsbet, who quickly dropped her own to the plate before her. "We have a new illustrator, and I am anxious for her to get started on some Books of Hours."

Davion rocked back as though she'd struck him. He then fidgeted nervously with his napkin, his eyes darting everywhere but toward the duchess. Finally, he stammered, "I am aware of our new talent, Your Grace," he said, his tone dark, "but the first items to be addressed are the repair of the pieces Philip brought back from Bruges this past spring. Many suffered damage from the elements. I had intended—"

"I understand your concerns, Lord Price. But as we are both well aware, reconstruction of damaged artifacts can take months, if not years to complete. I, for one, am not getting any younger." Her wry smile was self-deprecating and aggressively snide at the same time. "I wish for Lady Lambert to begin on my commissions as soon as possible. I trust you will be diligent in gathering the necessary materials—parchments, pigments and the like—while she works on the reconstructions. I believe, if I am not mistaken, we have plenty of gold for the tracings already in our possession." Then, in an undeniable close to the conversation, the duchess raised her hand to the servants waiting by the kitchen door. "We are ready for the main course now."

The subject was dropped as they proceeded to break their fast. Lijsbet could barely contain her gloating, taking care to keep her mouth either hidden behind the rim of her cup or behind her napkin when the smile snuck past her defenses. Earl Price ate in silence, moving as stiffly as a man wearing full armor. Again, he seemed... injured. His every movement was slow and careful. She tried not to stare. She'd have to ask the duchess about this later.

He was a young man, by God's breath. Yet every movement he made seemed painful, like an old man whose bones had worn thin.

The earl did not cast a glance her way, at least not that she was aware of. For that, Lijsbet was grateful. She certainly did not want to be caught staring at him. He might get the wrong idea, and that was the last thing Lijsbet needed.

She knew, however, her reprieve from dealing with this man was short-lived. He was, after all, her new overseer. He would be spending as much time in the scriptorium as she, no doubt breathing down her neck the entire time.

After the morning meal, Lijsbet excused herself to her chamber to change into clothing suitable for her workday—there was no sense risking damage of the lovely gowns Isabella had provided her from spilled ink or paint. Donning a simple, brown frock, she used a plain length of rope to tie around her waist, then secured her hair with a similar length of cord.

The day the duke had brought Davion in to meet her, Isabella had specifically instructed her to wear a proper gown and headdress. This, however, was not the most sensible way for her to work. Whether her overseer liked it or not, Lijsbet decided, the earl would simply have to accustom himself to her more practical, everyday attire.

*Davion*

Davion made a point to assure the duchess he would discuss the Book of Hours she had requested with the new artist this very morn. He then gathered the scroll on which he intended to begin categorizing the duke's collection, and set off for the scriptorium.

Standing in the doorway, he scanned the room. Dark, now that the duke had ordered heavy draperies hung. Even on such a bright, sunny day, the flickering torches cast dancing shadows across the stone walls. Again, only two scribes were at work, both monks dressed in their drab, horsehair robes. One, who was hefty and very short, glanced up when he stepped into the room, and nodded. Johannes, Davion thought the duke had called him. Brother Johannes.

The other man was tall and quite slender, and had not been in the room the day Davion arrived. He approached the worktable and had gotten halfway across the room before he realized the man had long, dark hair secured at the base of his neck. Odd. Monks usually kept their hair short around their tonsured crowns.

*The woman. This is the woman. What had Philip called her? Lilith?*

She jolted when he stopped an arm's length from her shoulder and said, "I did not recognize you in your artist's rags."

The eyes she turned on him were wide and flashing fire. She looked different dressed this way, without the sculpting seams of a woman's gown to accentuate her body. Her hair, pulled back from her face severely, contrasted with her delicate paleness. He had thought her younger than she appeared to be now, the first time when their eyes met.

She was no blushing maiden, this was plain. Beautiful, nonetheless. Striking, with high cheekbones and a pointed chin. It was her eyes, though, that still disturbed Davion. Much lighter than her mahogany mane, they were coppery, golden, like that of a hunting bird.

And in them he saw, at this moment, the same kind of predatory intelligence.

"I see no purpose in risking ruin to the fine garments the duchess has provided me," she snapped, tipping up her chin. "I am here to work, and when I work, paint and ink splatter." She narrowed those golden eyes at him, lowering her voice to an impetuous murmur. "Is there to be a dress code for those who work in the scriptorium, my lord?"

Davion took a step back, instinctively, and clasped his hands behind his back. "Nay, no dress code. I was simply surprised." He cleared his throat. "I did not recognize you... Lilith? Was that your name?"

Another spark of anger shot from her eyes and her entire body stiffened. "My name is Lijsbet. To you, my lord, I would think it proper you address me as Lady Lambert."

Davion began a slow pacing, back and forth in the space between Lijsbet's worktable and the wall. He kept his hands clasped behind him, and struggled to keep the corner of his lips from twitching. Her fiery temper was amusing to him, even though he realized it should do nothing but anger him.

He hated to admit it, but he enjoyed toying with her.

"Lady Lambert. Lady *Lijsbet* Lambert. That's a mouth full of 'L's. Could cause a man to become tongue tied." He stopped in front of her, close enough to smell the lavender scenting her hair, or her skin. 'Twas pleasing. He let go with his smile. "I believe I shall call you Lily. 'Twill make it easier, all the way 'round."

The quill she had been using when he came in clattered to the table and rolled down its angled surface to click sharply on the raised edge. Her fingers closed on that ridge of wood now, gripping so tightly her knuckles grew white. She was trembling, as well. Certainly not with fear. Rage, then.

*Good. An artist with easily aroused emotions renders much more passionate creations.* He wondered if her passion followed her out of the scriptorium door—

*Nay.* He must not think that way about a subordinate. How could an overseer possibly stay in charge with such rogue thoughts as these?

Long moments of silence stretched out, the only sounds coming from the scratching of the monk's quill on parchment. An occasional sputtering from one of the torches. Davion met her smoldering gaze and held it, refusing to be the first to look away.

When her lids slowly drifted closed, he knew he'd won this, the first of what he predicted would be many confrontations with the illuminator. This woman. *Lily.*

"Ye shall not disrespect me with an ekename. If you please, my lord, I shall like to be addressed as Lady Lambert," she hissed, never opening her eyes.

Davion drew in a deep breath and blew it out. "It does not please me, my lady. I shall seek the duchess' permission, of course. But I prefer to call you by the ekename." He unclasped his hands and motioned toward her abandoned quill. "Carry on, Lily. Finish what you are working on this morn. After the noon meal, I should like to sit with you in the duchess' solar and discuss this Book of Hours she has commissioned."

# Chapter Three

*Lisjbet*

"He's not really so bad once you get used to him."

Lijsbet's jumbled thoughts were racing so fast inside her head she almost didn't hear the monk's words. Blinking back into the present, back into her surroundings, she turned slowly in his direction. Brother Johannes, with whom she had become somewhat acquainted over the past few weeks, had turned on his stool and was studying her with a sympathetic expression.

"Lord Price is just young. He feels intimidated by us. All of us, I believe. In time, you will grow more comfortable with him," he added, a soft smile rounding out his rosy cheeks.

Lijsbeth huffed. "Lord Price seems to take added exception to me, Brother Johannes. Do you think it's because I'm a woman? Or because I'm so much older than he?"

Surprised by how his eyes scanned her body, from her eyes down and back up again, Lijsbet could feel the heat rise into her own cheeks.

*He's a monk. He's not supposed to be affected by my sex.*

Besides, there was little for anyone to see, hidden under the same, shapeless brown garment as he himself wore. Still, she reminded herself, he was a man. She supposed those particular sensibilities never left a person, no matter what kind of oaths they had taken.

The monk's eyes crinkled at the corners, though he managed to keep his smile in check.

"I do not believe Lord Price can ignore you are a woman, Lady Lambert. I do believe, however, in time you will realize it is not your charms he takes exception to." Johannes turned back to his work and finished his statement in a low voice. " 'Twill be your work he will take exception to."

Lijsbet wasn't about to allow an open-ended claim like that go unfinished. "And why is that? Do my talents as an illuminator not meet with his expectations? Or yours, for that matter?" She could not keep the haughty lilt out of her question.

She watched the tonsured head oscillate slowly, side to side. Still, he did not turn to meet her gaze as he spoke. "On the contrary. I believe your work is so fine, Lord Price may find your talents intimidating." He turned then to look directly into her eyes, his expression serious. "Take this as a warning, my lady, in your dealings with the young overseer: the earl is highly educated and of royal lineage. But unlike a seasoned warrior, he is fragile, in mind as well as spirit."

Lijsbet decided to skip the noon meal, as she often did, to finish re-outlining the damaged border on the manuscript leaf she'd been working on. This one, the duke had told her, was damaged during the Bruges uprising of 1437, during which the duke and his men were driven out of the city gates at dear cost. Only later, when the rebellion had settled down, was he able to retrieve the texts and a few paintings which had been deliberately vandalized.

It was not until Brother Johannes, along with one of the bookbinders returned to the scriptorium that Lijsbet remembered Earl Price's directive from earlier that morning.

*"After the noon meal, I should like to sit with you in the duchess' solar and discuss this Book of Hours she has commissioned."*

Setting all of her tools to rights on her table, Lijsbet slipped off her stool and smoothed the front of her coarse brown frock. Cringing, she realized she should have changed into something more suitable to hold audience with the duchess. Too late for that now. She straightened her spine, hoping her confidence would stand as strong and tall as well as she made her way to the door.

"Remember my words," Brother Johannes murmured as she passed his desk.

She flashed him a look, pausing in her step.

"Sometimes he who wears an invisible armor is protecting something much more delicate than is visible to the eye," he said.

Huffing again, Lijsbet made her way toward Isabella's solar.

The door to the sunny room was open, and Lijsbet blinked at the brightness her eyes were unaccustomed to. She was surprised to see the duchess and the earl sitting side by side in the chairs by the window, each holding a goblet. In the midst of what must have been a congenial conversation, she'd interrupted them both laughing when she entered.

*At me? Were they laughing about me, and my situation? My abilities?*

*Nay.* She must not think this way. What was the term? It was an ancient concept, common in Greek tragedies.

*Paranoia.*

*Nay.* She must be very, very careful to avoid feeling as though everyone, and everything, was in criticism of her.

"Good afternoon, Lady Lambert. I'm glad you could join us. I was concerned when you did not come to the hall for the noon meal." Isabella sipped from her cup, studying Lijsbet over the rim. "Are you well?"

"Yes, I am indeed well, Your Grace. I was engrossed in repairing the Bruges manuscript, and did not want to interrupt the work—"

"The work will always be there waiting for you, Lijsbet." Isabella set her cup down and poured wine into another cup on the table beside her. Holding it out to her, she continued, "You are lean enough without depriving yourself of a meal, my lady. I do believe you have withered further since your arrival at Coudenburg."

While the duchess spoke, the earl had risen and carried a third chair to form a small grouping near the window. After Lijsbet accepted the goblet of wine, he motioned gallantly to the embroidered seat, taking the one shaded by the velvet drape behind him.

"Sit, My Lady. We have much to discuss," he said. His tone, much friendlier than it had been this morn, bore a kind of joviality that made Lijsbet a bit nervous. The man was, obviously, very well acquainted with the duchess, as well as established in her good graces. Immediately, Lijsbet felt at a disadvantage.

"Lord Price tells me your work is enviable, Lijsbet. Quite a compliment from a man with such a vast knowledge of the arts."

Lijsbet blinked at the duchess' words. Mayhap what the monk told her was accurate. Mayhap the earl truly was impressed—even intimidated—by her talent.

*He has an unusual way of showing it.*

"I have been discussing with Lord Price the Books of Hours I wish to commission. He made, in my opinion, a wise suggestion to consider before we commence these projects," Isabella continued. "I know you did your training here in Tournai, under the tutelage of Rogier de la Pasture. I have the greatest respect for this master's school. However..."

Isabella paused and cast her gaze toward the earl, silently urging him to take over the conversation. As if expecting her direction, he picked up her line of thought seamlessly.

"The Tournai Master, as well as Robert Campin, are well known for their excellence in the execution of interior settings and careful detail." Price crossed one leg over the other and carefully folded his hands around his knee. "They are not, however, as concerned with the production of pieces on a smaller scale. With miniatures."

Lijsbet drew in a deep breath and tipped up her chin. The earl's words were true. She had been forever trying to explain to her mentors the difference between rendering detail on a large canvas versus on a piece of vellum—on a much, much smaller scale.

"You speak the truth, Lord Price. Still, I believe I have been able to adapt my skills quite effectively for miniatures. I'm sure you have studied my work." Her voice trembled as she spoke, and she hated herself for it.

Weakness. Insecurity. These were mortal enemies of any artist, particularly a female artisan.

Isabella refilled her cup, offering to do the same for the earl. "There is no doubt of your talent, Lijsbet. You have earned the respect of not only the earl, but of Duke Philip himself. 'Tis part of the reason you are here."

*Besides the fact that I am his bastard daughter. Or, would that be, in spite of?*

"Lord Price has spent time in Leuven. Some fine work is being done in that city by artists such as Dieric Bouts. Are you familiar with his work?" Isabella asked.

Lijsbet sputtered on a mouthful of wine. "Why, of course, Your Grace."

"There are also Books of Hours—fine, intricately decorated texts—being produced at the Groot Begijnhof. Were you aware of these?"

At a beguinage? A place for women devoting their lives to God? It made sense, Lijsbet thought. But nay, she was not aware they were creating Books of Hours. She shook her head.

"The duke and I would like to send you to Leuven for a time. To learn some of their techniques. You shall stay at the beguinage, where you will have quarters of your own, and be quite comfortable."

Lijsbet's head jerked up. She stared at the duchess, unsure whether to be insulted or elated by this opportunity.

But *her*? Staying in, essentially, a convent? It seemed a blasphemy. She was at a loss for words. In truth, nothing she could say would prevent her shame from showing through.

Finally, she sputtered, "Your Grace, I never expected—"

"I wish my Books of Hours to be as fine and elaborate as any of our day. Therefore, Philip and I have arranged an apprenticeship—a short one, but we feel 'twill be sufficient, considering your aptitude—in Leuven."

A frisson of excitement began to simmer in Lijsbet's chest. The opportunity of a lifetime. She could hardly believe what she was hearing. Her joy, however, was extinguished with the duchess' next words.

"Lord Price, of course, will accompany you. As chaperone, as well as to supervise the training you will receive."

Dropping back in her seat, Lijsbet nearly spilled wine all over her lap. The apprenticeship was a pleasant surprise. This last announcement was not.

"But Your Grace, if I will be staying with the beguines, why would I require a chaperone? Surely, Lord Price will not be allowed accommodations at the beguinage."

A glint of amusement sparkled in Isabella's eyes. "Nay, he would not. Lord Price has other business of his own in Leuven. He will be staying in a residence shared by some of the painters in the city. 'Tis one street over from Groot Begijnhof. For your safety, Lady Lambert." She paused, ducking her chin to rivet Lijsbet through her lashes. Her look conveyed more than her words. " 'Tis not a good idea for a woman to stay alone in a city filled with male artists, Lijsbet. Not all of your time will be spent inside the beguinage walls."

*Davion*

"We thought—the duchess and I—'twould be best for us to begin our journey as soon as possible. She told me, in her own words, she is not getting any younger." Price chuckled as he strode beside Lijsbet on their way back to the scriptorium. "So, when can I expect you to be ready to travel?"

Davion could feel the tension radiating off the woman beside him, even at the full arm's distance at which she kept herself. It was as though, he thought, she was afraid to get too close to him. As if she'd be tainted with his evil, or burned by some invisible fire she seemed to fear radiated from him.

*Just as well. If she so much as bumps me too briskly, the damage she may cause would be irreparable.*

When more than several seconds passed without her response, he repeated his question. "How long, Lily? How long until we can leave for Leuven?"

She halted so abruptly he'd strode ahead of her several steps before he realized it. He turned to face her. Hands balled tightly at her sides, a blush of red was creeping up her creamy neck and onto her sharply sculpted jaw. Her eyes, more the glowing gold of flame now than light brown, seared his own.

Almost painfully.

"I have only just arrived here at Coudenburg, My Lord. I've barely had time to settle my things in my quarters here." Her shoulders shuddered at the breath she sucked in. Then, again acquiescing as she had done with him once before, she blew out the breath. Her next words were soft and measured. "I can be ready as soon as need be, Lord Price. Let me know when the carriage has been arranged for."

*A carriage.* The duchess had been more than kind in offering this, a much more expensive mode of transportation, for their trip to Leuven. Isabella was aware of Davion's... idiosyncrasy. She knew that traveling by horseback was, for him, not only terrifying, but to his own mind, suicidal—even for such a short trip. Half a day's ride, for a normal person. Obtaining a carriage for such a brief trip seemed almost ludicrous.

Still, Davion knew he had no choice. The duchess understood this as well.

"Our ostler, Mathieu of Liege, will be traveling to Leuven himself a few days hence. But he will be traveling astride, and bringing a number of young horses on the trip back. Otherwise, I would have him escort both of you. But a carriage would only hinder the ostler's journey. 'Tis better this way," the duchess had said.

Davion was certain the court carriage would be the most lavishly padded, with a deeply cushioned interior. He was also quite sure that the distance from Coudenburg to Leuven would be taken at a much more leisurely pace than necessary.

Isabella had arranged, he knew, for Davion to speak in Leuven with a physician educated in the type of impairment from which he suffered. The man there had worked with similar cases in London, at the Bethlem Royal Hospital—a specialist institution for people suffering from illnesses of the mind.

# Chapter Four

*Davion*

The carriage was, indeed, lavishly appointed. Rich, burgundy damask covered the entire interior of the cabin, the seams edged with gold braid. Even the floorboards had been painted and, Davion mused, illuminated. A dark red background had been decorated with vignettes, hand-painted scenes of the countryside. Patches of lush green forest squinted against brilliant sunlight. Rolling meadows sparkled with spring color. A serene pond featured a pair of elegant swans.

'Twas almost sacrilege to plant his dusty boots atop the surface. Alas, he had no choice. Wedging his body into one corner of the thickly padded seat, Davion placed both feet flat on the floor to stabilize himself. A defensive posture, and one that would prove, he knew, to be quite uncomfortable after a time.

This journey would seem endless. One, very long day.

They left through the portcullis before sunrise, dawn just beginning to hint its glow above the hills to the east.

"I cannot believe you have chosen to make this journey so very trying," Lijsbet hissed soon after they had taken leave of the castle. " 'Twould have been fine with me to make the trip on horseback. With a pack horse in tow, we could have been there before None—"

" 'Tis what I required, Lily. I am sorry 'twill inconvenience you."

Even to his own ears, the earl's voice sounded strained. He simply couldn't help it. Travel was, for him, a treacherous feat, no matter how the trip was made. With both his feet braced against the floor, both hands pressed flat to his thighs, he closed his eyes and tried to slow his breathing. Still, every bump in the road, every jostle the carriage suffered, caused him to hold his breath.

He knew, after a time, the panic would pass. He would not be overcome by terror for the entire journey.

He only hoped.

"What's the matter with you? Are you ill?" Lijsbet's tone conveyed more annoyance than concern. He opened his eyes to see her staring at him as though he'd grown a second head.

"Nay, not ill. Simply not a fan of traveling, my dear Lily."

"Ugh!" she snapped. "About the ekename... I don't recall you asking the duchess' permission to call me by such a familiar."

One corner of his mouth quirked. He couldn't help it. "I did not. The subject slipped my mind. 'Tis not, dear lady, a *familiar*, as you call it," he said evenly. " 'Tis a way to keep my errant tongue from bumbling your name. Besides," he met her flashing golden eyes and held them, "the name fits you."

*Those eyes.* An unusual color, and filled with such spirit. Davion could not recall ever seeing another person with such eyes. He wondered absently if hers, after bending so close to the thin sheets of pure gold she used to illuminate vellum pages, had actually absorbed some of the precious metal.

He'd been dreading the journey. With Lily as his companion, however, his mind could surely find distraction from his usual concerns and terrors.

"Why does the ekename fit me? *Lily*?" She huffed. "What makes you say so? White lilies signify purity. I hardly believe you think of me in that way."

Davion narrowed his eyes, studying her.

*Those eyes. Those golden eyes. Unusual. Intense. Captivating.*

*Dangerous.*

"Nay, not white lilies. There is also a variety of the flower that is the color of flame, like the gold of your eyes. Like the gold of your illuminations." He paused, waiting for a reaction, though he saw nothing but indignance and shock. "Energy. Warmth. Confidence, mayhap to the extreme of pride. Do these not describe you, dear Lily?"

Refusing to answer him, she pressed her lips tight. Growling in frustration, she turned her body away and peered out the carriage window. The next several hours passed in tense silence, the only sounds coming from the creaking of the carriage and the snorting of the horses drawing it.

*Lijsbet*

*How dare he?*

Those three words repeated in her head, over and over, until she feared she might scream in frustration. An arrogant oaf, this esteemed English earl. One who made rash assumptions about a person he hardly knew. They had just now met, by God's breath! How dare he make such judgmental statements about her?

*But are they true?*

A little voice echoed from the far reaches of her mind. Lijsbet did possess, by necessity or design, confidence—in her work, in her intelligence. Aye, she was proud. It had been her only means of survival, of maintaining her sanity. Working in a studio overrun, and overseen, by men for most of her adult life, Lisjbet had had no choice but to develop a tough outer shell. She had not been granted the luxury of playing the gentle-hearted lady. Nay, from the time she was old enough to realize her station in life, Lijsbet Lambert knew she had two choices: toughen up, or be flattened to the cobblestones of life like an overrun rabbit in the street.

She'd been only ten years old when her mother finally admitted to her that her father had not, as she had been previously told, been killed in a battle with the English. Her father was very much alive, she learned, and doing quite well.

He was, after all, the Duke of Burgundy. Philip the Good.

At ten, Lijsbet still could not quite understand how she'd come to be. But the logistics were insignificant. The fact was, she was an illegitimate child. A bastard. A child produced by, yet not claimed—at least not publicly—by her natural father.

Two emotions overwhelmed her that night as she lay in her bed, a mere child with new, life-altering knowledge too big to comprehend, too painful to accept. She was a child, not only a mere girl but one with no father, and *no name*. Lambert was her *mother's* family name.

Lijsbet had been conceived out of wedlock.

The second revelation stung more than the first. Ever since she could remember, her mother had been her idol, her role model, the epitome of everything she hoped someday to become. Jutte Lambert was not just a commonplace wife, one who spent her days toiling away at the doldrums of everyday life. Jutte was an artisan, one who worked in one of the largest and most respected tapestry mills in Flanders.

Lijsbet's mother not only held the shuttle and the thread, she also designed the tapestries. She was respected by her peers, admired by her patrons. A strong and persevering widow, Lijsbet had believed, one who worked long hours to support her only daughter. Even if it was in a profession Jutte loved passionately.

Apparently, passion for the tapestries was not the only one Jutte possessed.

At ten, Lijsbet was far too young to judge her mother. But as the years passed, and she learned more about how the world worked, particularly between men and women, the less respect the young woman had for Jutte.

As it turned out, Lijsbet inherited not only artistic talent from her mother. She was also destined to follow in her footsteps in other ways.

Lijsbet secured her position in the workshop of Rogier de la Pasture with not only the talents of her hands, but those of her entire body. Just like her mother.

They arrived in Leuven in the early evening. Lijsbet could never remember feeling as fatigued as she did the moment she stepped down from the carriage—one, it seemed, that had literally crawled at a snail's pace along the road between Coudenburg and Leuven. Time had slowed and thickened, as had the tension in the carriage, sitting as she was across from the exasperating Earl Davion Price.

'Twas so thick, at times she felt as though the air was not fit to breathe. The earl was not only a pompous man, but he was incorrigible. She avoided speaking to him, to no avail. The man wanted to talk—constantly, it seemed, whether out of boredom or nervousness, she could not tell.

Yet pleasant conversation was beyond the capability of the Englishman. Every attempt he had made to converse with Lijsbet had ended in some sort of insult to her person, or in a riddle. A puzzling man, the earl was. For all of his dignity and arrogance, there was something about him Lijsbet sensed was fragile. It seemed he devoted all of his energy to protecting himself from injury. But why?

What had Brother Johannes said to Lijsbet as she'd left the scriptorium that day?

*"He is highly educated and of royal lineage. But unlike a seasoned warrior, he is fragile, in mind as well as spirit."*

At the time, Lijsbet had no idea what the monk was talking about. After spending many awkward, uncomfortable hours in a small space with the earl, she realized she still had no clue. Sighing as she took the footman's hand and stepped down onto the cobbled streets of Leuven, Lijsbet also admitted to herself that she didn't really care.

Why should she? He was to be her overseer. Her most critical observer. Why should she care what his weaknesses caused?

The carriage had stopped beside a massive red brick structure, one that seemed to stretch endlessly along the cobbled street in both directions. Peaked and stepped roof fronts punctuated each section, as did dome-topped doors made of wide, painted boards. A sense of unearthly quiet blanketed the narrow passageway between the buildings like a woolen cloak. Lijsbet was unsure if the silence comforted or chilled her, even as the late afternoon sun's heat radiated off the stones surrounding her.

She was not aware of her companion's departure from the carriage until she heard him release a long, shuddering sigh.

"Well, we have arrived, Lily. This will be your home for the next fortnight. Mayhap longer," he said. As he spoke, the arched doorway squeaked open and a woman stepped out, garbed in a plain black garment, one covering her voluminously from head to toe. Beneath the draped hood she wore a starched wimple, one so white and stiff it looked painful to the skin. Her face, youthful and plain, was the only part of her visible. Her smile, though, was spontaneous and warm—though most respectfully directed at the earl, not at Lijsbet.

A mere woman.

"Welcome to Groot Beginjnhof." A pale hand appeared from beneath the black cloak. "I am Sister Fenna, the mistress of this institution. Her Most Gracious Lady, Duchess Isabella forewarned us of your arrival, Earl Price."

Davion took the nun's hand—not a nun, Lijsbet reminded herself, but how then to refer to her? He made a show of brushing a kiss on the woman's skin but never made contact. Then he took a step away quickly, folding his hands behind his back.

He cleared his throat, appearing to have difficulty knowing what his next move should be. Then he waved one hand toward Lijsbet.

"This is the illuminator the duchess wishes you to instruct, Lady Fenna. Lijsbet Lambert. She trained in the workshop of Rogier de la Pasture."

Lijsbet cringed inside. Little did the earl know how literal his statement had been. She closed her eyes, struggling to maintain her composure.

Sister Fenna, however, stepped forward and grasped Lijsbet by the shoulders, peering into her eyes with a welcoming smile. "We have heard your work is outstanding, Lady Lambert. We look forward to sharing techniques with you. We expect to learn as much from you as you from us."

Lijsbet blew out the breath she'd been holding. This may not be as terrible as she'd feared. It was true, she looked forward to learning from the skilled miniaturists here at the beguinage. But the fact that they knew of and respected her work as well was a definite boost to her ego.

She stood taller and returned the mistress' smile. "I am most blessed for this opportunity."

The beguine's gaze drifted past her then to the earl. "I understand you will be staying at the artist's house, on Schapenstraat?"

"Aye. That's not too far a walk from here, is it not?"

Sister Fenna shook her head and pointed down the narrow alleyway. "If you go that way, you will come upon it immediately on the other side."

Price turned to the carriage driver. "Lady Isabella tells me she arranged for your overnight stay at the stables and tavern? You may return to Coudenburg on the morrow. Go on, then. I will not be requiring your services from here."

"But what of your wardrobe, my lord?" the driver asked, rumpling his cap between nervous hands.

"Drop them off at the artist's residence. I will be along shortly."

The mistress stepped forward. "Surely, Lord Price, you can join us in the common room for a cup of mead or ale? To refresh you after your long journey."

But Davion was already striding toward the alleyway Sister Fenna had indicated.

"Nay, Mistress, but I thank you just the same. I am fatigued, but prefer to settle my things at the artist's residence before nightfall." He turned to give Lijsbet a pointed look. "I will see you on the morrow, Lil... Lady Lijsbet. I return then, shortly after breaking my fast."

# Chapter Five

*Lijsbet*

*A fish flopping around on dry land.*

This was how Lijsbet felt inside the Groot Beginjnhof. She had arrived, it seemed, shortly after the evening meal had been cleared away, yet just moments before vespers. The sisters scurried about nervously, knowing their guest needed to be tended to: settled in her quarters and fed. Yet with the hour of the evening prayer upon them, all of their movements were rushed.

Lijsbet could not feel more out of place. This was a house of women devoting their lives to God. Even though she spent her days producing prayer books—Books of Hours—she never considered herself religious. She'd always felt herself unworthy. 'Twas the ultimate irony.

Now, with these friendly and accommodating women all hurrying to make her comfortable and quench her hunger and thirst, Lijsbet was even more uncomfortable than she had been riding all day in the carriage with the strange and annoying Earl Price.

She expected a narrow pallet in a dortour, with the other beguines. To her surprise, they led her to a bright room furnished with a canopied bed, a chest of drawers, and several cushioned chairs. Although the sun had already descended behind the tall building across the alley, Lijsbet imagined the two tall windows would provide plenty of light during the day. Extravagantly appointed, she thought, for the likes of a convent.

*Not a convent*, she reminded herself. *A beguinage*. Although the beguines were women of God, they were not women of the cloth. Not officially.

Sister Fenna, after directing the two women who carried up Lijsbet's wardrobe and paint box, turned to face her.

"I hope you will find this room acceptable, Lady Lambert. This is our guest quarters, the room we offer to the families of our sisters when they come to visit." She motioned toward a sideboard where a tray was set, bearing a loaf of coarse bread, a wedge of cheese, and some grapes. A pitcher and goblet flanked it. "We will provide you with a proper evening meal after our prayers have ended. For now, relax and enjoy what little we can offer you."

Before Lijsbet could reply, Sister Fenna turned and whisked out of the door, pulling it closed behind her.

She drew in a deep breath and blew it out with a sigh. A few moments alone, actually, was exactly what she needed. Scanning the room, she spotted a wash basin and another pitcher beside the bed. Aye, she needed to wash. Her face and hands, every inch of her exposed skin, felt gritty with the dirt from the road.

After refreshing herself, Lijsbet pulled one of the chairs over to the window, where she could reach the cheese board. As she nibbled on bread still warm from the oven, she studied what would be her view for the next fortnight.

*Mayhap longer*, the earl had said.

The street between the brick buildings was narrow. In one direction, the cobbled path twisted off to the left and out of sight. In the other, she could see clear through to a cross-street, where she caught glimpses of people and horses passing in the early evening light.

Was this Schapenstraat, the street on which the artists' house sat? She had gotten a bit turned around coming up the spiral staircase and winding through the halls of the abbey to get to her quarters, but she believed this was the street on which they'd arrived. The last time she'd seen Earl Price, he was making his way along the cobblestones toward that cross-street.

*Carefully.*

Lijsbet wondered if the man suffered from a sort of bone ailment, one that made him ambulate with such care. His every move was measured, taken slowly and with the greatest of caution. Any movement of his body, she realized, seemed to cause him pain.

She would have to ask Lady Duchess about this condition when they returned to Coudenburg. Surely, a man so young could not be suffering the creaky joints of old age.

*Mayhap 'twas not pain at all. Mayhap was fear. But of what?*

As if she'd conjured him by thinking his name, he was suddenly there, at the end of the alleyway. Lijsbet blinked and squinted to be sure 'twas not a trick of the light. Nay, 'twas him, dressed in the same bright blue tunic he'd worn on the journey in. And instead of walking away from her, he was now approaching.

Slowly, but definitely returning, she assumed, to Groot Beginjnhof.

What had gone wrong, she wondered? Had they not been expecting him at the artists' residence? Surely, he could not expect the sisters to offer lodging here.

When a soft knock sounded on the door, she jumped.

"Come."

Another pale, wimple-draped face peeked around the opening as the door swung open.

"Lady Lambert, the Mistress asks that you come to the main hall. She has asked cook to prepare you a proper meal." The woman standing inside the door was very young—a girl, really. Her flushed cheeks were very round, and although 'twas impossible to gauge her size under the yards of black cloth draped about her form, Lijsbet guessed the girl was quite plump. She curtsied, awkwardly. "I am Sister Fiona. Please, follow me to the hall."

Lijsbet followed the girl, who waddled her way through the labyrinth of hallways and down the steps until they came through an archway into a large hall. Here, everything was very plain and functional: wood plank tables and long benches, a hearth at each end, cold now for the warm months, and lancet windows set high. Torches set along the stone walls provided warm light but also sent a haze of smoke to hover in the air. The room, at the moment, appeared quite empty.

Through a door at the far end, Sister Fenna entered carrying a tray, followed by two other cloaked figures carrying platters.

"Come, Lady Lambert. Fruit and cheese are not enough to satisfy after your long journey. I have asked our cook to roast you a small bird, and heat up the summer potage." She set the platter down on the end of the long table nearest the kitchen door. "Please, sit. I will introduce you to some of our members while you sup."

As she settled on the bench, Lijsbet felt more awkward than ever, surrounded by a half dozen young women all cloaked in black, their faces the only thing visible beneath the white wimples they wore.

*I should have changed into my plain brown robe*, she thought ruefully, glancing down at the fine, bright blue gown in which she'd traveled.

The sisters did not seem cognizant of her discomfort. "This is Sister Aleida, Sister Renate, and Sister Wilhelmina."

As each woman cast a shy smile her way and dipped their chins, Lijsbet was unsure if she should extend a hand, or simply nod in like. She decided on the latter.

The last woman to exit the kitchen wore a stained apron over her black habit. "And here is our cook, Sister Rikila. She keeps us all well fed here at Groot Beginjnhof."

Not at all shy like the others, Sister Rikita stepped forward and extended a roughened hand toward Lijsbet. " 'Tis my pleasure to meet you, Lady Lambert. We are excited indeed to have a renowned illuminator to visit our workshop."

Lijsbet felt the color rise into her cheeks. "Ah, not such a renowned artist, Sister. I am but an apprentice in a trade requiring many, many years to master."

" 'Tis not what the Master, Dieric Bouts has to say about you."

All the women jumped when a man's voice echoed in the nearly empty hall. There, standing under the alcove at the front of the building, stood Earl Davion Price. Beside him was yet another sister whom Lijsbet had not met, who looked nervous and uncomfortable, wringing her hands.

In a small voice, she said, "My apologies, Mistress. Lord Price said you were expecting him. The gentleman comes from the Duke of Burgundy's castle. He arrived with Lady Lambert."

After a brief moment of shocked silence, Sister Fenna recovered and stood, making her way toward the earl with an outstretched hand. "Welcome, Lord Price. We did not expect you until the morrow, but you are welcome to join us now. Cook has just prepared a meal for our guest. I am certain there is plenty for two to share."

*Davion*

Davion had settled his belongings in his appointed room at the artists' house, then dined with the few in residence. He was pleased and surprised to find Dieric Bouts joining them at table. He had not seen Master Bouts since his travels to the region two seasons past. A tall, thin man with sharply sculpted cheekbones, Bouts had heavy lidded eyes that made him seem perpetually bored with the conversation. A man of few words but admirable talent with quill and paint, Davion remembered feeling ill at ease with the man on their previous meeting.

This time was no different. A mostly silent meal had been consumed with the only information exchanged between Davion and Bouts concerning his charge, Lijsbet Lambert.

Bouts' eyes riveted him. "I understand she is one of Rogier's most respected artisans."

But that was all he'd said. Blotting his mouth with a napkin, the artist then bid the other men good evening and disappeared.

Davion had tried to rest in the small, shared room to which he'd been assigned, but found himself pacing instead. He simply could not get Lily out of his mind. She must be going mad confined to a convent with all the nuns... or beguines, or whatever they chose to call themselves. He could not imagine Lily having much in common with these women. How awkward, how uncomfortable she must be.

He simply had to go back to Groot Beginjnhof to make sure she'd settled in well.

The tiny cloaked creature who answered the door actually attempted to turn him away. He was aghast. He was an earl, by God's breath! Why didn't these Flemings recognize royalty when they saw it? It had taken him several minutes of explanation, along with mentioning Sister Fenna's name at least twice, before the little woman ceased attempting to close the door in his face.

He was sorely tempted to shove his boot in the opening to prevent this, but thought better of the move. The door was heavy, thick wood, and the cloaked woman small, but rather quick. Risking damage to his leg was the last chance he intended to take.

'Twas not until he mentioned his position as curator for Philip, the Duke of Burgundy himself, that she opened the door wide enough for him to slip inside.

Now, here he stood facing a room whose smoky, shadowy corner was filled with women all garbed exactly the same way. Faces and hands were the only skin left uncovered. How would one ever tell one from the other?

Then he caught sight of Lijsbet, who was sitting beside Sister Fenna preparing to slide a small, roasted hen from a wooden plank onto a pewter plate before her. The look of surprise on her face matched that of the nuns... or beguines. Whatever they called themselves.

Except more than face and hands were visible on this elegant lady. She had her hair neatly contained, as she always did, but no headdress covering the shimmering mahogany tresses she'd woven into a braid wound on the top of her head. She still wore the royal blue gown she'd traveled in, the one with a deep, square neckline that exposed an admirable expanse of creamy pale skin. When their eyes met, he was again seared by the heat in them.

Davion wondered if he would ever see another kind of heat in those golden eyes, not one reflecting her ire.

His own thought shocked him. 'Twas the first time he had been drawn this way, so powerfully, to anyone. There had never been a possibility for him to develop a relationship with a woman. The risks were too great.

Relationships could lead to love. *Making love.* A rigorous exercise such as sex was out of the question for Davion. 'Twould leave him in pieces—literally.

Still, he wondered of it. Yearned for it. 'Twas only natural for a young man to notice women.

"Won't you join Lady Lambert in a late supper?" Sister Fenna asked as she approached.

He held up one hand. "Nay, I have eaten. But it looks and smells marvelous." He turned to address Lily. "Would the lady mind if I joined her while she eats?"

She sat taller and straighter, her spine as rigid as an arrow. Without taking her eyes from his, she raised her chin. "Is there a reason why have you returned this eve, Lord Price? Is there a problem with your accommodations at the artists' residence?"

He shook his head and strode to where she sat, sliding onto the bench opposite her. "Nay. I just thought... I was simply... I wanted to be sure you had settled in without issue." He paused, tipping his head. "I am your chaperone, Lily. 'Tis my responsibility—"

Lijsbet crouched low toward him and hissed, "I'm in a convent. How much trouble do you think I could get myself into in a convent?"

"Beguinage. I thought 'twas a beguinage," he whispered.

One by one, the other sisters, apparently sensing the tension between them, quietly took their leave. The mistress was the only one who remained, standing just inside the kitchen doorway. With her arms presumably folded under her cloak—no hands were visible—she stood as silent sentry, studying the scene with an impassive expression. Davion felt beads of sweat form on his upper lip.

*I am so making a mess of this.*

He cleared his throat. "Eat, Lily. You must be famished. The journey seemed endless, did it not?"

Her eyes still flashing, Lijsbet did begin eating, using her knife with added gusto and tearing the legs from the roasted bird with a savagery he found shocking. Mayhap somewhat exciting.

"I am hungry. And tired. And exasperated. I do not understand you, Lord Price. You have spent the entire day sparring with me in the carriage. Now, when I thought I would have an evening of peace, you have returned." She shredded the meat off the bird leg with her teeth, closing her eyes as she chewed. He watched her hum approval and swallow. Then she continued, "Exactly how much time, while I am training here in Leuven, will you be spending acting as chaperone? As overseer? Will I have you breathing down my neck throughout all the days?"

*Why does simply watching her eat please me so?*

As she laid down her eating knife, he reached for her. In one quick move, his hand darted across the table to cover hers. She blinked up at him in complete shock, but did not move. She did not pull away.

Her hand was soft and warm, and the contact sent tingles of pleasure up his spine. Davion Price was not a man who touched another person often—it was simply too risky. With Lily, though, he hadn't thought twice. It was as though he could not resist her.

"Lily, please. Do not view me as your adversary. It's true, the duke tasked me with certain responsibilities while we are here. But I had hoped... I had wished it could also be a time when you and I could become better acquainted."

"For what purpose?" The question was simple, her tone flat.

He wished he knew the answer.

"I have a great deal of respect for your work. I yearn to learn more about the time you spent at the Tournai school. We both have similar interests, Lily. I was hoping we could not only work together, but mayhap develop a friendship."

He saw the alarm flash in her eyes, and she snatched her hand away.

*Wrong thing to say, fool.*

Lijsbet threw her napkin down over her plate. "I would like to make one fact very clear, Lord Price. You are my overseer—my superior. I will work under your supervision. As far as a relationship any more personal than that, I must inform you: I am not interested. I am a very independent woman, and I intend to remain that way."

With that she rose, scanning the room until she spotted Sister Fenna. "Mistress, if you could be so kind as to escort me to my chamber. This abbey is very large indeed, and I fear I will lose my way."

Just before she disappeared under the archway, Davion called out, "I will return on the morrow, Lily. Sleep well." The look she shot over her shoulder could have shattered glass.

The very thought made Davion shudder as he made his way to the front door.

# Chapter Six

*Davion*

Master Dieric Bouts was at table very early when Davion came to break his fast. They were, it seemed, the only ones awake as of yet. Artists tend to work late into the night and sleep well into the morning, at least 'twas the rumor Davion had been told. 'Twas not how his scriptorium operated. The artisans who worked under him began early and worked until the days' assignments were complete.

Without so much as a greeting, Master Bouts blotted his mouth on a napkin and leveled his gaze on Davion.

"The Lady Duchess tells me you wish to speak with my acquaintance, the one who worked in the hospital in Bethlem." A long beat of silence drew the tension in the room as taut as the strings on a dulcimer. Finally, Bouts continued. "What, exactly, is it that ails you, Earl Price?"

*Too early in my day for this discussion*, Davion thought. *I haven't even taken a sip of my ale.*

Which he did, more to stall answering than due to a parched throat. He found he could not hold the master's gaze. 'Twas too intense. Too invasive.

" 'Tis a fear I have. A phobia I suffer from, Master Bouts. It's been plaguing me since I was a small child. I think it may have to do with the fact that my parents pampered me so." He found he could not hold the goblet aloft without liquid sloshing over the rim, so he set it down on the rubbed wooden table. "I am an only child."

"So is it a physical ailment, or a weakness of the mind? It is we, the artists, who have a reputation for the latter," Bouts said, ending on a chuckle that shocked the earl.

He didn't realize the man even had the capacity to smile. Davion had met Bouts briefly at an art showing in Amsterdam the year before. His impression of the man, he remembered now, was not favorable. Bouts wore his pride as a king wears his crown. As Davion sought to learn from the master, the artist treated him much as one treats an affectionate dog. The earl was, after all, merely a young student of the arts—not an artist himself.

Davion worried the napkin before him, keeping his eyes trained there. If he kept his hands moving, mayhap Bouts would not notice how badly they were shaking.

*Much too early in the day for this discussion.*

"I will arrange to have Dr. Vanderhoff meet with you here, at the residence," Bouts continued. "The house is empty for a good part of the afternoon while the artists are out working on location, or seeking models. Will this afternoon be soon enough?"

Davion felt the fabric laying on the back of his neck prickle with sweat. Meeting the doctor here, in a place where any one of the artists might encounter them? The very thought made him ill.

"Does Dr. Vanderhoff not have somewhere here in the city where he treats his patients?" he asked. He hated the quiver in his voice.

Bouts' expression grew serious. He folded his hands on the table in front of him. "What are you afraid of, Earl Price? Your employers, the duke and duchess, are already aware of your issue. Isabella herself was the one who inquired about Dr. Vanderhoff's reputation."

Davion pushed back his chair so abruptly it clattered to the tiled floor. The echo in the empty room sent frissons of fear up his spine.

*I must be more careful in my movements, upset or no.*

"I suppose meeting the physician here will be fine," he sputtered, beginning his pacing up and down beside the long table.

"Earl Price... Davion, come here. Sit and take some more ale. There is no reason for you to be so alarmed." He patted the table. His kindly, reassuring attitude surprised the earl again. Bouts had not seemed to be a very caring man.

Swallowing hard, Davion returned to his seat and watched the artist fill his goblet.

"We are all afraid of something, my lord. Some are able to conceal the fear better than others. Some let it bleed out onto canvas in shades of crimson and red madder."

This was a side of Master Bouts Davion had not known existed. In their previous encounters, he'd always struck the earl as a cold, distant man. One who lived inside a very private world walled from the outside world. Seeing the man's compassion made his throat feel tight.

"I appreciate your help, Master Bouts. In whatever way you can," he managed.

"There is one matter in which you can help me. I wish to meet your charge on this visit. This Lady Lijsbet Lambert. Her reputation precedes her." One of Bouts' pale eyebrows lifted conspiratorially.

Another emotion tickled Davion's skin now, but it had nothing to do with his illness or the shame of it. He narrowed his eyes and asked, "What do you mean, *her reputation*?"

"I mean to say, the masters at the Tournai school speak very fondly of her, and of her work. I hear 'tis some of the finest in the guild. 'Tis a shame her sex prevents her from becoming an active member."

Davion blew out the breath he didn't realize he'd been holding. "Yes, yes. Her work is superb. The duchess has commissioned several prayer books and insists they be illuminated by none other than Lil... Lady Lambert."

He cringed at his own slip of the tongue and prayed it had gone unnoticed. It had not.

Now both of Bouts eyebrows lifted as he sat back in his chair, folding his hands across his middle. "How long have you known the lady? And how well?" His questions were pointed, almost accusatory.

"I only came to Coudenburg a few days before we left to come here, to Leuven. I don't know the lady well at all. Just her work," he stammered.

"I see," Bouts said, staring at his hands. "Well then, I shall have to travel to the beguinage, to their workshop, to get to know her better for myself." He shot Davion a glance. "Her work, I mean to say."

Later, Davion's stomach roiled as he made his way through the narrow alleyway to the beguinage. He hadn't had any appetite and had refused the bread and boiled eggs offered him. The ale he'd consumed sloshed about like a small boat on the channel's rough waters.

Was it that, or was it Bouts' words that had him so riled? Both, he knew. Although he didn't know Lily well, she intrigued him. Unfortunately, what

Bouts said was probably true. Lily's reputation did precede her, and 'twas not one of virginal purity.

Davion suspected now that the Tournai master was finished with her, Dieric Bouts possessed some interest. He was, unlike de la Pasture, only a few years older than Lily.

The artist feigned interest in the woman's artistic talent. The earl was certain he was attracted to more than the skilled and colorful illuminations she created.

Davion did not know the details, only that Lily had spent the last ten or more years of her life as an apprentice in artists' workshops. She was nearing thirty winters old, and had never married. 'Twas rumored she had been the mistress of the Master of Tournai for most of her time there.

Rogier de la Pasture was older than Lily by more than a dozen years. Why would she wait so long to insist he consent to marry?

Alternately, mayhap a more permanent situation was not in the lady's plans. Isn't that how Lijsbet herself had come to be? Isabella had confided to Davion that Lijsbet was one of Philip's bastard daughters. That meant her mother must have been a mistress to the duke.

Did the daughter follow in the mother's footsteps? Did Lily truly have no intention to ever marry? Her words from last evening came back to him.

*I am a very independent woman, and I intend to remain that way.*

Mayhap an artist, and a mistress, was all Lady Lijsbet Lambert aspired to.

Of one fact, Davion was certain: the duchess had specifically designated him as Lily's chaperone for this apprenticeship period in Leuven. The mere term alone indicated 'twas his responsibility to keep her chaste, safe from unwanted attentions.

That included any from Master Dieric Bouts.

*Lisjbet*

Lily followed Sister Fenna and the other beguines down the long, narrow hallway linking the living quarters of the ladies to their workshop. *Their scriptorium*, Lijsbet thought. Her fingers tingled as they clutched the handles of her supply bag, which held all of her quills and colors. She could barely wait to get started—learning the ways of the Leuven beguines as to artistic process, and then trying her own hand at the task.

The sun had risen bright and hot in a clear sky, and warm bands of gold fell through the tall windows lining the street side of the scriptorium. This was different, she thought, *so* different from the workspace at Coudenburg. It was a poorly lit room when she arrived. But after Lord Price's arrival, he had turned it into a veritable dungeon. This room reminded her more of the workshop in Tournai, where light was considered a very important element in the design of the illuminations.

*That's what they are called, after all. Illuminations. That means light.*

Immediately, Lijsbet's spirits rose, spilling over into a new lightness in her step. Here she would learn some new techniques. Here she would take her skills of embellishment to a new level.

Sister Fenna led her to a long table where some of the beguines' latest works were laid out to dry. The unbound leaves glittered, the designs intricate, and their colors brilliant. Lijsbet sucked in a breath and laid her fingers on her lips.

"These are glorious, Mistress. Where did the sisters learn their skills?" she asked.

One side of Fenna's mouth quirked. "The Flemings have contributed much to our techniques, and to our process. Several of the artists. You have heard of Jan van Eyck, I trust?"

Lijsbet blinked. How could she have not? "Of course, my lady. He is considered one of the finest painters in all of the Lowlands. But of miniatures? I was not aware—"

"Not many people are. But van Eyck has completed a number of awe-inspiring works in a vast array of sizes and mediums. Have you no knowledge of the Turin-Milan Hours?" the Mistress asked.

Sister Fenna strode to the end of the long table, her arms folded under her robe. When she reached the last several leaves, she withdrew one hand, motioning toward the small texts.

"These, Sister Aleida, and Sister Wilhelmina embellished after a recent visit to van Eyck's workshop in Bruges. Although we do not profess these works are of equal skill, we do feel they reflect the realism and emotion portrayed in Jan's work." Her head jerked up, her hand coming to her mouth. "I mean to say, Master van Eyck's work," she clarified.

*They have worked with the creator of the Ghent altarpiece?* It was apparent the Mistress was also well-enough acquainted with Master van Eyck to use his given name. Lijsbet fought a wave of lightheadedness at the notion.

"I have never seen work so exquisite," she breathed. "But tell me, are you not concerned with damage from all the bright light streaming in through your wonderful windows? I had not considered the danger before. But my overseer, Lord Price, he keeps the scriptorium at Coudenburg in almost complete darkness for fear of the pigments fading."

The mistress tipped her head. "How do you work with insufficient light? On such miniscule projects?"

Lijsbet could not stifle an exasperated sigh. " 'Tis one of the most challenging aspects of working since the earl arrived. 'Twas not ideal before but now, 'tis nearly impossible to create by torch and candlelight." She flattened her lips.

Fenna smirked and rose her eyebrows. "I am the overseer here, and I believe 'tis true, sunlight can bleach the pigment—in time. But how can one create such intricate and minute details without sufficient light to see by?"

*Exactly my thinking.*

"After all, once complete, these are prayer books. They will see the light every day, at multiples times of the day."

A glow spread through Lijsbet's chest. She had worried over coming to the beguinage, being alone for a fortnight with women who embodied a way of life that was, truly, the polar opposite of her. But 'twas not true. As artists—as well as women who possessed an abundance of common sense—she had more in common with the beguines than she had ever dreamed possible.

Her visit here was an unexpected blessing, and Lijsbet was vibrating with excitement. She laid a hand on the rough woolen sleeve of Sister Fenna's robe. "Please, Mistress, show me where I shall lay out my tools, and let us get to work. I am eager to learn."

The mistress smiled. "First, allow me to take you through our entire workshop. We do not create only the inscription and embellishment here, but we also produce the vellum, measure and cut the quires, and perform the bookbinding."

Throughout the entire morning and up until the midday meal, Lijsbet allowed herself to become engrossed in what the beguines had to show her. She alternated between experiencing awe and, at times, a glint of jealousy. These ladies were talented! They had devoted their lives to God, but also to using all of the talents bestowed upon them. She intended to make use of every second in this scriptorium, absorbing whatever knowledge and skill she could.

Still, she could not shake the dark shadow lurking in the back of her consciousness. He had said he would come. In the morning, he had said. At any moment, her carefree interaction with the ladies of Groot Beginjnhof could come screeching to a halt. At any moment, *he* would come through the door and begin his scrutiny of her.

Yet by the noon meal, Earl Price had not arrived. As she followed the sisters to the main hall, Lijsbet found herself deluged by a barrage of warring emotions: relief, curiosity, followed by a growing concern.

'Twas already half the day gone. What had happened to the earl? Had some misfortune befallen him to prevent him from coming to the beguinage? Or had he decided, after her repeated and enthusiastic rebuffs, that he simply didn't care to see her?

Her stomach clenched in a tight little knot as she slid onto the bench in the hall next to Sister Aleida. She did not think she could eat. Not until she knew what was happening with her chaperone.

An odd reversal of roles, she mused. Yet she worried just the same.

The younger beguines spread an array of simple foods on the table before them. Dark bread, hard cheese, some dried fruits, and more grapes accompanied pitchers of some very nice wine. She savored the flavor on her tongue, and wondered...

"Sister Aleida, I noticed your grape arbors, through the windows lining the rear of the abbey. I'm assuming these grapes are your own?" she asked as she tore off a piece of crusty bread, still warm from the oven.

The beguine smiled proudly. "Aye, they are. And we make the wine here ourselves as well." She paused, shifting her eyes off to the side before continuing. "That is to say, the wine is *made* here at Groot Beginjnhof, but we do have some help from the monks at Affligem. They are magicians when it comes to wine-making."

Lijsbet rocked back in amazement. "You ladies are not only pious and talented, but versatile as well," she exclaimed. Raising her goblet, she called out, "To the impressive sisters of Groot Beginjnhof!"

Hesitating, the sisters glanced from one to the other. It was obvious that "toasting" was not a usual affair at the table of the beguinage. But one by one, they reached for their own goblets and followed Lijsbet's lead. She could not help but burst into laughter when Sister Fenna blurted, "Huzzah!"

Pounding in the front hall interrupted them. After a brief, shocked moment, Sister Fenna nodded to one of the younger sisters, who rose to answer the door. Lijsbet sucked in her breath, not sure if she was hoping the caller was Earl Price, or not.

# Chapter Seven

*Lijsbet*

The man's voice they heard echoing from the front hall was not familiar to Lijsbet. In a moment, the young sister appeared in the doorway with a tall, pale figure beside her. He was dressed richly, in flowing robes of crimson. The ermine edging his collar and cuffs were out of place for the summer season, obviously more of a status statement than worn for warmth. Sister Fenna rose with a shocked if not pleased expression as she approached the man.

"Master Bouts. To what do we owe such an honor?" When she reached him, she lowered to one knee, as though he were a king or other noble.

Lijsbet was puzzled. She'd heard of this man, this artist. She knew of his work, and that he was the guildmaster. But to be treated as royalty? *Why?* she wondered.

He was not a handsome man, with a squared jaw and strong, prominent features. His eyes, round and dark, scanned the room above the Mistress' head from under a prominent forehead and knitted eyebrows.

"I understand you have a guest artisan in your midst," he said. "I have come to meet this illuminator. This Lady Lijsbet Lambert."

Prickles lifted Lijsbet's skin like that of a plucked bird. The great Master Dieric Bouts was making a personal call on *her*?

Lijsbet stood and slid out from behind the bench. She glanced behind him, but he was alone. The earl had not accompanied him. Sudden panic clutched her chest. She worried her hands before her.

"It is I, Master Bouts. Has something happened to Lord Price? My chaperone?"

Bouts pursed his lips, his eyes narrowing. "Nay. The earl is otherwise engaged this afternoon. I did not think it improper for me to come visit you without him. Here," he motioned toward the beguines, "in the company of the sisters."

Her shoulders relaxed even as suspicion flooded her. "Will he be coming along later? He did tell me to expect him this morn. There is much I wish to show him about what I will be learning here at the abbey—"

"I did not come to discuss the English earl," Bouts cut in, his annoyance apparent. Then, as though a page had been turned to reveal a completely different man, the hard lines of his face softened. "I have come to see your work."

Although he sounded different, there was something about his expression that soured the wine in Lijsbet's belly to vinegar.

He took three strides on his long legs and was within an arm's length of her. She couldn't help but stiffen and take a step back. This man was presumptuous, to say the least. In a lower voice, his next words were meant only for her ears.

"I have heard much about you from the masters at the Tournai school, Lily."

Before she had a chance to react, the mistress stepped between them and beckoned to Lijsbet.

"Come, Lady Lambert. Let us take Master Bouts to the scriptorium and show him some of the leaves you brought with you to Groot Beginjnhof."

Lijsbet was relieved the mistress had intervened. She felt sure Master Bouts was about to reach for her hand, to kiss it. The thought made her skin itch under her brown frock. She was infinitely glad she had dressed for a workday this morn.

She certainly was not about to genuflect at his feet the way Sister Fenna had. He was a fellow artisan. A famed one, true. But Bouts was not royalty.

Technically, he and she were of the same social class. Lijsbet reminded herself of the fact as she followed the sisters down the narrow hallway, keeping her spine straight and her shoulders squared. She did, however, follow several steps behind Master Bouts. Her only show of respect.

As they entered the scriptorium, two of the sisters scurried over to open some of the windows. Although the sun no longer poured through the glass, it had already done its work. The room was warm and steamy, with the aromas of parchment and tempera thick in the air.

The scent, to Lijsbet, was a soothing balm. This was her place, her element. Her shoulders relaxed, and she breathed out a soft sigh. Everything she loved about life smelled just like this.

Earlier, the sisters had clustered around her as Lijsbet lifted out the half-dozen folios she'd brought with her from Coudenburg. These were her own work, though technically they belonged to Duke Philip. He had perused her portfolio when he'd come to Tournai last fall, and had chosen these leaves to purchase. The duke had intended, he told her, to combine them into a Book of Hours for his lady, the duchess.

At least, she'd assumed Isabella was who he was referring to when he said they were for "his lady."

In any case, Davion... Lord Price had suggested she bring them along to the Groot Beginjnhof so the sisters would have a better idea of what talents she possessed, and where improvement might be needed. She never would have guessed the Master Dieric Bouts would be evaluating them.

*And why?*

She stood back from the table, her arms folded tightly across her chest, as Bouts strolled the length of the display. From where she stood, she did not have a clear view of his face. She could not decipher his reaction. Approval? Scorn?

And, again, why did she care?

"These are exquisite, Lily."

*Lily. The earl's ekename for her.* Immediately the tension returned, turning her heart into a block of ice in her chest. She knew there was anger flashing in her eyes as he faced her, a smug smile on his face.

"Whomever trained you, they did a very, very good job."

They were words. Just words. Not even provocative words, but those supposedly concerning the quality of her artistic talent. Then why did they make her feel violated? Shamed?

When she met his eyes she knew exactly why. Because he'd intended them that way.

Lijsbet's palms began to sweat, and her eyes darted about the room in search of the mistress. The sisters had gone back to their work stations, but Sister Fenna was nowhere in sight. A wave of nausea washed over her.

"I was wondering if I might take you for a tour of the city later this evening," Bouts murmured, his voice a low rumble. "I would love to discuss—"

"Nay. I have come to Leuven to learn from the beguine sisters their illumination techniques. I am not here on a social visit." Lijsbet held her chin high and hissed the words. "Besides, I will not go anywhere without my chaperone."

Bouts clasped his hands behind his back, chuckling as he swept her body, head to toe. "Your chaperone doesn't seem to be watching you terribly closely so far. Is he?"

*How dare this man—*

"I would like you to meet some of the other artists staying at the communal house here. 'Twould be educational for you." He swept his arm toward the women working at their desks. "How do you think the beguines refined their methods so well? 'Twas with the help of fellow artists."

*Aye, whose names appear on the work as the creators. Male names.*

"Sister Fenna informed me." Was she being curt? She dared not.

Was she being overly sensitive? Suspicious without cause? Mayhap Master Bouts truly did have her artistic endeavors in mind.

"Really, Lily. There is nothing to fear. You will be treated as an honored guest. Just as you are here at Groot Beginjnhof." His voice was like freshly churned butter in the sun. Smooth and warm. Very inviting. But the use of the ridiculous ekename the earl had laid upon her irritated her.

"I have asked my chaperone, and now I am asking you, Master Bouts. I wish to be referred to as Lady Lambert. Not Lily."

Bouts twisted his mouth thoughtfully. "I see. My apologies, Lady Lambert." He hesitated, and the seconds of silence stretched out like a vast ocean.

"I was working with Sister Aleida before the noon meal, Master Bouts. If you are finished with your perusal of my work, I should like to continue."

Bouts dipped his head. "As you wish, My Lady. I shall return well before vespers to retrieve you. 'Tis best to come to the artist's house later in the evening, when more of them will be present."

With that, the intimidating figure turned on his heel and left the scriptorium. Relief washed over Lijsbet, and she swayed where she stood.

He had not given her a choice. He had not asked, he had ordered. To him, her opinion did not matter at all.

She should not be surprised. 'Twas how life was for a woman. Lijsbet sometimes cursed the saints she had been born one.

*DAVION*

Davion knew Lijsbet was probably expecting him. He had told her, after all, he would return to the beguinage this morn. Somehow, with the pending meeting with Dr. Vanderhoff weighing heavy on his mind, he could not face her. He knew she was safe and occupied with the beguines in their workshop. There was no reason for him to worry about her.

Except that there was. His conversation with Bouts this morn still churned in his belly. He would have to speak with the man at length on the matter this evening.

But first, he needed to face his meeting with the doctor.

Davion wandered the streets of Leuven aimlessly for several hours, fighting to avoid the wider, more brightly lit boulevards. Fortunately, Leuven was an old city with an intricate spiderweb of narrow cobblestone streets tucked between tall buildings. These streets, more like alleyways, stayed cool and damp most of the time, escaping the direct rays of the sun.

Just the way Davion preferred to remain.

The city was not very expansive, so there was no worry he would lose his way. Around the noon hour, the aroma of baking filled the air. Ahead, hanging over a small shop, he spotted a sign that read, "Bakkerijj Leuven."

*I shall buy some sweet treats for the house, and bring them back with me. 'Twill be easier to relax in my meeting with Dr. Vanderhoff with a cup of ale and a fritour steadying my hands.*

After selecting several varieties of the pastries the shop offered, Davion perched the wrapped parcel on his forearm and made his way back toward the artists' residence. By the time he reached the front door, however, his stomach had begun a writhing dance in his belly. The thought of eating any of the fragrant treats he carried waned. In fact, he was quite ill.

He heard low voices coming from the common room the moment he closed the door behind him. Dr. Vanderhoff, no doubt, had already arrived. He hoped he had not caused him too long a wait.

The kitchen servant appeared in the hallway.

"You have a visitor, Lord Price."

Davion handed the parcel of pastries to him. "Please, Jehan, bring some of these and some fresh ale to the common room for our guest."

He turned the corner to see a short, round man occupying one of the tall-backed chairs near the hearth. For a moment, Davion mistook him for a monk. Dressed in a drab, brown tunic and sporting a head of dark hair thinning in the pattern of a tonsure, Dr. Vanderhoff could easily have slipped into the role. When the doctor saw him, he rose and smiled, revealing round, very pink cheeks.

"You must be Earl Price," he said, bowing slightly. "The Lady Duchess speaks highly of you. Please, come." He motioned to the chair opposite him. "Join me."

# Chapter Eight

*Davion*

No sooner had Davion settled, carefully, in the cushioned seat facing Dr. Vanderhoff than Jehan arrived bearing a tray. He set out the platter of pastries, the pitcher, and two goblets, then scurried away. The silence in the room was oppressive, since Dr. Vanderhoff had not said another word since first greeting Davion.

"Please, Doctor," he said, his voice shaky, "help yourself to some of the treats I purchased at the bakkerij in town. They seem to be of a fine quality."

The round man's face grew rounder and his eyes lit up. "Methanks you. I think I shall."

After devouring one fritour and washing it down with long gulps of the ale, the doctor's eyes riveted Davion. "Isabella tells me you suffer from certain, shall we say, fears," he began. "Can you describe them to me?"

Davion drew in a deep breath and blew it out. He could feel Vanderhoff's eyes on him, but avoided meeting his gaze. It was easier to talk that way.

" 'Tis of no true import," he stammered, embarrassed. "I'm simply a bit more careful about protecting my body than some people think is normal."

The second fritour was lifted from the platter, half of it disappearing in one bite. "In what way? Are you afraid of cutting yourself? Bleeding, perhaps?"

Davion shook his head, although a memory flashed through his mind when the doctor said the word 'bleeding.' He shook the image away and shuddered. "Nay. I believe myself to be more fragile than most."

Dr. Vanderhoff lifted to pitcher to refill his goblet. "What do you fear will happen if you are not extra careful with your body?" he asked, then popped the other half of the fritour in his mouth.

The earl blinked rapidly. What *was* he afraid of, exactly? When faced with the spoken question, he was unsure of how to put it into words.

"Breaking," he sputtered. "I feel as though my arms, my legs, even my head could break apart. Shatter, to be precise. So I must take extra care not to—"

"So you suffer from glass delusion," Vanderhoff stated matter-of-factly. "Do you believe your body is made of glass?"

Davion's heart began beating against his breastbone so hard he feared what might happen. He often wondered if his rapidly beating heart would shatter spontaneously. But this doctor, he seemed to understand. He had a name for what the earl experienced. It was an exciting revelation.

He hoped the excitement alone did not cause his chest to shatter before discovering how he could cope with this fear.

"Aye, aye, that's exactly the feeling," he said, his voice tight. "This 'glass delusion.' Is it a common malady?"

Davion watched as Dr. Vanderhoff pointed to the last fritour on the tray. "You really should sample one of these. They are superb." The moment he shook his head to refuse, the doctor's eyes sparkled, and he snatched the pastry up.

As he chewed, he elaborated on this condition he called 'glass delusion.'

" 'Tis not very common, but some very prominent nobles have suffered from this delusion. It is recorded that the French king, Charles VI, was what we refer to as a *glass man*. He even had special garments tailored to protect his delicate body."

Davion cringed as a puff of pastry crumbs sprayed from the doctor's mouth. He closed his eyes and swallowed, glad his own stomach was quite empty.

"Did he, then? Shatter?" Davion asked.

"Nay. But he believed he could. Was obsessed with the notion. Spent most of his days motionless, wrapped in blankets to avoid breakage." The doctor's eyes swept Davion up and down. "Your case is not that severe, then. I see you are able to ambulate without any protective clothing."

Davion stared at Vanderhoff in amazement, a mixture of confused emotions flooding his senses. *He was not alone.* The thought was a comfort.

Others had suffered from this illness. In fact, it sounded as though the French king's case was much worse than his.

"What makes you think you are made of glass, Earl Price? That is what you believe, is it not?" The doctor was staring at him now, pastry-flecked hands folded over a very round middle.

"But I am," Davion said. "Can you not see—"

"I see a perfectly normal human body with the usual composition. A little pale in the face, perhaps, and a bit underweight. But I believe, dear boy, you are—physically, at least—made of the same components as I."

*Just in lesser quantity, if so*, Davion thought. *But he is wrong.*

He was shaking his head. "Nay, nay. You do not understand. I may appear normal, Dr. Vanderhoff. But I am far from like you, or most other men I know. If I bump into a door frame, you see, it could be catastrophic. If I sit down too abruptly, on a bench insufficiently cushioned, 'twould be the end of me. I know this."

Dr. Vanderhoff pressed his lips together. "When did this belief, or this *realization* that you are made of glass... when did it begin? Were you born this way?"

Davion sank back, resting gently against the chair's cushioned surface. He raked through his memory to find an answer, and could not. "It must have been with me at birth. I've known this as far back as I can remember."

Vanderhoff drained his goblet and swiped his mouth on a linen napkin. "I must explore your family lineage in more detail, Earl Price, before I can help you. 'Tis apparent you do not remember when this delusion began. It did, however, begin at some point in your young life, although you may not remember it." The man stood, and Davion realized he was as wide as he was tall. And aye, he could slip into any monastery and be mistaken for a monk.

"The duchess has provided me with your lineage. You were born on English soil, were you not? 'Twill take me a bit longer to research, then. I do still know many physicians at Bedlam." He tossed the napkin on the empty platter. "I will return. In a fortnight, no longer."

Before Davion could respond, he heard the front door open and slam shut. The voice echoing in the hallway was that of Master Dieric Bouts.

"Jehan! Jehan, we will be hosting a guest this very night. I wish the evening meal to be served before the hour of vespers. No later."

"Who is our guest, Master Bouts?" Davion stepped into the hallway, leading the departing Dr. Vanderhoff. Bouts looked right past him.

"Oh, dear Maerten," Bouts exclaimed, clamping his hand on the shorter man's shoulder. "So good to see you, my friend. Did you have a fruitful visit with Earl Price?"

"Aye, we did. I believe I have identified the earl's problem. Now 'tis simply a matter of digging down to discover the root." He grinned up at the painter. "Once we identify the root, we can dig it out and toss it away."

Davion wasn't sure if he appreciated being spoken about like a specimen—or a pesky weed—while he was standing in the same space. But Bouts and the doctor obviously knew each other quite well. In truth, the earl knew he should be grateful for Bouts' willingness to contact Dr. Vanderhoff, and to have him come speak with him.

After the doctor left, Davion repeated his question to the artist.

"Who is our guest for the evening, Master Bouts? Another artist from the guild? I look forward to meeting as many of these talents as I am able while I am here in Leuven."

Bouts' gaze eluded Davion as he continued down the hall. "I believe 'tis someone with whom you might already be familiar." Then he whisked around the corner and up the stairs without another word.

"Hmm," Davion huffed. Here was the Bouts he remembered from past visits. Abrupt, private to the point of rudeness. He would have to wait, it seemed, to discover who the guest was until the evening meal was upon them.

*Lijsbet*

To her consternation, Lijsbet found she could not concentrate fully for the rest of the day. Bouts' visit had shaken her. Angered her.

Mayhap frightened her.

She also could not help her mind to wander toward the whereabouts of her chaperone. Where was the earl? As a chaperone, he was failing miserably. Irritation prickled her scalp, and she scratched the itch away.

The art world was full of them, she mused. Perplexing, aggravating, confounding males of the species.

'Twas not until a slip of her quill caused an ink splatter on the margin of a page that she allowed her exasperation to show.

"By God's bones," she blurted as she tossed the quill down on the table, stomping her foot at the same time. She and muttered the oath softly enough, she hoped. She should not dare take God's name in vain in the presence of these holy women. Wiping her damp palms down her frock, she altered the oath, speaking louder this time. "In the name of all that is holy. I have succeeded in ruining a precious leaf of vellum."

Sister Aleida was at her side in a moment. "Oh, 'tis of no concern. Look, Lady Lambert," she said, pointing to the streaked splatter of black, " 'tis right where the acanthus vines would intersect in the pattern. 'Twill be quite easy to disguise."

Lijsbet smiled at the earnest face before her. "You are so kind, all of you here. I am not usually so apt to err," she began, and hated the fact her voice had grown thick with threatened tears. " 'Tis my first day with you. I will admit to being a tad nervous. I promise, I will improve in the coming days."

But the young beguine was searching her eyes for more than an apology for an error. Her pale eyebrows drew close together. "What is it, my lady? Are you not well?" she asked softly.

Sympathy was her undoing. The tears came, filling her eyes and spilling over. She folded her arms across her chest and turned away.

"I am well. The journey, it tired me. And I am, as I said, out of sorts in a new location. I shall be fine."

The beguine's hands closed warmly over Lijsbet's shoulders. "If there is anything we can do to make your stay here more agreeable, my lady, please tell us. And if there is a matter of specific concern to you, Sister Fenna is a very good listener."

Then she was gone, following the other sisters out the door of the scriptorium. The hour of vespers was nearing, she knew.

The hour of Master Dieric Bouts' returning as well.

Unsure if she could even find her way back to her quarters without guidance, Lijsbet headed down the long corridor linking the library to the main building. Her heart lurched when she heard soft footsteps behind her. Turning, her shoulders relaxed when she saw 'twas the mistress herself.

"What has you so out of sorts, Lijsbet?" she asked when she had reached her side.

Lijsbet sighed. As they walked slowly down the hallway, she pondered her options. Should she confide in the mistress about her concerns? Would that be a show of weakness?

Quickly, she decided showing weakness to the beguine sister would be of no consequence.

"The master's visit today," she began, "Master Bouts. It shocked me, but more, it frightened me. He is returning here this evening—very soon, to retrieve me for a visit to the artists' residence." She paused in her step to face Sister Fenna. " 'Twas not a request, but an order. You seem to know the master well, Mistress. Do I have need to be concerned by this?"

Fenna's lips pressed into a thin line, and she refused to meet Lijsbet's gaze. "I do know Master Bouts. He is an extremely talented artist. A very influential guild member. As for his personal life," Then Fenna locked eyes with Lijsbet, "be careful to make your intentions clear, Lady Lambert. Master Bouts is a man who has become very accustomed to taking what he wants." She paused, thinking. "Where is your chaperone? Surely, he would not approve of any excursions outside of the Groot Beginjnhof without supervision. Even in the company of the guildmaster."

"I agree. Yet he has failed to return as he said he would. I worry something might have become of him."

Fenna bit her lower lip. "I will not allow you to travel to the artist's residence with Master Bouts unaccompanied. Sister Aleida, or mayhap Sister Wilhelmina will go with you."

Lijsbet breathed out a sigh of relief. "Many thanks, Mistress. Now I shall freshen myself and dress appropriately for such a call." She cocked an eyebrow. "And modestly." As she strode off down the hallway, she lurched to a stop and turned. "Am I going the right way to my quarters?"

# Chapter Nine

*Lijsbet*

Lijsbet chose the plainest of the gowns she'd brought with her, one fashioned in cotton damask in a dusky blue color, the pattern barely recognizable in subtle monotones. Cut simply, the gown did not fit her as well as some of those the duchess provided, and bore no ornamentation of any kind. In fact, the cloth buckled and draped about her waist. She had, in truth, become thinner in her few weeks at Coudenburg. What else could one expect with a major life change?

'Twas a gown she'd brought with her from Tournai, worn many times and somewhat out of fashion. Faded, even. A modest neckline with long sleeves left a minimal amount of skin exposed. And now, several measures too large. Perfect, she thought, for a woman wishing to emphasize her trade more than her femininity.

She heard voices in the front hall shortly, a man's voice mingling with those of the sisters as they filed into the chapel for the hour of prayer. The master had arrived, just as he'd said. A fist of tension closed around her throat.

As she made her way down the winding steps toward the front hall, Lijsbet's heart hammered against her breastbone so violently she had to pause every few steps to catch her breath. *Compose yourself,* she thought. *Take care on the stairs.* 'Twould not be seemly for her to tumble down the steps and arrive at the artist's feet in a heap.

Straightening her spine, she took the last few steps slowly. *Dignity. Independence. Strength.* These were the traits she wished to portray to the Flemish painter. To all the painters she would likely meet this evening.

As her slipper hit the stone pavers on the ground floor, however, she realized the voice she was hearing 'twas not that of Master Bouts. 'Twas that of Earl Davion Price. Immediately, she was overcome with an elixir of confused emotions.

Relief. Curiosity.

Annoyance.

*Earlier I expected Earl Price, and 'twas Master Bouts. I now expect the artist, and 'tis the earl.*

"I see you have not become food for the crows," she murmured as she stepped out into the hall. Davion's head shot up, and when their eyes met, another emotion overcame Lijsbet. 'Twas one not particularly welcome. Warmth flooded her, starting in her chest and spreading out all over.

She should not be reacting this way to Lord Price. Her overseer. Her chaperone. A very young man.

A very young *Englishman.*

Yet she could not hold back the smile. "I was concerned for your welfare, Lord Price," she said in a softer tone, searching his eyes.

His initial pinched expression eased, and he reflected her smile. "My apologies, Lady Lambert. My afternoon was taken up by other matters. But I am here now." He stepped forward and motioned toward the door. "I know 'tis late, but would you like to join me at the artists' residence for the evening meal?"

Lijsbet nodded silently.

*So Master Bouts has sent him to retrieve me.* She breathed a bit easier.

"Do you mind if we walk the short way over to the artists' residence? 'Tis a lovely evening."

"Nay. I could use some air."

Sister Fenna stood near the doorway beside Sister Wilhelmina. "You shall not be needing my beguine to escort you, then." 'Twas not a question, but a statement. She bowed toward the earl.

As soon as they reached the bottom of the beguinage steps, Lijsbet slipped her hand into the crook of the earl's elbow. She felt him stiffen.

"Is there something wrong, my lord? If you'd rather I not hold onto you—"

"Nay. Nothing is amiss, my lady. 'Tis my honor to escort you. I have missed you today." As they crossed the street and reached the entrance to the alleyway, he smiled down into her eyes. "Lily."

They began their trek down the narrow cobblestone street leading to Schapenstraat. An early twilight cloaked the alley. At first, the earl's arm had felt like a piece of iron, but she felt him relax as they stepped out of the last long rays of sunlight. She glanced over at him and saw the furrows on his brow had smoothed.

"I am very pleased you came for me instead of Master Bouts," she began. "I was uncomfortable leaving the beguine without a chaperone, but Sister Wilhelmina—"

The earl stopped short and turned to face her. "What do you mean? What of Dieric Bouts?" The furrows reappeared, this time hovering over narrowed eyes.

Lisjbet blinked in surprise. "I do not understand. Master Bouts said he was coming for me before vespers. There are some artists at the residence, he said, he wanted me to meet."

A muscle worked in his jaw. "When did you speak with Master Bouts?" His words were tight.

"He came to the beguinage earlier today. To see my work, he said. He had heard much about me from the masters of Tournai—"

"Aye. He said the same to me." Davion's voice was low, ominous. "I was not aware he was coming to the beguinage today, or I would have been here."

The question tumbled about in her head, and she tried to hold it in. Alas, she failed.

"Where were you, Lord Price? I do not mean to press into your personal affairs, but I felt very uncomfortable meeting a man without you present. Even with the sisters there."

*Scolding? Had I sounded as if I was scolding? Mayhap I was.*

The earl's shoulders lifted and fell on a deep breath as he walked on. "It shall not happen again. I promised Duke Philip I would watch over you here in Leuven. And watch over you I shall. I apologize I was kept away this day."

In a quieter voice, Lisjbet asked, "What does he want of me, Lord Price? Master Bouts is an artist of large pieces, massive oils for framing. What interest would he have in miniatures? Does he illuminate manuscripts as well?"

At that moment they saw a figure turn the corner into the other end of the alley. Tall, with robes swishing about his ankles, he looked to be a noble.

Even in the fading light, Lijsbet recognized the bright red of the surcoat she'd seen earlier. 'Twas Master Bouts.

So, he had not sent the earl to retrieve her. He'd simply been a few moments too late.

Davion's entire form turned rigid beside her, and his steps slowed. "Allow me to speak with Master Bouts in private, Lily."

He patted her hand and left her standing against the red brick building flanking the alley. She wrapped her arms about herself and leaned against the cool wall. When he and Bouts practically collided a few dozen yards ahead, she could hear them speaking, but could not make out the words.

*Davion*

"I see the dutiful chaperone has decided to take up his duty after all," Bouts hissed, stepping closer to Davion than made him comfortable. Hating himself, he was forced to step back.

"What interest do you have in this illuminator, Bouts? Have you decided to switch to miniatures? Has the market for altarpieces and portraits fallen off of late?" Davion knew he was inviting trouble. His tone was irreverent and his words inflammatory.

*But he came after Lily behind my back today.*

There is only one reason this man would be so interested in the lady, and the thought made Davion's stomach clench.

One corner of Bout's lips curved up mockingly. "You speak bravely for a such an insignificant man. Such a *fragile* one," he taunted. "You do realize I could destroy you right here, right now, right in front of your charge's eyes. *Lily's* eyes."

"What do you want with her?" Davion was trembling all over, but not with fear. With rage.

Bouts shrugged and crossed his arms over his chest. "I am simply interested in her. I studied a few of her pieces today. She is quite talented," he said with a smirk, his tone sardonic.

"If the lady had not sufficient talent, the duke would not have taken her on for his workshop."

Bouts barked out a laugh. "We both know why the duke took the woman into his employ, Price."

Davion blinked, shocked. *So he knows her status as well.* The earl did not realize the circumstances of Lisjbet's heritage were so well known.

"Some are prone to say—like mother, like daughter. She's already proven the fact in Tournai, has she not?" Bouts jeered and shook his head. "Don't tell me you haven't considered the possibility of, let us say, some socialization with the lady yourself."

The earl clenched his fists so tightly he feared they would crack. At that moment he wanted, more than life itself, to connect one of those fists with Bouts' jaw.

'Twas impossible, he knew. 'Twas also uncivilized, and beneath his status. But it could very well destroy him.

"I have vowed to Duke Philip to protect Lady Lambert while she is in Leuven, and this I intend to do. Now, if you don't mind, I am escorting her to the artists' residence to introduce her to the other guild members, and to share a civilized meal. Do you take issue with this plan?" Davion asked, his tone frigid.

Bouts unfolded his arms and looked past him, motioning for Lijsbet to approach. " 'Twas my thinking as well. We both have the same intention on this point. Let us escort Lady Lambert to the evening meal."

'Twas the tensest meal Davion had ever endured. For one, 'twas his own first meeting of many of the artists—five in all, including Bouts. For another, although the lavish spread of dishes on the table was appetizing, none, it seemed, held the men's admiration as much as Lady Lambert.

He wondered how she could stand being stared at by so many pairs of eyes. Male eyes.

Then again, he thought back to her history—she'd lived and worked in artists' workshops most of her life. 'Twas a fact, not many artists were female. That made her the lone flower.

And a lovely one she was. He could not blame the men for devouring her with their eyes, even as the slices of mutton and highly seasoned vegetables grew cold on their plates.

*A perfect lily. Tall, regal, strong.*

The wine flowed freely, and Lijsbet drank her share. The more she drank, the less shy she became. By the meal's end, she was laughing and exchanging stories with all of the artists—some of them quite influential guild members.

All the while, Davion sat, carefully centered on his cushioned chair, watching her.

*I am as bad as the rest. I cannot not keep my eyes off her.*

Lijsbet possessed the rare kind of beauty produced by contrasts: dark, shiny hair that absorbed as much light as it reflected, framing porcelain skin that looked to be as soft as a flower's petal.

A lily's petal. Aye, she may not be fond of the ekename he'd dubbed her, but it did fit. *Lily.*

Her hands were smooth and soft-looking too, with long, elegant fingers that fluttered in the air before her as she spoke. When she wasn't sparring with him, he noticed her voice was light. Lilting. Feminine. 'Twas her eyes, though, that drew every man at table's gaze, seeming to mesmerize them.

Not brown, not hazel, but golden brown. *Ochre*, he thought. Her eyes looked to be painted with the color yellow ochre.

Unusual. Striking. Again, against porcelain pale skin and rich mahogany hair, a study in contrast.

Davion had learned all about color and its use at university during his studies of art. He couldn't help but compare Lijsbet to a finely executed painting. Classic, elegant, yet innovative, all at the same time.

The sound of his name called him back to the conversation. 'Twas Lily herself. He realized he'd been staring. She was riveting him with those ochre eyes, and none too kindly.

"Earl Price. Are you well? You have not eaten a bite," she said, blotting her mouth with a linen.

Davion glanced down at his plate. She was correct. The food he had heaped upon it was untouched. Begrudgingly, he lifted his eating knife.

"I am well. Not terribly hungry. I visited a bakkerij this morn and overindulged on fritour. Has ruined my appetite, 'twould seem." He frowned down at his plate, then replaced his knife in its slot on his belt. He glanced toward the kitchen, where Jehan stood, a cloth over one arm. "Jehan, please bring the treats to table."

A deluge of emotions warred in him. He had never experienced these feelings before, not until he met the puzzling Lady Lisbet. His only concern, up until now, had been studying art, and taking care not to destroy his own body.

What was happening to him? What was this flare of hot emotion threatening to burn a hole clear through his chest? The flames leapt higher every time Master Bouts leaned toward Lijsbet, spoke her name, or laid his hand over hers.

Davion had not much experience with the ladies. He went from the living the life of a spoiled, aristocratic child—an only child—to that of a dedicated student of the arts. In University, he had few friends—'twas far too risky to be in contact with many people. Most did not understand him anyway, assuming him to be yet another rich noble's son with an ego bigger than his brain.

At just barely twenty-one, the earl was shamed by his secret truth: he had never been with a woman. He was, in the male form, a virgin.

This was unheard of, and a most embarrassing state of affairs. But there was nothing to be done for it. Nothing he had ever wanted to be done for it. He had his studies, his obsession with art, with history, with improving his status in the eyes of the guild members. Earl Price had been satisfied with his life.

Until now.

Yet the truth hung over him like the blade of a guillotine. 'Twould be impossible for Davion to develop a relationship with a woman—any woman. Romantic liaisons meant physical contact. Embraces, entangled limbs, and more. He knew he was far too fragile to engage in these activities.

'Twas a painful pinch in his heart, the realization of how lonely life would remain. Unless he could be cured.

Would Dr. Vanderhoff be able to cure him?

As the flames of jealousy burned in his chest and pangs of loneliness echoed throughout his being, Davion realized that, for the first time in his life, he wanted to be different than the man he had been. He yearned for human contact. He wanted Lily.

Was a heart made of glass capable of love?

# Chapter Ten

*Lisjbet*

Lijsbet found her initial reaction to Master Bouts—distaste and fear—had faded since their first meeting. Sitting at table with other men of the trade, as she was quite accustomed to, eased her discomfort. Mayhap the master meant no transgression by his overt friendliness. Mayhap she had been too sensitive, too defensive.

The wine, she was certain, helped ease her discomfort as well.

Having her chaperone by her side also steadied her. The earl certainly was an eccentric, there was no doubt. Although Davion was behaving oddly this night, even more so than usual. Still, she couldn't deny the fact she enjoyed the warmth of his body beside her, the scent he carried as proudly as his title.

Not such a bad situation, her ending up under his supervision, she decided. He was well-educated and knowledgeable in the arts, as well as a member of the nobility. The earl was also very pleasing to look at, although much too young for her to consider as more than a colleague.

The evening passed quickly, and before Lijsbet had a chance to get to know all of the painters with whom she'd dined, 'twas time to return to the beguinage. A mixture of disappointment and some other emotion overtook her when the earl's fingers touched her arm and he murmured, "The hour grows late, Lady Lambert. We should return to Groot Beginjnhof."

What was the other emotion? Whatever 'twas, it warmed her from the inside out, and she felt her cheeks grow warm. Too much wine, mayhap.

As she stood, the room tilted a bit. Aye, she had imbibed to excess. She should be more careful about that in the future. The habit had gotten her into trouble more than once in Tournai.

At the door, Master Bouts made a spectacle of lifting her hand to his lips, lingering there longer than necessary. Lijsbet could barely contain the urge to shrink away from his touch. Even now, although she had come to feel easier around him, she mistrusted the man. His hands, she noticed, even his lips, were cold.

Bouts acted as though Earl Price was either not present or had waxed invisible. He growled, "I should like to see you again, Lady Lambert. Mayhap alone next time." He slanted a look toward the earl as he stepped closer to Lijsbet's side.

"The light is fading. 'Tis time to depart," Price said curtly, slipping his hand under Lijsbet's arm.

Twilight had cast the streets into deep shadows. The alleyway leading back to Groot Beginjnhof was, thankfully, lit by widely spaced torches. Lijsbet breathed a sigh of relief. The thought of passing through the dark, narrow passageway had her skin lifting into gooseflesh.

"Did you enjoy meeting the guild members, my lady?" Davion asked. He had not released her arm, and seemed to be carefully pacing his steps to stay in time with her own. Lijsbet released the breath she hadn't realized she'd been holding.

"I did. Thank you for escorting me, Lord Price. I do believe the evening would have been fraught with discomfort had you not been by my side."

Admitting so prickled Lijsbet's pride, but 'twas true. Master Bouts unnerved her. Even though she had lived and worked among male artists for most of her life, never before had she feared for her safety. For one of the very few times in her life she could remember, after today's earlier meeting with Bouts, Lijsbet had known this kind of fear.

Earl Price's tone was low and ominous. "I do not trust the man myself, sad to say. He has an excellent reputation as a painter, and much prestige and influence with the guild. But as a man..." The earl paused in his step and turned to face her. "I beg of you, Lily. Please use my given name. I would much prefer you call me Davion."

Lijsbet laid her free hand on her throat, where she could feel the clamminess of her skin and the rapid pulse beating beneath. Was it the dampness of the evening, or the effect of the wine? Or, mayhap, the warmth of the long, comforting fingers curled around her arm? She met his gaze.

Even in the dim light, their brilliant blue color was unmistakable. Such a contrast against hair as dark as the night. The torchlight sparkled in them, and for a brief moment, Lijsbet swooned.

*Aye, God's breath. Too much wine.*

"My lady, are you unwell?" Davion's grip on her arm tightened as she swayed. She lifted her hand to her brow.

"Just a might dizzy," she sputtered. "The wine, I think."

*Davion*

Davion was completely out of his element. Not only was his experience with the opposite sex lacking, but with his condition, the thought of helping someone else in danger of falling seemed impossible.

Yet he must. This was his charge. His *Lily*. He did not hesitate.

She did not flinch when he wrapped his arm around her waist and slowly backed her up to the brick wall to steady her.

"Shall I call for help, Lily?" He glanced in one direction, then the other. They were quite alone in the alley, without a soul to be seen. "I cannot leave you here, unattended, to go for help. If you cannot continue, my lady, I... I shall have to carry you."

No sooner had the words left his lips than he froze. Where had that come from? *Carry her?* Was he daft? The simple act of lifting her slender form into his arms would shatter the long bones of his arms to shards on the ground. Yet for once in his life, Davion was speaking without thinking, without worrying, without panicking. His duty was to protect the lady, as he had promised the duke. And protect her he would.

He did, however, breathe a sigh of relief to hear her next words.

"Nay, nay," she sputtered. "I just need a moment." Her eyelids fluttered closed.

Time stretched out as darkness grew thicker around them. The only sounds came from the sputtering of the flames on the torches, punctuating each breath he took. He rubbed his hands up and down her arms.

"Does this happen to you often?" he murmured, unable to hide the concern in his voice.

She shook her head. "Nay. Much has happened in the past days, and I did not sleep well at the beguinage. Strange surroundings." Her golden eyes opened then and locked on his. "And you, Earl Price. You have an unsettling effect on me." She spoke barely above a whisper.

His gaze fell from her eyes to her mouth, full and lush. A fiery ball formed quickly in his middle. The tension in the air between them was palpable, almost crackling as were the torches lining the alley. Davion's breath grew shallow, and a bead of sweat trickled down his back beneath his tunic. Paralyzed, he knew not what he should—or could—do next.

"Davion?"

*She had used his given name.* 'Twas almost permission, he thought. He wanted to kiss her, and badly. Knowing he could not pained him.

"Yes, Lily? What is it?" He could barely hear for his own heart pounding in his chest, which normally frightened him. His body was so frail, so fragile, so prone to splinter into shards at the slightest touch—

She did not give him a chance to form another thought. Before he could deny her, try to explain, make excuses. Before he could draw the next breath, Lijsbet had lifted herself onto her toes, laid one hand gently on each shoulder, and pressed her lips against his.

Davion's breathing ceased and he held himself very still. Her touch was gentle enough, but he'd never been touched this way before. He'd never dared. As a result, he had no idea how much pressure his skin could endure before the stress cracks began. Before the inevitable breaking apart of his glass exterior commenced.

The heady scent of wine on her lips made his senses spin, his world tilt on its axis. This too, was a luxury Davion knew little about. He had never permitted himself more than a single glass of any drink that might dull his senses. He simply couldn't take that chance. Imagine, him, staggering drunk, only to smash himself to bits with a simple bump into a doorjamb?

This sweet aroma, though, and the sensation of warm flesh upon his own was tantalizing. A drug in itself. When he felt the tip of her tongue run along his lips, he shuddered all over. Was this what he'd been missing out on all of his life? God's bones, 'twas almost worth the risk.

All of his senses screamed that 'twas definitely worth the risk.

Slowly, carefully, he slid his hands around her waist, marveling at the realization that his fingers encircled her nearly completely. Like a bird, she was fine-boned, seemingly delicate—at least physically. Mayhap she would understand the need to be gentle.

He parted his lips on a sigh, and she breached them. Aye, she tasted of the wine, hot and tempting, sweet and inviting. She tilted her head for better access, than began an exploration of his mouth he'd never imagined. Tongues, tangling. Trembling all over now, his knees wobbled.

A moment ago, he feared he'd need to help Lijsbet stay on her feet. Now, 'twas himself he worried for.

Her hands wandered up until they were locked behind his neck, her fingers combing into the short hair on his nape. Tingles shot down his spine, circling around him, consuming him.

"Nay," he breathed, panting, as he took a step away. "I cannot, Lily."

The hurt look in her eyes shot through his heart like an arrow. "But why, Davion? We are both adults. I am no innocent maiden, and answer to no one."

Shaking his head, Davion ran his fingers through his short-cropped hair. "I am your escort, your chaperone, Lily. I promised the duke—"

"You promised the duke to protect me from harm. I do not see you as a threat, Davion. You cannot deny the attraction that exists between us." She stepped closer then, close enough for her soft body to press against his.

"Nay, I cannot deny I want you, Lily. But 'tis not only my position as your chaperone. I have a... a condition," he began. He was stammering now, embarrassingly so. "The duchess arranged for me to see a doctor here. 'Twas where I was this afternoon, when I should have been with you, watching over you."

Tiny furrows appeared between her eyebrows and she tipped her head. With the back of one hand, she brushed his cheek, sending another shudder through him. "What is it, Davion? An illness? An injury?"

As much as his body urged him forward, his mind clenched tight. Folding his arms, he turned away from her. "I cannot risk injury, Lily. Mayhap after future visits with Dr. Vanderhoff, I will be better able to cope with this incapacity."

He felt her hands on his shoulders. "I am sorry, Davion. I did not realize you were ill. Forgive me." Then, almost under her breath, he heard her say,

"What a shameless wench you must think of me." She released his shoulders, then clasped his hand gently in hers. "Come. Walk me back to my quarters."

*Lijsbet*

They spoke no more words until the front door of Groot Beginjnhof stood before them. Lijsbet had been silently berating herself with every step since their encounter. 'Twas true, he must think her a shameless wench. Not only had her reputation followed her from Tournai, but now she'd proven her brazen nature. She should be overcome with guilt.

Yet, by God, she was not. She was no man's woman, but her own. Why should she feel guilt for expressing desires born unto her from nature? Her pride was wounded by his rejection, true. But she believed him when he said 'twas not that he did not desire her. She could not help but wonder about his *condition*. She'd noticed how carefully he moved, as if afraid of breaking some part of his body. But what part? Its entirety, 'twould seem.

She wished she could ask Isabella, since the duchess obviously knew of his illness. He'd said as much—the duchess arranged for him to see a physician.

With a small sigh, she turned toward Davion after rattling the brass knocker on the door.

"I hope I did not offend you this eve, Lord Price," she murmured. Better to resume more formal address for now.

Still, standing there in the dark, his scent surrounding her in a dreamlike fog, Lijsbet could not help herself. Again, she lifted onto her toes to press one quick, gentle kiss on his lips. He did not back away.

Of course, 'twas at the very same moment the door swung open, revealing a wide-eyed young novice whose hand quickly covered her mouth.

# Chapter Eleven

*Davion*

Davion wandered away from Groot Beginjnhof in a daze. Lily had shocked him, pleased him greatly, but also frightened him. She knew not of his physical impairment. She was not aware he could not return her amorous advances.

He dared not.

God knew he wanted to. Lily had awakened in him a dragon he'd managed to keep sleeping all of his young adult life. Now, he could almost hear the dragon's roar.

He was a man with natural desires. 'Twas unnatural for him to deny them. Yet to indulge could mean the destruction of his entire being.

As he made his way down the darkened alleyway back to the artists' residence, the earl pondered his options. Dr. Vanderhoff told him he would return within a fortnight. 'Twas too long a time. He and Lily may not even still be in Leuven then. There must be another way.

Yet his only way to contact the doctor was through a man he was quickly coming to despise. Master Dieric Bouts.

When he returned to the artists' house, he found only Bouts and one other artist—Petrus Christus, another young painter who had taken over the workshop of the famed Jan van Eyck, eight years prior. Davion shrank in their presence, fully knowledgeable he was in the company of some of the most respected artist guild members. He found them sitting in the common room, sharing goblets of drink and discussing a woman.

"As talented as she is attractive," Bouts was saying. "At least, 'twas the opinion of Rogier."

"Hmm, so I have been told. A bit high strung, but not prone to make many demands—"

The earl soon realized the woman of whom they spoke was Lijsbet. His entire body tensed, and he cleared his throat to announce his presence. Both men looked up, not a trace of embarrassment apparent on their faces.

"So. I see you have returned. So quickly, Earl Price! We both felt certain we would not see you until the morn," Bouts spewed. Davion noticed his speech was slurred.

"And why might you assume that?" he asked.

Both men chuckled. "Come now, Price. We all know the lady's reputation—and I use that term loosely. The Master in Tournai spoke very highly of her, well, her attributes." Bouts paused to refill his goblet. "So talented is she, the master actually spoke briefly of considering breaking with custom. Admitting her to the guild." He took a long drink, then belched.

*Disgusting.*

Davion's age, he quickly realized, put him at a distinct disadvantage here. While Lijsbet was cohabitating with the Master in Tournai, he was still yet a boy, a student at university. Rumors of this sort would have never reached his ears. Now, the mere thought of these two arrogant men discussing Lily with such disrespect made his skin twitch with ire.

She was, he reminded himself, eight years his senior. He had just met her. He was, in truth, nothing more than her overseer. Why did this talk upset him so?

Choosing to dismiss the subject entirely, Davion stepped forward and snatched an empty goblet off the sideboard. As he filled it, he asked, "Master Bouts. Dr. Vanderhoff indicated he would be returning within a fortnight. Where, may I ask, may I contact him in the meantime? I have important matters to discuss with him."

Bouts' eyebrows rose. "Why, in his residence on the north side of the city, of course. I can give you the address. I cannot guarantee he is to be found there. He travels quite a bit."

The wine tasted bitter on Davion's tongue, almost making him wonder if it had gone sour.

"If you would be so kind as to share his location, I would be very appreciative."

With a scrap of parchment in his hand bearing the information he requested, Davion forced himself to swallow what was left in the cup, then turned to leave. "I bid you gentlemen good evening. The days' events have tired me."

"Price," Bouts bark stopped him in the doorway. "What did Dr. Vanderhoff have to say about your condition? Did he believe he could help you?"

A long, silent moment hung on the air before Davion responded. With his back still to the room, he murmured, "The doctor wishes to gather more information about my heritage. Although I do not see as how this could enlighten him on my condition, I have no choice but to wait."

"Ah, but perhaps it could shed some light on the matter," Bouts continued. "I have known your family for quite a long time. Since you were a child, although our paths never crossed again before you left for University."

Davion turned slowly to stare at the artist. Had the answer to his illness lain here, right before his eyes all of this time? Did Bouts know something about his family that could help put things to right?

His heart sank when he saw the artist's eyes drop to his cup, and he began shaking his head. " 'Tis a shame, truly, the tragedy your family endured. But 'tis not my place to speak of it. These things are better discussed with a man who possesses training in the field."

Davion clenched his fists, then thought better of the move, making a deliberate attempt to relax his fingers. "What tragedy, Master Bouts? What do you know about my family history?"

His narrowed eyes were cold as they studied the earl's face. "Only rumors, dear boy. All I have heard are rumors. I would not wish to taint the doctor's plan of treatment for you with unsubstantiated tales that may, or may not, be true." Bouts drained his own mug, then wiped the rim with a linen and rose to leave. "I'm afraid you'll have to obtain what information you require from Dr. Vanderhoff yourself."

That night, as he tossed and tangled in the bedclothes on the narrow cot in his quarters, Davion drifted in and out of a restless sleep. Snatches of a dream—a nightmare, a memory?—taunted him, remaining just out of his reach. Sounds echoed in his brain. Wails of grief, a woman's grief. *His mother.* A sickly scent, pungent herbs and the unmistakable miasma of death. Sunlight spilling relentlessly through glass. *Stained glass.* He bolted upright to a scream he realized had come from his own throat. His roommate, grumbling in his sleep, barked a curse and turned his back toward the earl.

His entire body was soaked in sweat, and his heart raced so fast he could barely hear for the blood rushing in his ears. There was a heaviness in his chest, a feeling as though he had sinned, or committed a serious crime. 'Twas barely dawn, only the faintest hint of pink peeking over the rooftops of the houses across the street. Quickly, Davion rose and dressed. Then, clutching the address of Dr. Vanderhoff in one sweaty hand, he crept from the room and down the stairs to the street.

He'd been plagued by nightmares before, all of his life, it seemed. Many ended the way this one did. 'Twas the root of his fear, he was certain. But why? Where had these fears, or memories, come from?

Dr. Vanderhoff may be able to help him sort out their meaning. Something, he was sure, had happened to him, mayhap when he was a small child, to instill this fear within him. Yet time after time he examined his own skin. No scars were evident, anywhere.

Deep in his heart Davion knew, however, the frailty of that skin. How fragile 'twas. How careful he must be in all he did.

The streets were empty and quiet as the light grew, a hazy sun appearing in a sky streaked with white and blue. Like a painting, he thought. Davion, although he possessed no talent nor any desire to produce the fantastic works of art the painters did, could certainly appreciate their inspiration. 'Twas all around them, everywhere, if one simply stopped long enough to look and take notice.

What of the miniaturists, he wondered? What possessed artists like Lily to produce images that, even if they did contain vignettes of real-life scenes, were entangled within a jungle of acanthus leaves and mysterious figures. Where did the inspiration come from to depict bizarre animals that did not exist in the real world? And always hiding, hiding within a dense tangle of vines.

Davion pondered this, and thought to ask Dr. Vanderhoff what he thought of artists compelled to create such tiny, intricate yet mysterious masterpieces.

*Lisjbet*

The sisters at Groot Beginjnhof were quiet around Lijsbet the following day, not nearly as friendly as they had been initially. She was certain news of the scene on the doorstep had by now spread through the abbey like the plague. Even the Mistress, Sister Fenna, had not made eye contact with her at table this morn.

They, too, must all think her a shameless wench. Would they cast her out? After all, this was a cloister of women who had pledged their lives to God. Being caught in the doorway in the act of physically accosting a man—had Davion considered it an accost?—this surely must brand her a sinner.

She took her time with her bread and cheese, and was the last to leave the table. Sister Rikita, the cook, came from the kitchen to collect the empty platters just as Lijsbet was leaving.

"Goedermorgen, Lady Lambert. Did you sleep well?" she asked.

Lijsbet blew out a breath. "Nay. 'Twill take me time to accustom myself to a new environment."

The cook crossed her arms, cocking a hip as she studied Lijsbet. "Don't be bothered by the sisters' avoidance of you, my lady. Aye, we all heard of your tryst on the steps with your chaperone. But 'tis no business of ours what you do with your life. You are a free woman."

Lijsbet blinked, surprised at Rikita's forwardness, but instantly comforted by the woman's words. "I am sorry to have caused any disruption," she said. "I will admit, I do feel quite out of place among you, who are women of God."

Rikita snorted, a gruff, unladylike sound. "We are not nuns, my lady. We are beguines. Has no one explained to you the difference?"

A few moments later Lijsbet found herself seated on a bench in the kitchen garden beside Sister Rikita. Both held a copper tin of ale in their laps. Rikita slurped nearly half of hers, then wiped her mouth on her sleeve. Lijsbet fought to keep her eyebrows from lifting.

"We of Groot Beginjnhof are not, you see, formally recognized by the church. We come to the beguinage voluntarily and take no vows. We are free to leave at any time. In fact, some resent our rather, shall we say, unconventional status." Her mouth quirked up at one corner. "Now 'tis true, as long as we live here and claim status of a beguine, we cannot marry. We live a life of prayer and serve the poor, but we are forbidden to preach or teach. We are frowned upon by some. But remember, unlike the nuns," she drained her cup and hit Lijsbet with a stern stare, "we are still women, not merely vessels of holiness."

Lijsbet did not understand. She'd always thought the beguines were just another sect of nuns. She met Rikita's gaze. "So, you do not condemn me for my actions?"

Again, Rikita snorted and shook her head. "If anything, I would wager the young postulate who encountered you with the earl may have experienced some jealousy. As many of us might. But we do not judge."

"Then why were the sisters so silent this morning? Even Sister Fenna refused to meet my gaze."

"We do not want to interfere with your life, my lady. How you decide to conduct yourself with Earl Price—with any man, or woman, for that matter—is none of our business. You are our guest, not a new member of our group." Rikita rose and held out her hand to help Lijsbet to her feet. "I'm sure you will find nothing has changed of the atmosphere in the scriptorium this morning. In fact, I believe one of the sisters wanted to show you a new process she has been developing for applying the gold leaf to the illuminations."

Surprised, relieved, and a little numb, Lijsbet made her way to the scriptorium where she found, as Rikita had said, a young postulate waiting for her at her work bench.

Even as she struggled to keep her concentration on the process Sister Benoit was attempting to teach her, Lijsbet's mind wandered. 'Twas as though she could not free her nostrils of Earl Price's unique scent. Could not wash the taste of his lips from her own. Could not erase the feelings she had experienced when her body was pressed so close to his.

'Twas lust, of that she was certain. But is that all 'twas? She found herself with an ache in her chest resembling affection, the same which she had developed for the Master in Tournai for all those years. Dangerous emotions, these. Yet with the earl, 'twas different. He was younger. He was English, and would be returning, she felt certain, to his homeland when 'twas time to claim his earlship.

Davion, although her overseer, was not, she acknowledged, forbidden to her. A mature woman—spinster, even—had nothing to hide, need ask no permissions. Lijsbet was free to pursue a relationship with the man, if he were willing, without commitment. Without the faintest glimmer of hope for a lasting relationship.

Without hope for love.

Even with this knowledge, the yearning, that which had begun as a spark of irritation with the contrary nature of the man, had begun to burn quietly within her. 'Twas growing, like a flame to which dry leaves were fed. In like manner, the desire felt dangerous.

Why should she not pursue him?

He was younger, for one. Mayhap that was his reason for balking at her advances. Mayhap he saw her as an old woman. A spinster. Something within her told her, though, 'twas not the case.

He had reacted to her kiss. Not that any young, healthy man's body would not react to a woman's kiss, but...

*Healthy.* Was he? He spoke of an illness. Was it of body or mind?

As her fingers played delicately over the thin wisps of gold she applied to the illuminations, Lijsbet made her decision: she would discover the cause of Earl Price's illness. 'Twould help make her future path clear when it came to pursuing a relationship with him. Mayhap, whatever ailed him, she might help him to overcome it.

Although never a very religious woman, Lijsbet whispered a silent prayer that whatever Davion Price's problem, 'twould not keep the two of them apart.

# Chapter Twelve

*Davion*

The residence at 625 Noordeinde was a two-story, brick structure closely flanked on one side by an almost identical building. On the other side, a gate blocked the view of a narrow alley, mayhap a terrace. Davion studied the wrinkled paper in his hands, matching the number to that on the metal plate beside the door. He stood this way for what seemed a very long time, alone in a street that remained, thankfully, quiet and vacant.

He stepped up onto the stoop and rattled the knocker. Behind one of the two multi-paned windows facing the street, he saw a lace curtain stir. Footsteps followed.

The entry swung wide and the doctor himself stood inside the doorway, his generous form nearly filling it. He squinted at Davion before recognition took hold. Then he bobbed his head.

"Earl Price. I was not expecting you." His voice sounded gravelly. Davion wondered if he'd awoken the man.

"I need to speak with you, right away," Davion began, worrying the paper bearing the address between his fingers. "I realize not enough time has passed for your research to have even begun. But after speaking with Master Bouts last evening, it seems information may be easier to come by than we thought."

The doctor's lips pressed together, and he stared at Davion for a long moment. Finally, as if just realizing his lack of manners, he stepped aside and motioned for the earl to enter. "Come in, Lord Price. I am sorry. I was rather distracted. Deep into some reading."

Moments later Davion found himself perched on a straight-backed, wooden chair in the front room of Vanderhoff's house. The seat was cushioned, for which he was grateful. Sweat washed over his skin as he endured the doctor's scrutiny.

"What is it Master Bouts could tell you, Earl Price? I was not aware he had any training in such matters, regarding what ails you." Vanderhoff narrowed his eyes.

Davion shook his head. "Nay, no information on my condition. He alluded to the fact that he knew information about my family." He paused. "He said they were only rumors, but he had knowledge of some tragedy my family endured."

Vanderhoff reached up to run his fingers along his jaw. "I see. I had forgotten about this. When Master Bouts first contacted me, he asked me if I knew what happened to your sister. If the tragedy might be a causative for your distress." He shook his head, his jowls wobbling. "A terrible shame. Word of the accident spread quickly through the nobility, clear across the channel."

Instead of feeling fragile, Davion's entire body now went to stone. He stared at Vanderhoff, his jaw working. He was unable to make the words come out. Finally, he stuttered, "I... I am an only ch-child."

Vanderhoff sat forward in his chair. "You do not remember your sister, Diana?"

The room began to spin. Davion's vision waxed and waned, as though the light in the room fluctuated from dim to bright. Vanderhoff's face became blurry, gradually melting, like a candle left too close to the hearth. Soon his facial features were no longer distinguishable. A pale smear between two slashes of dark. Davion grabbed for handles, but the chair had none. He could not afford to fall. He could not—

When he opened his eyes, Davion saw only a blank ceiling above him, one where the plaster had cracked. The pattern resembled a spiderweb, spanning from one side of the small room to the other. He had no idea where he was. He lay there for a moment, confused and afraid to move. Was this the room in the artists' residence? He'd not noticed the poor condition of the plaster before. But then, it was always dark when he'd retired.

The sound of a door creaking startled him so badly, he cried out. Yet he dared not leap up. Carefully turning his head in the direction of the noise, he saw the figure of Dr. Vanderhoff, who looked every bit as frightened as Davion felt.

"Lord Price, are you well? I have sent my assistant to fetch a barber-surgeon. I feared you may have injured yourself when you fell." Dr. Vanderhoff's voice was breathy and hushed. Furrows dug deep between his eyebrows.

"When I fell," Davion repeated. "What part of me suffered a fracture?" A hint of panic made his voice sound high-pitched, even to his own ears.

Dr. Vanderhoff's head shook, jostling his jowls once again. "Nay, I do not believe you damaged any bones. But you did hit your head rather sharply on the hearth. You did not move at all for a very long time. I feared," he paused to cross himself in haste, "I feared you might be dead."

Now the doctor was standing over Davion, who still lay prone on a narrow, hard pallet. A painful pulsating, he realized, emanated from his right temple. He raised a hand to his forehead, expecting to feel the keen edges of broken glass. "Not dead." He was shocked to feel smooth skin under his fingers. He examined his hand. No blood, either.

As if reading his mind, the doctor said, "You didn't even break the skin, though you may have a nasty bump by the morn."

Confusion whirled Davion's mind into a frenzy. This was impossible. He could not have fallen, rapped his head onto the unyielding stone of a hearth, and come away whole. He would have cracks, if nothing else.

*And what had caused him to fall?*

The moment the question flashed into his mind, it evaporated into a hazy mist. He blinked fast, trying to catch it, to remember his last thought. 'Twas no use. 'Twas gone.

Slowly, Davion pushed himself to his elbows.

"No, pray thee," Dr. Vanderhoff held out both hands. "Pray thee lie still until the barber-surgeon arrives."

Ignoring the doctor's plea, Davion swung both feet to the floor. He held his arms out in front of him, lifting the cuff of each sleeve in turn. No cracks, no breaks. Not even a scratch.

How was this possible?

"Are you well? Are you in any pain?" the doctor asked.

Davion touched his head again, gingerly, in the spot where there was the dull ache had now escalated to sharp throbbing.

"The skull. The bone is probably crushed under my skin," he murmured to himself. "But then, why am I not dead?" He glared at the doctor. "How can this be?"

At that moment voices reached them from beyond the doorway.

"Dr. Bakker is here. Be still, pray thee." Vanderhoff scurried out the door, wringing his hands. He returned shortly, accompanied by a tall, thin man with craggy features beneath cloud-white hair.

"What has happened here?" The man's voice was surprisingly deep for such a lanky form. He looked to be older than Vanderhoff by some years. He came to Davion's side and crouched beside him. "Where are you injured, my lord?"

"I struck my head, I am told," Davion replied. He fingered the tender spot above his temple. " 'Tis no blood, but I fear the glass beneath is quite ruined."

Davion tried to ignore the look that passed between the two men. As if he had spoken in an unknown language, or said something profane.

As if he were mad.

*Lijsbet*

Lijsbet worked side by side with Sister Mila on a prayer book until the bell for sext tolled. All the beguines who remained at their tables, along with Mila, scurried out. Prayer before the noon meal, apparently, she thought. They'd been so engrossed in their work, time had accelerated.

*I will continue working until the hour of prayer is finished. There is one more detail I want to add to this page.*

It was not one she had felt comfortable drawing with Sister Mila by her side.

In all of the beguines' illuminations she'd studied, she remembered seeing not one unusual creature. Plenty of birds, some deer, and an occasional hare. But no beasts. All real-life animals. Nothing from the dark of the forest, from the places where men were afraid to tread.

This one had begun its existence as a boar, but gained the wings of a dragon and the talons of a hawk somewhere along the way. She was in the process of adding a beard, but not of the kind found on a dragon. *A man's beard*, she thought with a smirk.

In black ink against the pale vellum, 'twas hardly noticeable. But once she finished adding a rainbow-hued coat and sparks of gold to its eyes, the mythical beast would truly come alive. Or so it would seem.

Lijsbet loved tucking these creatures within the vines of her borders. Rare were the eyes who even noticed her tiny beasts, hiding in the thicket. Yet somehow, putting them there made her feel a sense of justice. Of completion.

Her artwork dare not come close to the sacred text. 'Twould, however, declare its importance anyway. Silently.'Twas her signature, the one she was forbidden to add to her creations.

As she worked, using the sharpest point of a small quill and ink, her mind wandered back to her chaperone. Earl Price. How, she wondered, was he spending his day? Was he thinking of her the way she was of him?

The figure she drew was of a beast not known in this world. A *babewyn*, the Master of Tournai would have called it. He did not disapprove of her fondness of inserting these tiny aberrations into the Books of Hours she illuminated for the school. In fact, at first, they amused him. He would taunt her about them, deep in the night when their two bodies could come no closer.

*"Where do these visions come from, my beloved? Do they flash across your mind as you work? Why are they so small and ugly?"* He would tickle her then, *walking his fingers like the creatures' legs down from her chin to her neck.*

"Are you coming to the noon meal, Lady Lambert?"

With a sickening scratch, her quill jolted, sending a splatter of ink onto her work desk. Looking up, she saw Sister Mila standing beside her, eyes wide and mouth open. She raised her fingers to her lips.

"What have you done?" the young beguine gasped.

"I have seen such drawings before," Sister Fenna said. She stood behind Lijsbet, looking over her shoulder. The other beguines were clustered around her, all craning to see what she had drawn.

*Too close,* she thought. *I can feel their breath upon my neck.*

"Some of the monks from Ghent draw these. Unnatural looking creatures, are they not?" the Mistress continued. Her dark eyebrow rose as she glared down at Lijsbet, though her tone bore no ill will. "What possesses you to insert them, so small and so hidden they may go unnoticed?"

Lijsbet knew, simply by the way the Mistress said the words, that Fenna knew exactly why she dreamed up and tucked the babewyns into her illuminations. In Books of Hours. Books entirely devoted to prayer.

"Of what devotional significance have these?" Fenna asked, tilting her head. "Or are they simply distractions of the artist's mind?"

Lijsbet fidgeted, avoiding the mistress' glare. "Every artist deserves to add his own personal touch to his work. Or hers," she sputtered. "Do you not agree, Sister Fenna?"

The quirk at the corner of her lips betrayed the mistress, and Lijsbet's shoulders dropped on a whooshing breath. Thanks to God, she would not be cast out of Groot Beginjnhof for adding her signature beasts to the illuminations.

Part of her was surprised. Another, pleased. 'Twould be a disaster to earn the scorn of the beguines for augmenting her illuminations with such imaginative—mischievous, mayhap *ungodly* creatures.

'Twould also be very confusing, especially now. She had not drawn their ire for kissing a man on their front steps, so surely they would not shun her for this tiny transgression.

The atmosphere in the scriptorium changed so suddenly, Lijsbet could hardly believe she was still within the beguinage. Suddenly the sisters were more than cordial; now they became outright friendly. There was conversation in the room, random chatter that had not gone on before. The reverent hush Lijsbet had assumed was usual for a place such as this had been lifted. A lock had been broken.

The beguines suddenly saw Lijsbet as more than a guest, a fellow artist. More than just the daughter of the duke. To them she had suddenly became human.

They saw her as a woman, just like them.

'Twas not until the bell rang for vespers the thought of her chaperone, Lord Price crossed her mind again. The day was nearly over, and he had not come to see her. To check on her, as was his duty.

A sadness clutched at Lijsbet's heart, followed quickly by anger. 'Twas her usual progression, she mused. The easiest way to lay balm to a wound was to sheath it in anger.

Lord Price had abandoned her again. Two days in a row. How dare he? She would remember to mention this to the duchess upon their return—

Or should she be worried 'twas her actions of last eve keeping him away? She had offended him, scared him off. Shocked him, surely. She had, very effectively, extinguished whatever spark may have existed between them.

Her anger was not enough to keep this worry away. 'Twas a calamity of her own doing. She should be cross with herself, for her own actions.

An endless loop, this. Resentment, then anger. Worry, then anger again. She shall never sleep this night, Lijsbet thought.

*I must go to the artists' residence. This very night.*

# Chapter Thirteen

*Lisjbet*

"Sister Fenna, may I have the luxury of Sister Wilhelmina as a chaperone this evening? I must leave the beguinage. It appears Earl Price has abandoned me yet again."

All conversation at table ceased when she spoke the request, and every eye turned upon her. Lijsbet was not surprised. She knew it would probably have been wiser to ask in private. But she had made up her mind; she was going through the alleyway to the artists' residence tonight, chaperone or no.

The mistress blotted her mouth and laid her eating knife on the edge of the pewter plate with a click. Her gaze slid from Lijsbet to Wilhelmina, and back again. She was measuring her words, surely.

"Where is it you need to travel? At such a late hour? 'Twill be dark soon. 'Tis not safe—"

"I know 'tis an unusual request, but I shall not be gone long. I must go to the artists' residence. I must see if all is well with Lord Price."

Realization washed over the mistress' features, followed by an expression Lijsbet clearly read as sympathy. She tipped her head. The pity made her stomach clench.

*She thinks I'm chasing after the man.*

"What reason do you have to believe something has gone amiss? Mayhap Lord Price had other business to attend. Mayhap he means simply to allow you your independence."

Lijsbet was shaking her head. "Nay, you do not understand. He has an illness. A condition. He shared this with me last evening." She laid down her napkin and rose, smoothing her coarse, brown frock as she stepped away from the table. "I must go, Sister Fenna. I would rather not go alone."

The Mistress' eyes flashed again to Wilhelmina, who pushed to her feet.

"I will accompany you, Lady Lambert. 'Twill be my pleasure."

Sister Wilhelmina, if not for her high-pitched, lilting voice, could well have been a man disguised under the robes of a beguine. She was a massive woman, towering over Lijsbet by almost a head. Broad as well, Wilhelmina had large hands and feet. 'Twas difficult to decipher much more under the habit and wimple, but Lijsbet saw no facial hair, nor any on the backs of her man-sized hands.

Wilhelmina may be a woman, but one very well suited to serve as protector to one traveling alone through a darkened alleyway at dusk.

*I must remember never to anger Sister Wilhelmina. Her fist is bigger than my head.*

"Lord Price seems a very likeable sort of man," Wilhelmina said as they made their way toward the alley. "Soft-spoken. Respectful. I admire those qualities."

Lijsbet picked up the front of her frock and quickened her step, hoping her companion would follow suit. Even though Wilhelmina's legs were much longer than her own, the big woman seemed to be taking her time this evening.

*She probably doesn't get out of the beguinage very often.*

"He has manners," she said, adding, "but he can be a difficult taskmaster. On our first meeting at the scriptorium in Coudenburg, I grew to dislike him quickly."

"You don't seem to dislike him very much now."

Lijsbet cringed. Not only bold of body, but Wilhelmina was also unafraid to speak her mind.

"Nay. I have changed my mind about Lord Price. But he is not well. He told me so. The duchess arranged for him to see a doctor while he is in Leuven."

"Oh, I hope 'tis nothing too serious," the big woman replied. She then fell silent, and Lijsbet quickened her step a bit more.

Even with torches burning every twenty or so steps, the alleyway was like a tunnel that sucked light from the very air. It was a warm evening, but Lijsbet could not stop the shudder quaking her shoulders as they neared the middle of the long path. Would she have dared make this journey alone?

*Aye.* Lijsbet had done many things in her life she found frightening, or distasteful, because she had been compelled to by her situation. Tonight, her sense of urgency overcame any worry for her safety. Which, she acknowledged, was probably not the wisest course of action.

"I am grateful you consented to accompany me, Sister," she said. "This trip has the potential for being intimidating."

She saw the corners of the woman's mouth curve. "Ye shall have no fear with me by your side."

Within minutes they were on the steps of the artists' residence, and Lijsbet rapped on the door. Silence was followed by footsteps. When the doorway yawned open, the house servant—Jehan, she remembered—stood before them. His expression was discomforting. A young man of slight build, he looked more like a boy to her than ever this evening. A boy who had experienced a bad dream.

He blinked round, pale blue eyes at them. "Ah. I was hoping 'twas Master Price returning."

Lijsbet stiffened. "So, he is not here, then?"

"Nay. Master Bouts received word about an... incident. The master has gone to retrieve him."

"From where?"

"From Dr. Vanderhoff's residence. I am sorry. I know nothing more." Jehan appeared suddenly uncomfortable, as if afraid he'd shared too much information. He began to close the door, but Sister Wilhelmina's outstretched arm held it fast.

"Where does this physician live? His address?" Lijsbet snapped, a hint of panic eking its way out through her usually stony facade.

Jehan shook his head. "I know not. I am sorry," he repeated. "I cannot help you." His gaze, which had been darting everywhere except at her face, now lifted to the street behind her. His shoulders relaxed. "Ah. They return."

Lijsbet turned to see three men approaching in the twilight, slowly. Earl Price looked paler than usual, and kept his eyes trained on the cobblestones before him. He was flanked on one side by Master Bouts. On the other, a short, round man Lijsbet assumed to be a monk supported him with a hand curved about the earl's forearm.

"Not food for the crows yet, I see?" Her words were sharp, but betrayed by her tone. The earl glanced up, and 'twas then she saw the raised, reddened area at his temple. She covered her mouth with one hand. "What has happened?"

*Davion*

Davion was still unsteady on his feet—a definite worry for the likes of him—so he did not hesitate to accept Dr. Vanderhoff's offer of help to get back to the artists' residence. The barber-surgeon, after determining no significant damage had been suffered due to Davion's fall, had prescribed an herbal powder for the earl's headache and left.

Davion, however, was not convinced there was no damage, even if unseen by the naked eye. His skull, surely, wore a latticework of cracks now, much like that in the ceiling of Dr. Vanderhoff's guest room. 'Twas simply a matter of time, he was certain, before additional and more serious symptoms surfaced.

He was not prepared to face Lady Lambert. What was she doing here? Did she have some need of his services? Surely he was in no condition—

"The earl suffered a spell. Of dizziness. He slipped from his chair and bumped his head. Nothing serious, we have been assured." Master Bouts wore a stiff, grim expression. "Is there anything we can do for you, Lady Lambert? The barber-surgeon encouraged us to get the earl to his bed for rest at once."

Lijsbet blinked and took a step back, bristling at Bouts' curt attitude. "No, nothing I need. I came out of concern for the earl," she said flatly. "Plainly, my presence here is unnecessary."

*And unwanted.*

Yet as she took hold of Sister Wilhelmina's sleeve and turned to leave, Davion's words stopped her.

"I am sorry I left you unattended for another day, Lil—" He glanced up at Bouts, then at Dr. Vanderhoff. "Lady Lambert. If these gentleman have no objection, I'd like to invite you in for a bit of wine before your return to the beguinage."

Both of his companions dropped hold of his arms like they were hot pokers. Bouts stepped through the doorway and swept an arm inside. "Since the earl has apparently recovered quite completely, please do come in, ladies."

Lijsbet's gaze flickered to the sky above them, fading to twilight as they spoke, then up at Sister Wilhelmina. "I suppose we can visit for a few moments. 'Tis not dark yet."

*Lisjbet*

To Lijsbet's relief, Dr. Vanderhoff left them at the door, and Bouts disappeared shortly after ordering Jehan to bring drink to the guests. They sat in the common room, where she watched as Davion made his way slowly to the most generously cushioned seat. He still looked quite unsteady, causing her stomach to clench. Jehan brought a tray with goblets and a pitcher, which he left on the sideboard. Before the earl had a chance to rise and serve them, Lijsbet lurched to her feet to serve.

"Tell me, Lord Price. What was the cause of your dizzy spell? Was that why you were with Dr. Vanderhoff again today?" She poured modest splashes of the wine into each of the goblets, lifting them to hand to Davion and Wilhelmina. "Did it have to do with your illness?"

Confusion clouded the earl's features, heightening her concern. A bump on the head could, she knew, be a very serious matter. But from what Dr. Vanderhoff said, the barber-surgeon didn't seem to think 'twas the case with the earl.

"I don't believe so. I had gone to see Dr. Vanderhoff this morning to discuss his research of my family history further. We were in the middle of a perfectly normal conversation when suddenly, the room began spinning around me." He blinked, long, dark lashes fluttering once over luminescent blue eyes. "After that, I don't remember more."

Lijsbet pressed her lips together. This illness of his seemed more than a physical ailment, she felt quite certain. She wondered what they had been discussing when his spell began. Unfortunately, the doctor was long gone now, or she would have asked.

"How do you feel now?" she asked, tipping her head. "The swelling on your head. Does it not pain you?"

Davion began to nod, then stopped himself and closed his eyes. "Aye, it does. What I fear most is what damage is hidden beneath the skin."

*But the barber-surgeon was not concerned.*

Glancing out the window, Lijsbet noticed the rapidly fading light. She swallowed the contents of her goblet in one gulp and reached for

Wilhelmina's hand. "I'm afraid then we will have to make our way back to the beguinage. I do not look forward to traversing that long alleyway in the dark."

Davion went to rise, then closed his eyes again and sat down. "I would offer to escort you, but I don't think I would be of much use this evening."

Lijsbet cast a sympathetic glance at Davion. "I wish I could stay and tend to you. Unfortunately, I cannot." Lijsbet called for the house servant, who appeared in the doorway. "Jehan, could you please see Earl Price to his quarters? I'm afraid the good sister and I must take our leave."

As they strode quickly toward the alleyway, arms linked, Sister Wilhelmina said, "Odd. 'Twas told to me the earl was charged to look after *you*. Seems to me your roles may be reversed."

Lijsbet was at a loss for words. What Wilhelmina said was absolutely true. The odder point was this: Lijsbet did not mind the role reversal at all.

She had never been one who had needed taking care of, even as a girl. Her mother had been too busy, too distracted with her own life to pay much mind to an unplanned girl-child clinging to her skirts. Lijsbet learned early on, if she was to stay safe, and make a path in this life, 'twould be on her own.

Mayhap 'twas why she resented Earl Price so. In the beginning. Not so now, though.

They had reached the midpoint of the alleyway—to Lijsbet, the scariest spot—when they heard footsteps approaching from behind them. Lurching to a halt, Wilhelmina spun about and squinted in the flickering torch light. Her posture, rigid at first, softened.

"Oh, not to worry, my lady. 'Tis just Master Bouts. Probably wanting to ensure our safe passage to the beguinage."

'Twas his claim, when he caught up to them. But Lijsbet felt uneasy, noting the gleam in Bouts' eyes, the suppressed smirk on his lips as he chose to walk close beside her. A little too close. He did see them safely to the door of Groot Beginjnhof, but he did not leave.

"Sister Wilhelmina, I would like a word with Lady Lambert before I take my leave, if you do not mind. 'Twill not take long."

Wilhelmina cast a questioning glance at Lijsbet, who wrapped her arms around herself. The evening was not cold, but suddenly she was. She could refuse. She had no chaperone present. Yet Master Dieric Bouts was one of the most powerful artists in the guild. Her career, her future, could well lie in the hands of this man. The shiver that shook her came not from cold.

After a moment's hesitation, she bobbed her head at the beguine, who stood with one foot on the threshold.

" 'Tis fine, Sister. I will be along shortly."

After the heavy door clicked shut, panic rose into Lijsbet's throat. What was she thinking? Alone, in the dark, with this man who looked at her as if she were the most tempting of the meats on a roasted platter.

Keeping her arms hugged around her, she glared directly into Bouts' eyes. "What is it you want, Master Bouts? The hour is late, and I am weary from a long day in the scriptorium."

To her horror, Bouts smirk broke into an unabashed grin, and he stepped closer to her. With the back of one hand, he stroked her cheek. She jerked away.

"Your proximity offends me, my lord. If you have nothing to say, 'tis time for me to retire—"

"Yes," Bouts growled in a low voice, " 'tis exactly what I had in mind."

Staggering back a step, Lijsbet nearly fell when her slippered heel slipped off the stoop. Bouts grabbed her arm, feigning an attempt to steady her. But he did not release her.

"Being weary did not seem to hinder your late-night sessions in the scriptorium in Tournai. At least, 'tis the news I gathered from the master there."

Lijsbet's temper flared. Clenching both fists at her sides, she stepped back up on the stoop, moving so close to Bouts she could smell the wine on his breath. He stood his ground, towering over her, studying her lazily with hooded eyes.

"You offend me, my lord. I resent what you are implying, and will make sure my chaperone—as well as the duke—know of your insolence."

A cold dread washed over her when Bouts threw back his head and laughed out loud. "Do you think the duke will have issue with my attempts to woo you, Lady Lambert? The *duke*? I daresay, if you were not his daughter, he would have beat me to the task."

He still held her upper arm, his grip tightening. Fear bubbled over the anger as sweat broke out all over her body. This man couldn't accost her here, in public? On the steps of a beguinage?

How powerful a guild member *was* this Dieric Bouts?

The thumk of a bolt unlatching made them both lurch. Relief laid a soothing mantle over Lijsbet as the door of the beguinage swung open, revealing the imposing form of the mistress, Sister Fenna.

Although not as big a woman as Wilhelmina, Sister Fenna was not petite by any standards. The expression on her face in this moment had the power to sour fresh milk.

"Lady Lambert, is all well? We heard voices," she snapped, glaring directly at Bouts.

"All is well," he hastened to answer before Lijsbet could utter a word. " 'Twas laughter you heard. We were having a pleasant conversation, the lady and I." His broad smile made Lijsbet's stomach lurch. She flinched as he trailed his fingers along her arm before releasing her. Then he stepped down off the stoop and bowed his head. "I bid thee both farewell." And then, riveting Lijsbet's gaze, he added, "Anon. *Lily.*"

# Chapter Fourteen

*Lijsbet*

Lijsbet arose early the next day, intending to ask for a private audience with the mistress. Although Sister Fenna did not appear to be much older than Lijsbet, for some reason, she felt the woman had perhaps gained a good bit more wisdom in her years than she had herself. Wisdom, at the moment, was a trait Lijsbet sorely needed.

Sister Fenna was, fortunately, the first to take a seat at table that morning. Lijsbet took the liberty of seating herself directly across from the mistress, who studied her with a curious expression.

"Good day, Lady Lambert. You are up before the sun this day." The mistress smiled as she poured herself a goblet, then offered the pitcher to Lijsbet.

"Aye, my lady. I wish to speak with you this morn, if possible. In private."

Fenna nodded silently, her gaze drifting toward the pair of beguines just entering from the hall. "Follow me to the kitchen garden after your meal," she murmured.

Which Lijsbet did, discreetly rising as soon as the mistress and following her through the kitchen and out the door at the rear of the beguinage.

Brilliant sunshine flooded a lush kitchen garden, a garden that appeared to flank the entire length of the building, from what Lijsbet could see, in either direction. Small plots of herbs and various vegetables surrounded the kitchen entrance. Fenna motioned for Lijsbet to follow her along a stone-paved path that wound around the planting beds. In the distance, she could see a broad swath of raised trellises, heavy with grapevines.

*Ah yes,* she remembered. *They make their own wine here, from their very own grapes.*

Thick with a canopy of broad, flat leaves, the air under the arbor was cool and pleasant. Several benches dotted the area. Lijsbet imagined this was a wonderful place where the beguines came to rest or pray. One of the alcoves formed by the meandering trellis was lined with a U-shaped turfed bench, lush with green grass—an exedra, Lijsbet thought. Fenna sat and motioned for her to take the flanking seat.

She arranged the skirt of her habit around her, then folded her hands in her lap and leveled a gaze on Lijsbet. "What is it you wish to speak about, Lady Lambert? Are you displeased with some aspect of your stay here at Groot Beginjnhof?"

Lijsbet shook her head. "Nay, not at all. This is a wonderful place, mistress, and your sisters are very welcoming. Inspiring artists. I have learned so much already." She paused and cleared her throat. "What I wish to speak of is of a more personal nature."

Fenna's eyebrows lifted. "Of Lord Price, then?"

"Aye," Lijsbet began slowly, "but also of Master Bouts. You seem to know the master quite well. I have concerns about him, mistress." Lijsbet held Fenna's gaze for a long, silent moment. "He followed Wilhelmina and I back from the artists' residence last eve."

"Aye."

"Well, you know he asked to speak with me in private. You heard his laughter."

*How can I phrase this without offending? Fenna seemed friendly with Master Bouts.*

She took a deep breath for courage and blurted out the words in a rush. "Bouts was rather forward with me. He insulted me. He also... he propositioned me."

Fenna crossed her arms over her chest, studying Lijsbet with an expression she could not read. Judgement? Nay. Surprise?

Nay, she realized. No surprise at all.

Finally, she spoke. "Master Bouts and I have a history, you might say. Before I came to the beguinage. He is a man of somewhat loose moral codes. He also possesses a very high, shall we say, appetite." She paused and lowered her gaze to the ground. "As a matter of fact, it's the very reason I entered the order. After entertaining the artist for a number years, then realizing he had no permanent arrangement in mind, I became something of a lost soul."

Fenna turned her face away, but before she did Lijsbet saw the sheen of tears in her eyes. Her heart clenched for the woman. They had so very much in common.

"I know exactly the way you feel. My situation in Tournai was much the same. When I escaped, I chose not to enter an order, however. I still have hope of making a life for myself, with or without a man." Lijsbet's voice grew thick with the last words. "Now, though, I will probably resign myself to a solitary life."

"What of Earl Price?" Fenna riveted her eyes once again. " 'Tis plain to see. The attraction between you is obvious. The choice of whether or not to pursue the liaison is solely for you to make."

Lijsbet rocked back. "Is it that obvious? I believed myself more capable of masking my emotions."

She was surprised to hear the mistress' soft laugh. "The signs come not only from you. I believe the earl is quite taken with you, Lijsbet. I realize he is young and hails from England, but that could only work to your advantage. Do you not believe so?" Her lips quirked on one side.

Lijsbet sighed. "The problem is, the earl has an illness. He has not confided in me as to its nature, but I do not believe 'tis of his physical being."

Fenna leveled her gaze on Lijsbet. "Oh, I can assure you, 'tis not physical."

Lijsbet blinked. "How do you know?"

"Dr. Vanderhoff is not a barber-surgeon. He is the kind of doctor who deals with ailments of the mind."

Lijsbet's heart sank. Was Davion a lunatic? Had not the duke thoroughly investigated a man he was taking on as the overseer for his art collection?

Fenna leaned forward and laid a hand on Lijsbet's wrist. "I can guess where your mind is going, my lady. Rest assured, I do not think whatever ails the earl is something that cannot be easily managed. I also have no concern the earl would pass this illness on to his children."

*Children. Not a concern for me.*

"How on earth would you know that?" Lijsbet breathed, pressing her fingers to her throat.

Fenna patted her arm. "Let us say I have some knowledge of a trauma the earl's family suffered, early in his childhood. I believe it marked him. Left him with a scar invisible to all but him."

"What was the tragedy?"

"I am sorry, Lijsbet. I know not anything more. Dieric may have heard the details, but I fear if you press him for answers, he will expect... payment in some form."

A shudder racked Lijsbet's shoulders. "Not from me."

"My advice to you is this: follow your heart. Mayhap you can help the earl overcome his ailment. Talk to him. Let him know he can trust you. It is a fact many flaws of the mind can be cured by the heart." Fenna rose. "Take your time. Enjoy the solitude in this place. Peace may help guide you." Turning, the mistress disappeared around the leafy corner.

Sighing, Lijsbet reached up to tuck an errant strand of hair behind her ear. As excited as she had been to come to Leuven, to learn new techniques in illumination from the beguines, she was suddenly overwhelmed with the desire to return to Coudenburg.

Isabella would have the answers she sought.

Yet they had only been in Leuven a few days. Still nearly a fortnight lay ahead before their departure. Surely, she would not discover the cause of Davion's ailment from Bouts. Fenna seemed to know little more. Dr. Vanderhoff may not be willing to confide in her. After all, she was no kin to the earl. She was simply his charge.

Fenna's words echoed in her mind: *Many flaws of the mind can be cured by the heart.*

Was hers the heart called to action for Earl Price? She could not help but wonder.

*Davion*

Davion lay on his pallet long after the sun rose, long after his roommate had dressed and left the room. The hour for breaking of the fast was well past. Shock seemed to immobilize him. By all his beliefs, he should now be dead. Yet he was not. Still, dare he risk rising? Moving about? Was it safe, even now?

Upsetting him most was the fact he could remember nothing about the incident the day before. His memory was empty, like a fallow field, shorn clean and plowed under. One minute he had been sitting on the rather uncomfortable, straight-backed chair in Dr. Vanderhoff's front room, and the next he was studying a spiderweb of cracks in the ceiling.

Finally, when the rumbling from his midsection would allow him to linger no longer, he rose slowly and dressed. Mayhap Jehan had a leftover crust of bread and some ale in the kitchen. In truth, he could not remember the last time he had eaten a meal.

The kitchen was smoky, the hearth roaring under a large iron pot. The air was heavy with the aroma of baking bread, along with the earthy aroma of boiling vegetables. His stomach grumbled audibly, actually beginning to cause him pain.

Was that part of him made of glass as well? He prayed not.

"Good morrow." Jehan greeted him from the other side of a long worktable, where he was busy chopping leafy greens. "Can I get you something to break your fast, my lord?"

"Aye, if you please. I regret I did not come to table at the appointed time."

Jehan waved his hand in the air. "In an artists' residence, meals have no appointed times. 'Tis whenever the muse grows lazy, and the man hungry," he said with a laugh. "I have a fresh loaf cooling now. Some ale while you wait?"

Davion sat on the wooden bench flanking the worktable against his better judgement. Normally, such a seating arrangement would frighten him to pieces, literally. However, after the events of the day before, the earl was suddenly not quite so fearful of shattering his body into splintered shards that reflected light like flashes from the sun off a wind-tossed lake. In truth, he was feeling a bit bolder today, a bit more brazen. Mayhap 'twas merely the ache in his head causing him to throw caution to the wind. But sit he did, carefully, arse to oaken plank.

'Twas not the most comfortable seat, he quickly realized. But he was hungry, and he felt obligated to sit with the gracious Jehan, who was willing to provide him with warm bread and mayhap a bit of butter and honey. The ale was warm but quenched his thirst as he waited.

"Do you paint?" Jehan asked, in between the slashes of his cleaver on bunches of green herbs.

"Nay. I studied art at university. I am the overseer of the art collection at Coudenburg. For Duke Philip," Davion replied.

Jehan nodded, laying down his knife and scooping the chopped greens into the pot hanging over the fire. "Are you the guest of Master Bouts? He is a great painter. Many come to Leuven to learn his techniques."

"So I am told," Davion said, shifting his backside gently on the hard seat. "Is the bread cool enough to cut yet?"

"Oh, my apologies. I'd forgotten." Jehan pulled a cloth off the loaves cooling at the end of the worktable. "Would you like some cheese? I'm afraid the pottage is not yet cooked well enough."

"Nay. Butter?"

A sly smile lit up Jehan's face. He leaned across the table and spoke in low tones. "The master instructs me to covet the butter, for his consumption alone, and for his *special guests*. But he is not here this morn. He will never know."

Davion tipped his head. "Does he not consider me a special guest?"

"Nay," Jehan laughed. "A special *lady* guest. Master Bouts entertains many."

The earl's appetite suddenly waxed to nausea. He was not interested in the private affairs of Dieric Bouts. But this confirmed his suspicions as to the painter's intentions toward his charge. Toward Lily.

He stood, holding out his hand. "I have decided, Jehan, to take the bread with me. I must be leaving. I am late already. No butter needed. Many thanks for your kindness."

Davion ate the bread in small bites as he made his way to the beguinage. 'Twas his duty to check on the lady, one he'd failed to perform for two days running. Today he would take charge of his responsibility and prove to Lily he was a reliable man. A man who cared.

One who cared, he realized, quite a bit.

A young beguine answered the door with whom Davion had not been introduced. She smiled when he introduced himself.

"Ah, Lady Lambert is in the scriptorium. She will be pleased to see you."

And she was. Davion was surprised at not only her enthusiastic reaction to his arrival, but to the warm tingle coursing through his veins upon seeing her again. He stood a bit taller, straightening his shoulders as he approached her workbench.

"Are you well today? Your head, thought. I see the swelling persists," Lily said, creases forming between her dark eyebrows. She raised her hand toward his temple. "Does it hurt badly?"

His head did throb still. He would not admit this to the lady, however. He tipped up his chin.

"Nay. As if it ne'er happened. What is it you are working on this day?"

Lily smiled as she slid the folio toward him. The illumination was nearly complete on this leaf, he noted, the gold leaf dried and color applied. Her work, he admitted to himself, was outstanding. Davion doubted he could draw such finely detailed vines and flowers. The colors were brilliant, luminescent, standing up boldly even against the gold detail.

"These are magnificent, my lady," he said. "The depth is superb. As if one could climb in between the vines, if small enough."

A warm smile spread across her face. " 'Tis my life's pride, this work. I studied many years. The journey," she paused, searching his eyes, "has not always been an easy one."

Those golden eyes. They bore straight into his heart, he could not deny it. How could this have happened, and so quickly? Years of loneliness melted away when Lily was standing beside him, so close he could smell the lavender scenting her hair. He wondered if her skin smelled the same way. Warm, heady lavender.

He wanted to know. Now. Today. *Tonight.*

"Lord Price, are you well? You did not answer my question." Those creases had reappeared between Lily's eyes, and she lifted one hand to touch his cheek.

*Too much inside my own head.* This had been his problem all of his life, Davion thought. *One cannot relate to another person unless you come out from behind your own thoughts.*

He caught her hand and pressed his lips to the soft, smooth skin. "I am, very well, Lily. Your concern touches me."

Suddenly aware they were not alone in the room, Lily glanced nervously about her. The beguines all seemed focused on their work, paying them no mind. She smoothed her hands down the front of her frock.

"A walk, mayhap? I could use a short respite. Such close work wears upon my eyes at times." Lily took his hand, a gesture that sent tingles up his arm.

She was always so gentle in touching him. "Come. 'Tis a lovely, sun-drenched day."

As they stepped out onto the street, Davion winced and shielded his eyes with one hand. "If you do not mind, Lily, I prefer to walk on the shaded side of the street."

She studied him curiously. "Does your skin react to the sun? I know many with fair skin who suffer from this."

"Nay," he began. Then he continued, "Well, aye, I suppose it does. 'Tis warm. You don't mind?" he asked.

"Not I. A lady's skin should remain as pale as bleached parchment." She paused, lowering her head. "Not that I shall ever hold the title of lady."

Davion stopped walking and turned to face her. "Why not? You are as gracious a lady as I have ever met."

Lily released his hand to wrap her arms about herself. "Do not tell me you are unaware of my history, Lord Price. If the artists have not spoken of it, surely the duke has."

He tipped up her chin. "We all have history we would rather forget. It seems," he chuckled and shook his head, "in my case, I have done exactly that. As for your history, 'tis none of my affair. Nor am I one worthy to judge you."

As he watched, the lines in her face relaxed, and color rose into her cheeks. 'Twas as though she was becoming younger and more beautiful, before his very eyes. Kind words, he realized, not often came Lily's way.

A pity, truly.

" 'Tis kind of you to say so, my lord," she replied, blushing. "As for your history, is that what the doctor believes caused your ailment?"

Davion began slowly walking. " 'Tis what he believes. Some tragedy, one I do not remember, befell my family when I was a child. I have no memory, yet I seem to carry a scar—"

"What kind of scar, my lord?"

The tightness in his throat commenced, the same feeling he got whenever someone probed his personal affairs. He calmed himself, taking a deep breath slowly. It seemed she was simply showing interest, not probing. Yet how could he possibly explain his fears? She would think him mad.

He decided he could not, feeling his shield closing, like plates of an invisible armor.

"A malady I hope soon to be free of," he said. He stopped and turned back toward the beguinage front entry. "I will allow you to go back to your work now. I wanted to come check on you, ensure you knew I was thinking of you. Do you have need of anything?"

She was staring at him with those eyes, swallowing him, it seemed, body and soul. Shaking her head slightly, her mouth curved up into the most endearing smile. "I am pleased you came by."

"May I come see you again later? After the evening meal?"

Again, a blush of color made her face seem to glow. "I should like that. Aye. I would like that, very much."

# Chapter Fifteen

*Lisjbet*

He arrived shortly after the evening meal had been cleared. Lijsbet was just rising when the knock on the front door sounded. Glancing down, she realized she was still clad in her brown frock. She frowned as she smoothed her skirt.

*I should have made time to change my dress.*

"You look lovely, Lady Lambert. A true artisan." Sister Fenna watched her from across the hall. "There is a small parlor of sorts, down the front hallway. You may entertain your guest there. 'Twould not be proper to bring him to your quarters, even though he is your chaperone." The glint of humor in Fenna's eyes made Lijsbet smile.

"Thank you, mistress. You are most kind."

"I shall have Rikita bring wine and some dried fruits," the mistress said, disappearing into the kitchen.

She answered the door herself, and could not help her breath catching upon the sight of him. Aye, Davion Price was a very handsome man, indeed.

He looked freshly bathed, his short hair still wet, shiny black like a raven's wing. The tunic he wore was black as well, edged with red braid. In one hand he clutched a cluster of flowers.

The earl seemed surprised she had answered the door. He hesitated a moment, then held out the bouquet toward her. "Good evening, Lily. I brought you some flowers to brighten your room here at the beguinage."

Warm tingles began on her scalp and spread downward, making her feel floaty and buoyant.

Rogier had never brought her flowers.

She shook her head to free herself from the memories. That was *then*. 'Twas history. Mayhap history best forgotten.

"So very thoughtful of you, Lord Price." Lijsbet took them, then stood there, not quite knowing what to do next. She wasn't even sure where the room the mistress had spoken of was located. Fortunately, Sister Rikita appeared in the hallway carrying a tray.

"This way, my lord, my lady," she said, jerking her head down the hall in the opposite direction from that which led to the scriptorium. "I will bring you another pitcher for those colorful blooms, as well." She winked, surprising Lijsbet.

*Nay, these women are not nuns. In truth, far from the ladies of the cloth.*

Lord Price followed, pausing before the chapel. The door was inset with an elaborate stained-glass panel, and since there were candles lit within, colorful light danced in the glass. The earl froze, eyes wide.

"Is something amiss, my lord?" Lijsbet asked.

"Nay. Nothing. The light, through the glass. It seems almost alive." He put his head down and continued down the hall, his steps quick and jerky.

The guest solar, though small, was cozily furnished. Two high-backed chairs, upholstered with faded tapestry, faced each other before a multi-paned window looking out onto the street. A bench, also padded with tapestry, filled one wall. Rikita left the tray on the table, then returned moments later with a pitcher half-filled with water. She took the flowers from Lijsbet.

"I don't believe I've seen this color on this type of flower before," she said, awkwardly attempting to arrange the blooms. "They are lilies, aren't they?"

Lord Price stood, his hands clasped behind his back, near one of the chairs. "The man in the market square said they were calla lilies," he murmured. "Golden calla lilies." Although he was answering Rikita's question, his eyes never left Lijsbet's face.

Embarrassment flooded her, and she had to look away. "Thank you, Sister Rikita. I will bring the tray back to the kitchen when Lord Price departs."

"All right then." Rikita scurried toward the door. Before closing it behind her, she winked again at Lijsbet.

*Sassy one, this beguine.*

"Please, sit with me, Lily. Tell me about the pages you worked on this day." The earl had filled both cups with wine and was holding one out toward her. "I would like to see more of your illuminations in the coming days."

Lijsbet took the wine and sat. "My apologies for my attire, Lord Price. 'Twas little time between working and the evening meal."

"I believe we agreed to use our given names." His gaze burned into her own. "Lily."

Her mouth was suddenly so dry, her tongue seemed bound to the roof of her mouth. Why was she so nervous around the man? She sipped the wine, rich and sweet.

"Aye, we did. I finished a page bound for a section of a Book of Hours for the duchess. For the Hours of the Virgin." She tried to suppress the sly smile she had worn the entire time she had been working on the finer details of the page.

Dedicated to the Virgin Mary, this section of the prayer book usually contained only the most sacred animals. A lamb, most commonly. Not in those illuminated by Lijsbet. Here, especially, she enjoyed hiding her bizarre, fanciful creatures within the acanthus vines.

"You were working on that leaf when I visited earlier, where you not?"

Lijsbet nodded slowly. Had he noticed? He had not seemed to examine the leaves that closely.

"I saw your mythical beasts. Very clever detail. Do you insert these in all of your illuminations? Or just those destined for the Hours of the Virgin?" His tone was serious, yet the quirk of his lips revealed more.

Lijsbet struggled not to smile herself. "Nay, not just for that chapter. I sprinkle them all through the books I illuminate. I consider them my... my signature, you might say."

"Very clever. Admirable. Especially when one never knows if the identity of the true artist will ever be revealed."

*Exactly.* She tipped up her chin. "Most never see my creatures."

"I have a reputation for being very attentive to detail. 'Tis, after all, a trait needed by one in my profession." The earl sipped, then set his cup down on the table. "I was correct. The color of your eyes is like golden calla lilies. Ah, but yours tend more to that of a flame."

Even as he said the word, heat flared in Lijsbet's cheeks. *He was embarrassing her.* She didn't think she was still capable of that emotion. She was not sure if the fact pleased or perplexed her.

"Kind words, Lord... Davion. An even kinder gesture. Very gallant. I have heard the English men know gallantry. Like knights. I've heard them referred to as knights in plain tunics."

"Is it a knight you seek, my lady?" His voice was barely a rumble, one Lijsbet could barely hear over the pounding of her heart.

Her head jerked from side to side. "No knights for me. I am a simple artisan. I seek a simple life."

"A simple match, then, as well?"

She blinked, thinking back to the day when she held herself taller, prouder, prancing through the streets of Tournai on the arm of the great master painter. Mayhap his prestige had played a part in her attraction for him. 'Twas not for the handsome cut of his face, for he was older, much older than she. He had lost his youthful allure years ago.

Rogier de la Pasture was old enough to be her father, a fact of no consequence to her.

*Then.*

"Aye. A simple match, if one at all," she murmured. "I am quite used to being alone. My work suffers if I am distracted."

Creases folded between his dark eyebrows. "I am not a renowned artist, nor even an artisan. My title in England means nothing to me. Might I make a simple enough match for you, my lady?"

Her initial reaction was shock. How dare he? She hardly knew him. Yet there was no denying the attraction between them.

*The choice of whether or not to pursue the liaison is solely for you to make.*

The mistress' words echoed in Lijsbet's head. 'Twas the question he was asking. Was she willing to take this chance again?

His eyes were mesmerizing, locked onto hers in a way that riveted her to the spot. She could barely hear for the blood rushing in her ears.

*'Tis plain to see. The attraction between you is obvious.*

"Aye. Mayhap." Her words were a whisper. "But we've only just met."

Slowly, Davion rose and came to her, taking her hand and bringing her to her feet. "We have time, then. All the time in the world to get to know each other better."

His lips lowered to hers and she felt his breath upon her skin, warm and tender as a breeze. How could she deny this attraction? The more important question was, why should she even try?

Cupping her face in his hands, Davion ravished her mouth. His scent, his taste drove her desire higher with each passing moment. An ache began in her core. There was no denying the fact: she wanted the earl. Selfish or no. Foolish or no.

'Twas inevitable.

When he drew back, he seemed to be searching her face for something, but what? Mayhap he had reservations because of her age.

"My lord, you do realize how much older I am. I am no blushing maiden. I am, in truth, a spinster—"

She had barely gotten the word out when he laid a finger on her lips. "I never want to hear that word from your lips again. 'Tis blasphemy, for you even to think it so."

Lijsbet took Davion's hand and led him across the small chamber to the padded bench.

"Sit with me, my lord."

The light coming through the window, waning even as they arrived, faded to black. No candle lit the room. The only illumination radiated from distant torches lining the street.

His gentle touch thrilled her. She had not been treated so reverently before. Slowly, he brushed the back of his hand across her cheek, his eyes never leaving hers.

Somehow, Davion's attentiveness and patience was even more exciting.

Absently, Lijsbet wondered if the door was locked. His hands, she realized, had not explored any farther than her shoulders. Was he shy? Waiting for permission?

"I am pleased I please you so. I wish to please you, Davion."

Even in the faint light bleeding in through the window, Lijsbet could see the panic in his eyes. His muscles went rigid under her hands.

"I cannot. Not here," he stammered.

*Ah. He has issue with intimacy in the beguinage. Understandable, but—*

He turned away before Lijsbet finished the thought. Taking a rushed step toward the door, he stopped suddenly, remembering his manners. He faced her, holding out both hands.

"My apologies, Lily. 'Tis not the place, nor the time. I must speak with Dr. Vanderhoff first. I must know my limitations."

"Limitations," she murmured.

He dropped his head and whooshed out a breath. "You do not understand, Lily. And in order for this to happen, you must come to understand. But first, I must know more about the condition from which I suffer myself."

She felt his hands land lightly on her shoulders in the dark. His lips softly brushed on hers. "I must go," he whispered.

# Chapter Sixteen

*Davion*

*How would it even be possible?*

The question hummed through the earl's brain, over and over again, all through the night as he tossed about on the narrow pallet in his quarters. If Lily were willing to give herself to him—he was quite sure she was—where could they be alone? He was sleeping in the shared room of a public house. She was staying in a beguinage. No chances in either location for them to explore the possibilities he felt existed between them.

In Coudenburg castle, he had his own private quarters. But nearly a fortnight lay between now and their return. Davion had waited to explore a physical relationship with a woman all of his life. He did not want to wait any longer.

Before, his fear had kept his natural urges in check. Worry over shattering into pieces is more than enough to keep one celibate as a priest. But after surviving his fall at the doctor's residence, Davion realized he may not be as fragile as he had thought. Surely, if he proceeded slowly...if he explained to Lily his condition, and his delicate nature...

*If she were willing.* Once she discovered he knew nothing about lying with a woman, would she still want him? Would she show him the way?

He must know.

But first, Davion wanted to speak more with Dr. Vanderhoff. Their conversation yesterday had been cut short by his fainting spell. He still was unsure what had caused it, but mayhap if he returned to the doctor's house now, he could question him. Davion dressed quickly, then rummaged through the pocket of yesterday's tunic. There, crumpled in a corner, was the paper bearing the address.

Leaving the artists' house with urgency in his step, he turned right and headed to the north of the city.

This time he suffered no uncertainty when he reached the doctor's residence. He rattled the knocker, then turned to watch for movement of the lace curtains. He saw none. But in a moment, he did hear footsteps, and the door swung open.

"Lord Price. Glad to see you are up and about this morn." 'Twas the doctor's house servant, he assumed, a man he had not met on his previous visit. Slight, wiry, and very blond, the man looked to be considerably younger than the doctor. A son, mayhap?

"I was wondering if the doctor was in this morning," he asked. "I know I come unannounced again, but—"

"Nay, I'm sorry. But father has gone out to visit with another patient. Is there some message I might leave for him?"

Ah, so 'twas a son. Davion should not have been surprised. But Dr. Vanderhoff looked so much like a monk, he never thought of him as a father. The doctor was not at home. He could not help the weight of disappointment from turning his mouth downwards.

"Nay. Do you know what time he is expected to return?"

The young man was shaking his head. "He may not be home until the morrow. He planned to go to Antwerp to send off a message on the ship bound for England."

*I wonder if this was in regard to my family history?*

"Very well. Please tell him, upon his return, I would like to see him. Mayhap I should come by tomorrow afternoon?"

"I will tell him," the young man said. "Good day, Lord Price."

Squinting against the now harsh sunlight, Davion crossed the street to walk on the shaded side. Why he was so averse to bright sunshine, he did not know. 'Twas how he had been ever since his childhood. He found the warming rays, those others considered pleasant, offensive. Almost painful.

He sighed. If Dr. Vanderhoff was just today sending off a missive, an answer could not possibly be expected before many days passed. Mayhap not even before they were scheduled to leave Leuven.

Davion planned to visit Lily this eve to declare his feelings for her. To propose a romantic relationship. One complete with the emotional as well as the physical complications. To go one step farther than he'd been able to the night before.

If he intended to pursue Lily, to woo her, he would be forced to take the chance that his body would withstand the strain. He decided quickly, 'twas worth the risk.

In truth, he had not a clue what his next move should have been. If it had even been possible. The earl had never courted, nor bedded, a lady before. He realized, with a sudden seizing in his chest, he had not the slightest idea how to proceed.

But who to ask? Especially here, in Leuven, where he knew few people? Bouts could surely instruct him as to the physical pursuit of a lady, but the very thought of speaking of such things with the artist turned his stomach. Walking slowly back toward the artists' residence, Davion was so invested in his own deep thoughts he nearly ran into a man walking in the opposite direction.

"I cry your mercy, dear sir."

The voice startled him, and immediately Davion staggered aside, terrified of colliding with the tall man who had spoken.

*Too much inside my own head. God's bones, I need to be pay heed. Could well have been the end of me.*

"I beg your pardon, my lord."

It was not until Davion looked up that he recognized the lanky man with long, dark hair. 'Twas Mathieu, the ostler from Coudenburg.

"Why, Mathieu. I had forgotten you were coming to Leuven," he sputtered.

Mathieu's wide smile warmed him. 'Twas good to see a familiar face.

"Aye, I am here on a most pleasant shopping excursion. Nothing pleases me more than selecting young stock for the duke's stables. There is an ostler here near the city who starts young colts, then sells them. I have Admiral La Laing with me, but he is off visiting with some friends this morn."

Davion let out the breath he had been holding. " 'Tis good to see you, man. I regret nearly colliding with you."

*And mayhap creating a starburst of glass shards in the street.*

"Won't you join me?" Mathieu asked. "I am headed to the Café Fiere for a mug and a bite."

Aye, 'twas wondrous to see a familiar face in this strange city. Davion did not know Mathieu very well, as he himself had only come to Coudenburg a few moons past. But the ostler was a friendly type who easily made himself seem more than an acquaintance. Davion had happened upon him in the bailey several times. He'd learned the ostler was also Philip's falconer—a prestigious position indeed—and was blessed with a lovely wife and daughter.

*A wife and daughter. Surely the man knew something about courting a woman.*

They found a corner table in the nearly deserted café on a side street near the city center. 'Twas late for breaking the fast, and early for those seeking a meal and drinks with friends. Davion was pleased.

'Twas not the kind of conversation he wanted to pursue in a crowded tavern.

"How is your stay going, Lord Price? I know the duke is excited to know what his new illuminator is learning." Mathieu paused to pull a leather thong out of his tunic pocket, securing his long hair off his face. Hair, Davion noticed, that had begun to shimmer with tiny strands of silver.

The earl did not know how old the ostler was, but had heard the man's wife was younger than he by a number of years. Their daughter, Meadows, Davion guessed to be about seven or eight years old. He'd seen her flitting through the bailey with some of the other children of the court's ladies.

"Lil... Lady Lambert is thriving at the beguinage. The sisters there have quite an impressive scriptorium. They produce some amazing work. Unfortunately, due to the nature of an all-male guild, I'm certain many of their illuminations are attributed to other artists." Davion nodded to the serving wench who brought them both a mug of ale.

Mathieu narrowed his gaze on the earl, then winked. "Lily, you say? Aye, I think the ekename fits. She's an attractive woman." The ostler paused to swill a good third of his mug, then swiped the foam from his mustache with two fingers. "She is unmarried as well, I understand. At least, 'tis what the duke tells."

Davion leaned forward, gently resting his forearms on the table. With both hands wrapped around the mug to keep them from visibly shaking, he lowered his voice. "Aye. She has a history in Tournai, but I understand 'tis over now. This does not concern me. I like Lijsbet... Lily. I like her very much."

"Then I say you should pursue her, man. Beautiful, talented, and a daughter of the duke. What more could a man ask for?" Mathieu was openly grinning now.

" 'Tis a fortunate coincidence indeed, meeting you here in Leuven," Davion continued. "I was hoping you might be willing to share some advice with a somewhat," he paused, looking away, "less experienced man." Davion sipped his ale. His mouth was so dry he feared his tongue would shatter. "I'm quite embarrassed to admit this, but most of my life I spent sequestered. An only child of royalty, then a serious student at university. I have not much experience with the gentler of the species."

This time Mathieu's laughter echoed throughout the café, and Davion cringed. Glancing about, he was relieved they were still quite alone in the room. Embarrassment flooded him, and he felt the heat rising up his neck.

"I am sorry, I was not laughing at your situation, my lord. I was laughing at your referring to Lady Lambert as a gentler of the species."

Davion bristled, expecting another slur of Lily's reputation, like those he'd suffered from Dieric Bouts. Mathieu, however, read the anger in his eyes. He held up both hands.

"I mean no insult. The lady is not only beautiful and talented, but from what I've seen, anything but gentle in nature. On the contrary, Lady Lambert seems quite high-spirited." Mathieu winked again. "A lot like my Eva. I like that trait in a woman."

The earl blew out a breath. "She is that." He fiddled with the handle of his mug, nearly toppling it. He jumped when Mathieu's big hand appeared and righted the vessel before ale sloshed over the rim.

"Just come out with it, my lord. We are both mature men. 'Tis nothing we can discuss that should embarrass either of us."

Davion swiveled his head, first one way, then the other. Then, leaning closer over the table, he murmured, "I would like to court Lady Lambert. But I haven't a clue as to how to proceed. You see, I have never... I mean to say, I have no experience with—"

"You are a virgin, then," Mathieu blurted out. Instead of a smirk or chiding tone, all Davion saw was genuine concern. "Do not worry yourself. I was as you once myself. Now I am a father of one with another on the way, and I had no one to teach me either. But nature and instinct take care of most things all on their own."

Davion blinked. *Nature. Instinct.* Do creatures in the wild fear they will shatter certain parts of their bodies in the act? He thought not.

"Look. We both know Lady Lambert is, let us say, more experienced in this matter. I am sure if you explain to her your concerns, she will be most patient and kind."

"Or she will shun me altogether." Davion grumbled the words.

"Or she will shun you," Mathieu repeated. "If that happens, my advice to you is this: you are much better choosing another to pursue." The ostler drained his mug and motioned for another when the servant brought his platter of bread and sausages. "If the woman cares for you as you seem to care for her, she will not shun you."

Later, as they parted ways in the street, Davion could not thank the heavens enough for what seemed a divine intervention. Seeing Mathieu here in Leuven was exactly what he needed. Now, the problem left for him to solve with Lily was the how and where.

The *if* still existed. But as Mathieu said, if the lady shunned him, he needed to set his sights on another.

Davion said another silent prayer that his plea for Lily's affection would not be rejected. He began to whistle as he strode back toward the artists' residence, hardly noticing the glare of direct sunlight washing over him.

Now, quite painlessly.

It seemed almost impossible that just days ago, the thought of pursuing a relationship with a woman was beyond his most wild imaginings. Now, instead of a mere dream, the quest had become his goal. He could not wait to get started.

# Chapter Seventeen

*Lisjbet*

Lijsbet was so engrossed in putting the finishing touches on the illumination she'd been working on all afternoon, she did not even hear the bells chime for vespers. The beguines moved so silently, she did not realize she was alone until a last ray of of late afternoon sun reflected off the brass candlestick on her worktable, momentarily blinding her. Blinking and looking about her, she chuckled.

When her mind was thrown into her work, the building, she mused, could catch fire and burn down with her inside. She would not realize anything was amiss until the smoke obscured her vision.

And her focus was piqued. Her creativity had sparked and burst into flames after Lord Price's visits the day prior. In the scriptorium, his compliments on her work seemed genuine. But 'twas more than his approval of her artistic talent. The earl seemed genuinely interested in her. *Her*, as a woman, not as a mere object, a toy with which to quench physical desire. When he looked into her eyes, Lijsbet saw more than a young, handsome English aristocrat. She saw a sensitive man with wounds invisible to the naked eye. A man who seemed to be reaching out to her, mayhap for her help.

Mayhap for something more.

She hoped 'twas the latter.

Hurrying to her quarters, Lijsbet decided that today, she would shed the drab, brown tunic she wore in the workshop. She would freshen herself with scented water from the basin, brush and re-braid her long hair, and don a gown—a real gown. One of the few she'd brought with her from Coudenburg.

She came down the stone steps just in time to see the sisters filing out of the chapel after the prayer hour. Several paused and looked up at her, surprise evident on their faces. Fenna and Wilhelmina flashed her broad smiles.

"You dress for the evening meal tonight," Fenna chided. "And what is the special occasion?"

Lijsbet felt the color rise into her cheeks as she lowered her gaze. "Lord Price will be returning this evening. I thought mayhap 'twould be a pleasure for him to see me as more than a charge."

As they headed for the main hall, Fenna took Lijsbet's arm and leaned close. "The gardens are lovely in the evening. I will ensure the other sisters have no cause to wander the arbor tonight."

Again, heat flooded her. Embarrassment, along with pleased surprise. Imagine, being given permission for a private moment with a man in the vineyard of a beguinage—by the mistress herself!

Although the meal smelled wonderful, Lijsbet found she could barely eat a bite. Excitement churned in her belly, spreading warmth all through her body. 'Twas a warm night, but when she felt the trickle of sweat snake its way down between her breasts, she knew she could not blame the season. Still, she refused to admit the truth.

*'Tis the blasted gown. 'Tis a much heavier weave than the brown frock I usually wear.*

He arrived just as the meal was ending. When the bell sounded, Lijsbet leapt to her feet, waving off the young beguine nearest the entryway.

"I will go. I believe it's my chaperone, Lord Price."

She was shocked and disappointed when she opened the door to see the tall, imposing figure of Master Dieric Bouts on the steps.

"Good evening, my lady. I was hoping to find you here," he said with a sly smile. "You are looking quite lovely this eve. I was hoping you might join me for a walk along the town square. The air is excellent tonight."

Lijsbet stiffened. "I fear I cannot, Master Bouts. First, I am not permitted to go about without my chaperone. Also, he is expected here, any moment." Then, with a sudden burst of mischief, she added, "Of course, if you would like to wait, I could ask Lord Price to accompany us."

Bouts' mouth twisted as though he had taken a handful of salt. " 'Tis a pity. Alas, I am not interested in keeping company with your English earl. Just you, Lily."

Lijsbet narrowed her eyes, her hands fisting at her sides. "Well then. I will bid you good morrow."

She stepped back to close the door, but caught the glimpse of a figure emerging from the alleyway. 'Twas Lord Price. Relief mixed with joy and trepidation. She had seen how Bouts could be confrontational with her chaperone. She hoped an incident was not brewing.

Following her gaze, Bouts turned. "Ah! So the wayward chaperone returns. Just in time, good man. I was about to whisk your charge off to ravish her."

The sparks of anger in Davion's eyes were visible even from twenty paces away. He said not a word until he reached the steps of the beguinage, where Bouts still stood, holding his ground. Lijsbet watched as the earl stepped close to the painter, glaring up into his face.

Davion was, already, a hand's breadth shorter than Bouts. With the painter standing on the stoop, his advantage was amplified further. The earl, however, did not hesitate.

"I will ask you to step aside, Master Bouts, and allow me passage. But not until after you have apologized to the lady for the slur you just uttered."

Lijsbet brought her fingers to her mouth. This was not the shy, timid earl she thought she'd come to know. His fists were clenched, elbows drawn back. Nothing about his stance, or his tone, conveyed fear.

Bouts, apparently, was equally as shocked. He stepped down off the stoop, awkwardly, nearly losing his balance. "Well, well. Dr. Vanderhoff has been able to pump some life into you, it seems." He turned toward Lijsbet. "I pray thee forgive my impudence. In truth, I spoke in jest. Anon, Lily."

With that, Bouts turned and strode back toward the alleyway, leaving both Lijsbet and Davion staring after him. The earl looked at Lijsbet.

"That was somewhat of a surprise," he said. "I did not think the great guild master could be so easily discouraged."

"Neither did I." Lijsbet's words whooshed out on the breath she had been holding. "But I am glad. Very glad. So nice to see you, Davion. Please, do come in."

*Davion*

In truth, Davion was as shocked as was Lijsbet. 'Twas as though a lock had been broken inside him—in a good way. Although the fear of breaking apart still hovered in the back of his mind, somehow 'twas not as debilitating.

*Aye*, he thought, *Dr. Vanderhoff is helping me already.*

When he finally came out of his thoughts to look at Lily, really *look* at her, she took his breath away. She was no longer plain in her shapeless brown frock. The blue gown dipped low across the tops of her breasts, and nipped in sharply at her tiny waist. She was slender, true, but in a gracefully feminine way.

He followed her through the hallway to the small parlor where they had met last evening. As before, the small table held a tray with a pitcher, two goblets, and a pewter plate, this time with small cakes. Lijsbet waved him in and closed the door behind her.

"Sister Fenna and I were not sure you would have eaten the evening meal. 'Tis not much, but if you are hungry—"

"I am hungry," Davion said, without a glance toward the cakes. He stepped close to her and lifted a wisp of her dark hair off her brow. "But not for bread."

Lowering his head, he brought his mouth down over hers. When his lips met her soft, warm skin, stars burst behind his eyes. Slowly, he brought his hands up to cup her face. She leaned into him, the heat from her body setting his on fire. When her lips parted, Davion thought surely he would lose his mind.

*Hungry? Aye, very.* She tasted like manna, that prophetic heavenly bread spoken of in the sacred texts. A food with the promise to satisfy a hunger Davion had never known he possessed. Now, 'twas all he could think about. As they embraced, it seemed their kiss stopped time.

*Mathieu was right. Instinct, nature takes over.*

"You placed a spell on me that first day I saw you, toiling over your worktable in the scriptorium at Coudenburg. How could I resist? Your beauty is timeless, ageless. I also would like to believe it is more than skin deep." Davion peered into those strangely golden eyes, so intent on his. Her scent overwhelmed him, as if he were enfolded in a bed of lavender.

"I felt it too, this attraction we have. Although I will admit, on first meeting, I did not like you very much." Her lips, pink and swollen from their kiss, turned up into a trembling smile. "I believe mayhap 'twas my instincts, warning me. Holding me back from liaisons such as this." Lowering her gaze, she looked away. " 'Tis been a source of trouble for me in the past."

He tipped up her chin. " 'Twill not be a source of trouble with me, Lily. My intentions are honorable. In fact, mayhap we should court, in a proper way, until such time as you decide if a more permanent arrangement would suit you."

Her laugh was sad. "I have waited long enough. All I ever wanted was to find someone who understood my strange passion in art. I always thought 'twould be another artist. An expert in the study of art would make as good a match, I think, or better." She kissed him again, soft and chaste.

Davion stepped back and reached for the pitcher, which he saw was filled with rich, red wine. He poured some into each of the goblets, then handed one to Lily. "To celebrate the beginning of a liaison—in the art of the heart?"

He was surprised to see tears brimming in those golden eyes. "Aye, celebrate we will." She sipped from the cup, then added, "The sisters make their own wine here, at Groot Beginjnhof. From their own grapes."

Davion savored the wine on his tongue. "Very nice. Their own grapes, you say? Where is their vineyard?"

Lily's slow grin held infinite promise. "The arbor runs all along the back of the buildings. The vines are thick now, the clusters fragrant. Would you like to walk with me?"

The earl refilled their goblets, and Lily took his hand and led him out the door and down a dimly lit corridor. All was quiet in the beguinage, with no one about. Too early for compline, Davion thought. The women must be allowed private time after the evening meal to pursue their reading or needlework.

*Prayer. They were women of God. Probably prayer.*

Lily's hand was warm and held his firmly. At the end of the hall, a narrow door led out into a garden. Such a garden, Davion had never seen.

The space between the buildings spanned no more than twenty-five or thirty feet. From brick wall to brick wall, however, not a bare patch of ground existed. Some areas were cordoned off with stones for planting beds.

Here was no kitchen garden. Flowers of many colors and varieties fought for dominance, their colorful heads swaying gently in the evening breeze.

"What is this place?" Davion asked. "Are these herbals?"

"Aye, some are. But most of the herbs are in the kitchen garden, down the other end of the row. This spot is simply a flower garden, a place where the sisters grow color and beauty to bring joy to their souls."

"Like the calla lilies?"

She dipped her head. "Aye. Like the calla lilies."

Still holding his hand, she followed a pebbled path that wove between the beds. In the distance, Davion saw arches spanning the space between the buildings, covered with leafy vines.

The path led them into the labyrinth beneath the grapevines.

"From the street, one would never know this space existed," Davion said, studying the lush growth over his head. Heavy with clusters of ripening grapes, 'twas easy to see how the beguines could produce as much wine as they might dare to drink. "I am impressed."

As they followed the path, ducking in places where the vines hung low, Davion noticed small niches cut into the sides of the arbor. These were fitted with seating, either iron benches or ones woven from the woody cuttings of the vines. What charming spots, he thought, to enjoy the warmth of an afternoon, shaded from the sun.

" 'Tis a wondrous place," Lily said, reading his thoughts. "I had no idea 'twas here until the mistress brought me through earlier today. The most special seat, though, is through here."

She ducked under a place where the vines looped very low, nearly obstructing the entrance to yet another alcove. Here, the bench lining the spot was turfed—an *exedra*, lush with soft, green grass. The seat was U-shaped, wide, and deep—almost deep enough for one to stretch out for a nap.

Lily spun to sit on the grassy surface, gazing up at him with glistening eyes. The leafy canopy enveloped them in cool, green twilight.

"Come. Sit with me, Lord Price. Davion."

# Chapter Eighteen

*Davion*

Davion surprised himself with the feeling that with Lily, he felt safe. Even without specific knowledge of his impairment, she had taken careful notice and acted accordingly. She respected his space. When she kissed him, she did so gently. She held his hand securely, but tenderly—*as if it were made of glass*.

Davion had never confided the nature of his condition with Lily. Yet she somehow knew.

Standing here before her in this hidden alcove, Davion suddenly realized there was nothing holding him back. Nothing preventing them from going forward. Nothing except his sudden and overwhelming fear.

"Lily I... My condition," he stammered.

Closing her eyes, Lily shook her head and patted the grassy seat beside her. "I simply want you to sit with me, Davion. Talk to me. Allow me to come to know you better."

Relief flooded him. Doing as she asked, the earl took a seat beside her. 'Twas, as it looked to be, soft and comfortable.

"Are you at ease in the artists' residence?" she asked.

Davion considered the question. "At ease? No, I cannot say I am truly relaxed. Not anywhere."

Lily tipped her head. "Why?"

Davion gazed off into the tangle of vines above their heads. "Since I was a child. I do not remember ever feeling at peace. Unafraid."

"What do you fear?" she asked.

He sighed. "You can see how carefully I must conduct my body. It may not seem so to look at me, but my condition, it leaves me in danger of damage. At all times. Everywhere."

Lily released his hand, which had become moist from her touch. His skin chilled, sending a shiver up his arm. To his embarrassment, she saw his reaction.

"Do you find my touch repugnant?" She sounded curious more than upset.

"Nay, nay. Quite the opposite, my lady. 'Tis just." He stood and began pacing the width of the alcove, worrying one hand over the other. "The issue is not only my condition. 'Tis simply, I feel I may disappoint you, Lily. You are... you are more worldly than I."

Her laughter resonated around him, tiny arrows prickling his skin.

"I meant it not as a judgement," he continued, "nor a statement of opinion. We all have histories. We all have parts of our lives we prefer not to linger in memory." He turned to face her. "Do you, my lady? Do you wish your past did not exist?"

She raised her shoulders and let them drop on a sigh. "I cannot say. If not for the last years in the workshop, I would never have developed my talents as an artist. I learned much. Illumination is my passion. One cannot discount the positives. There was, however, a cost. As you, I am sure, are aware."

"Did the Master of Tournai make no promise of marriage?"

She was gazing off into the vines, now, as he had been. A quick shake of her head told him 'twas a subject she would rather not explore. "Nay. I simply continued to wait. To hope."

"Many men, it seems, are ruled by their bodies, not their minds. Or by their hearts. Some seem not to possess one. A heart." He searched her face. "Master Bouts, for example. I believe he would like to take the same liberties with you as your previous master." Try as he may, he could not keep the acid from his tone. "His intentions, I'm quite certain, are no better."

" 'Tis true. He has become all but abusive with his attentions, I am sorry to say."

Davion flushed with anger. "Has he harmed you?"

"Nay. But he would like to take advantage of my less than virginal history. I shall not allow it."

Davion returned to his seat beside her. " 'Tis not how you think of me? Do I take advantage?"

Her eyes caused his heart to seize. Then she slowly began shaking her head. "Nay, my lord. If at all, I have been the one to take advantage of you."

Before another thought formed, her lips were on his again. Still gentle, still tantalizing. She tasted of wine, rich and sweet. Her kiss blotted out all other thought. She made him feel weak, yet at the same time awakened within him a beast he hadn't known existed.

Lily spoke to a part of him that wanted to remain hidden, secluded, safe. At least, always had until now. She opened in him a gate to desire. A place he had found forbidden.

As his excitement mounted, his heart beat with the same frantic tempo as the pounding in his head. Davion came to a sobering realization. There was no holding back the beast any longer.

*Lisjbet*

A curious man, to be sure, this Earl Price. He was a living contradiction. So seemingly confident in his work, in his reputation, she had assumed he would be a horrific taskmaster. At first, he had seemed so. Until the glimmers shone through. The cracks in his carefully maintained facade revealed a more vulnerable side to the man.

She wondered what caused his pain. His fear. His "condition," as he called it.

At the moment, she did not care. She was following this undeniable attraction to a man who was, in truth, the total opposite of the man she had thought she loved. For whom she had wasted so many years of her life. Because of whom she had gained the reputation as a less-than-proper lady.

So be it. Within the brotherhood of artists, their world, *her* world, rumors grew like bread rising, and the men talked. Not all they said about her was true. Still, at this point in her life, she had nothing more to lose.

Except, perhaps, her heart. But she was not planning to risk that again. Lijsbet was certain she could share her body without falling in love. This time.

His scent mingled with the sweetness of the grapes in the air, and he tasted like sin. Not an apple, but forbidden fruit, nonetheless. She could not help herself.

"I want you, Davion. 'Tis no secret."

*Aye, you may own me then, as did the Master. My body. Ye shall own my body alone.*

"I must be careful," he stammered, breathless.

She ran her fingers along his jaw. Such an incredibly handsome man. One so regal. After all, in his homeland, he was an earl. The question popped into her mind and was spoken before she could stop the words.

"How can such a prestigious, titled man have remained chaste to such an age?"

She felt his body stiffen. "I am an earl. I am heir to lands and title. But I am not a political man. I care not for the trappings of prestige. They are just as they are called—trappings. Traps that keep one from living for fear of imminent destruction." He took her by the shoulders. "Do you not see? An arrow or mace can down a man, even a knight. But for an earl, one wayward comment, one failed negotiation, and a noble can lose it all."

Lijsbet did understand. She worked in a guild of the most sensitive creatures on the earth—artists. Aye, she was one of them. Only she had learned to protect her sensitive nature, like a knight donning his armor.

Had she not?

She tipped her head. "You do not plan to return to England, then? To claim your title and lands upon your father's death?"

"Nay. At this point in my life, I hope to remain under the employment of the duke. Mayhap for the rest of my days."

*This complicates matters. I thought, at some point, he would be going away. I must be very, very careful.*

Davion drew back until she was gazing into a pair of the bluest eyes she had ever seen. A handsome man, indeed. Regal. *Young.* He was looking at her with the most perplexed expression.

Lijsbet had never become involved with a man younger than she, nor one of his innocence. She felt her face heat. A compliment to her, she thought. His reaction to her tickled her pride.

Mayhap she was not such an old, worn-out spinster after all.

# Chapter Nineteen

*Lijsbet*

The next weeks passed quickly for Lijsbet, who divided her concentration between two passions. Learning from the beguines their techniques of illuminations fascinated her. Her art consumed her days.

The nights had come to belong to Earl Price.

Since they had no other options, the vineyard became their love nest. Sister Fenna found ways to keep the other sisters out of the gardens after vespers. Although the two women never again discussed Lijsbet's activities with Lord Price, an understanding grew between them. Lord Price... *Davion* arrived each night at sunset for their stroll under the arbor. And other activities.

Yet, with the end of their stay in Leuven approaching, Lijsbet could not help but wonder how their relationship would change and if it would continue, once they returned to Coudenburg.

He was, after all, her overseer. She'd been down this path once before.

Still curious about his strange aversion to harming himself, she questioned him most every evening. He seemed less and less willing to discuss the matter. *The doctor should be hearing of my family history soon,* he would say. How that would explain his problem, Lijsbet could not imagine.

Two days remained for their scheduled departure from Leuven. The duke, he had told them, would send a carriage. As the time drew nearer, Davion became more and more anxious.

"I cannot leave until Dr. Vanderhoff receives the letter from England," he said one night as he paced in the niche before her. "I should have sent word—"

"What is it the doctor can possibly find out in a letter that would help you with your condition?"

Davion ran his hand through his short hair. "The tragedy. Whatever it was that happened in my family when I was a child, but I do not remember. I *cannot* remember." He turned, his expression frantic. "I must know. Every night, every time we embrace, I fear I will come away damaged. That I will cause you harm from splintered shards of glass." He shuddered. "The fear remains, Lily. I have learned to overcome the paralyzing worry, but only for brief times."

Lijsbet stood and went to him, stroking his cheek. "You are making progress, even without the doctor's help. Can you not see?" Her voice was gentle.

He gazed into her eyes, the moment stretching out between them. She felt pity for him, but could not believe he would not overcome this silly fear on his own. With her help, mayhap. She was no doctor, but she understood life, and knew more about men and their motivations than she cared to admit.

In addition to pity, and the obvious attraction for him and his body, she found herself developing a fondness for him.

Mayhap 'twas better if he remained in Leuven when she returned to Coudenburg. Mayhap some time apart was in order. She had been successful, thus far, in holding her heart in check. She worried, however, that he was becoming overly enamored with her.

Since he had confessed to her that she was his first love, Lijsbet understood the infatuation. She did not want to mislead him. Their affair was physical only, and must remain that way.

"There is another matter," Davion murmured, his throat thick. "What if you become with child? We are not married, nor have either of us discussed any kind of future together."

Contrary to how most women would react to this unspoken denial of commitment, Lijsbet whooshed out a breath.

*So, he has no intention to make our affair long-term. A relief, to be sure. Isn't it?*

"Lily? Do you not worry with pregnancy? I am not father material."

She blinked up at him, jolted from her own thoughts. Then she began to shake her head.

"I kept company with the Master of Tournai for over five years, Davion. I did not become pregnant. I believe I am barren."

*But what if 'twas not her barrenness, but the master's problem?* A little voice in the back of her head whispered an ominous warning. *Davion is young and healthy—*

"Nay. I am barren. 'Tis no cause for concern."

"It cannot have been a fortnight. So soon?"

Lijsbet paced in Sister Fenna's quarters after being called there for a message from Coudenburg. Even before entering the mistress' chamber, she knew what the missive would say.

"A carriage will come for you and Lord Price the day after next." Fenna pointed to the letter lying open on her desk. "I shall be very sorry to see you leave, Lijsbet. I have grown fond of your company, even in this short time." She stood before the window of her chamber wringing her hands. "Lady Isabella is fortunate indeed to have you working in her scriptorium."

Lijsbet stopped and met her eyes, her own filling with tears. 'Twas true, she had grown fond of the mistress as well. She loved staying here, and working with the sisters. For the first time in her life, she had developed a sense of belonging. A sense of family.

Mayhap a life as a beguine would not be the worst way to spend one's days.

"You have been more than kind to me, Mistress. I cannot tell you enough how much I appreciate your support, as well as your discretion."

Color tinged the mistress' cheeks. "You are being given a second chance. I have enjoyed helping to make this possible." Fenna's eyes crinkled at the corners. "Will you and the earl marry?"

Lijsbet closed her eyes and shook her head. "Nay. He is too young and still fears for his health. In fact, he may be sending me back to Coudenburg alone, remaining here in Leuven until news comes to the doctor who is treating him."

Fenna blinked. "Oh. You would go back unchaperoned?"

"The journey is completed in less than a day. The driver will be a vassal of the duke. I am sure he can be trusted." Lijsbet sighed. "I would delay my departure, but a message may not reach Coudenburg in time to stop the carriage from coming."

Fenna sat and motioned for Lijsbet to do the same. "Is he no better?" she asked quietly.

"He functions, but with great caution. He retains this paralyzing fear that he is made of glass. That he could shatter into pieces." She shook her head. "Have you ever heard of such a malady?"

The mistress leaned forward with knitted brows. "Yes, I have heard of this delusion. I believe one of the French kings suffered from it. Is there no cure?"

"Davion and his doctor suspect the fear stems from an incident in his youth. One he cannot remember. The doctor believes, if that memory can be unearthed, the fear would disappear. Be explained, if nothing else." Lijsbet pressed her lips together. "Some time apart may be good for the earl and I. My heart has been broken once. I do not intend to make that mistake again."

"I understand your fear, very well." Fenna crossed her arms and gazed out of the window.

Grey skies overhead cast a steady misting rain over the brick buildings and cobblestone street. Lijsbet wondered absently if 'twould rain for the return journey. The dreariness outside made her heart feel even heavier than it already was.

"Is there no worry of a child?" Fenna asked, and Lijsbet jolted. " 'Twas what ended my time with Master Bouts. He was grateful I lost the babe before anyone even knew. He told me plainly he would not marry." She leveled her eyes on Lijsbet's. " 'Tis a chance you take, my lady. Would Lord Price claim the child?"

Shaking her head in jerks, Lijsbet rose and began to pace once more. " 'Twill not happen. I am barren. I never conceived before, and I was with the master nigh on five years."

Fenna's eyebrow rose. "He is an older man, Lijsbet. Lord Price is in his prime."

"Nay. It cannot happen. Even if it did, I would not insist he marry me. Marriage is not in my future. I have already accepted the fact." She stopped and faced Fenna. "I am an artist, an illuminator. I am a woman, but not one who can bear the earl any sons. Nor do I wish to surrender the independent status I have enjoyed. I would not make a good wife. Lovers is all we can ever be."

Fenna blinked, shocked. "Independent? You were the mistress of an artist for most of your adult life. How can you say you were independent?"

The mistress may as well have plunged a dagger into Lijsbet's belly and twisted it. She spoke the truth, a truth the illuminator had been denying to herself all of these years. Quick tears rose to her eyes, and she blinked furiously to will them away.

*One must never cry. 'Tis a sign of weakness. Especially for a woman.*

### Davion

The day the carriage was due from Coudenburg, Davion rose before the sun. He dressed and left the artists' house as quickly as he could, making his way north through the quiet streets to Dr. Vanderhoff's house. If the doctor had not received news from England yet, Davion would have no choice. He must remain in Leuven until his condition was identified, and with God's grace, cured.

'Twas the only way he could pursue a life with the woman he loved. With Lily.

*Loved.* Was that the emotion he was feeling? There was no way for him to know. Lust, surely. Affection and respect as well. But how does one define love?

Every time thoughts of her drifted into his head, 'twas the word ringing in his ears. Every time he saw her, and his heart leapt a little in his chest (he still worried for that), 'twas the emotion he was convinced he felt. She must know. He must tell her.

Now. Before they parted for God knew how long, Davion desperately wanted Lily to know his feelings for her. Even if only for a few days or a fortnight, they would be apart. As improbable a chance as it was, the earl wanted Lily to understand how she had captured his heart, so she would give hers to none other.

He'd awoken the doctor's son from a deep sleep, he was certain. The boy answered the door after a long pause, with Davion having to rap the knocker three times. His blond hair stood up in haphazard tufts on his head, and it appeared he had pulled on his braies quickly, as they were askew on his hips.

"I am sorry, Lord Price. My father has gone again to Antwerp. I do not expect him until later today."

Davion's heart sank. Even if the doctor returned early, 'twould not be early enough to allow him to accompany Lily back to Coudenburg. The consultation also would take time. Days, mayhap.

Hurrying back along the streets until he reached the passageway to Groot Beginjnhof, the earl felt as though his tender heart was breaking. It could, he knew. But he had always thought the cause of such injury would be a physical blow. He had not been aware that affection, adoration of another person could cause the hair-like cracks he could feel forming with each beat of his heart.

Dew still sparkled wet on the grass when Davion arrived. Glancing about, he saw no carriage. Not yet. Surely it could not have left already. He mounted the steps and flipped the knocker.

Almost immediately, the door swung open and she was there before him. His heart threatened to burst inside his chest. Fresh-faced and bright-eyed, Lily was wearing the same lovely blue gown she had their first night together. Memories came rushing back, and Davion felt heat flood his cheeks.

"I am so relieved I arrived in time," he breathed. "Still no news from the doctor, Lily. I shall have to remain in Leuven."

Lily blinked slowly, then nodded. " 'Tis of no consequence. The driver from Coudenburg can be trusted. 'Tis not a very long journey." She paused to reach out and run her fingers along his jaw. "Soon, you will return to Coudenburg. Do not look so sad, my lord."

The softness in her voice made his throat seize. He had not realized 'twould be this painful. In such a short time, he had grown so fond of her company. Her beauty. Her soft body.

The clatter of the horses' hooves echoed throughout the narrow street. As the carriage drew near and slowed, the wheels squealed angrily. Over Lily's shoulder, Davion saw two young beguines carrying her bags and artist's case down the hallway. He reached for the largest bag as they stepped out onto the stoop.

Time, which had seemingly been winding tighter and tighter for the past fortnight, popped free and spun wildly ahead. Davion felt as though he blinked once and opened his eyes to see the carriage receding down the street on which it had come. All he had left of Lily was the taste of her lips on his own.

He had not had a chance to tell her he loved her.

They had not a moment alone. Even after she had hugged each sister in turn, the embrace with the mistress lasting the longest, the beguines did not disperse. Her baggage stored, the driver had stood ready, only a pace away, waiting to help her into the carriage. When Davion took her into his arms, he wanted to hold on forever. Finally, after a brief, chaste kiss, she pushed him away and turned to board. Even as the carriage rolled away, she held up her hand in farewell, but would not meet his eyes.

*'Tis over, then. Our time together here in Leuven has been no more than a temporary distraction for Lady Lambert. An affair, just as her time with the Master of Tournai.*

*How many others?*

# Chapter Twenty

*Lijsbet*

Lijsbet's eyes and throat ached from keeping her emotions in check. She had decided she could not, *must* not, do anything to show the earl her true feelings about leaving without him. Leading him on would not be fair. Theirs had been an affair of a physical kind, nothing more. Even if she chose to share her body with him again when he returned to Coudenburg, 'twould be temporary.

It must be.

Only after they had left the cobblestone streets of the city and wove out into the countryside did Lijsbet allow the tears to come. Her heart ached, and her anger flared.

*No strength. Simply another weak woman. I must gather my wits and restore my resolve.*

The emptiness deep inside her would not listen. It throbbed like an open wound all the way back to Coudenburg.

Lady Isabella was standing on the steps of the keep when the carriage barreled up through the bailey. Her smile made the duchess appear younger than her years. 'Twas a comfort to Lijsbet that Isabella was happy for her return. She so yearned to belong, somewhere.

Furrows appeared between the duchess' pale eyebrows when she searched the carriage to discover Lijsbet was alone.

"Whatever has happened?" she asked, her tone frantic. "Where is Lord Price? Is he well?"

"The doctor," Lijsbet began as she stepped down from the carriage. "He waits for news from the doctor."

An hour later, seated across from the duchess in her solar, Lijsbet clutched the goblet in her hands and took a deep breath. 'Twas not her place to ask such a question. She was no kin to the earl. He was simply her overseer, a man for whom she worked.

*If only.*

"Lady Duchess, may I ask the nature of Lord Price's affliction? I spent a good deal of time with him on this journey, and I can see how... something affects his every move."

Isabella pursed her lips. "I hoped he might have an answer before now. Surely, he told you the name of his condition. *Glass delusion.* Many nobles suffer from this affliction." She sighed and leaned heavily on the arm of her chair. "For most, it is the manifestation of fear, of losing their status, their wealth and titles. These, however, do not seem to concern Lord Price. At least, consciously. I had hoped Dr. Vanderhoff might be able to identify the root of the earl's issue."

Lijsbet nodded silently. She knew he feared breakage, as he called it. In the beginning he had worried he would injure her with sharp fragments of his own body. She had heard tales of the *glass men*, as they were called, but never believed they truly existed.

"Is there a curative? Will he recover?" she asked.

" 'Tis my hope." She smiled sadly into Lijsbet's eyes. "He is a good man, Lady Lambert."

That evening, they were both seated in the great hall when the duke burst through the doors. He was away, Lijsbet learned upon her arrival, and had not been expected to return soon. Yet here he was, grinning like a madman as he strode across the big room toward the duchess. Once beside her on the dais, Philip lifted her hand and kissed it.

"I have a gift for you, dear lady."

Isabella tipped her head. "What is the occasion?"

"A good husband needs no reason to lavish gifts upon his bride."

At this Isabella's eyebrow rose. Their relationship, Lijsbet knew, was one more of political convenience than of the heart. What was the duke's motivation for this sudden outpouring of affection?

"No decent noble would not have at least one portrait of his beloved. I know you do not like to be away from your castle here, and painting a portrait takes much time. So I bring the artist to you." Philip swept an arm toward the doorway.

Lijsbet gasped when the man who stepped through, a red velvet cap in his hands, was none other than her former lover.

The Master of Tournai. Rogier.

"I present to you," Philip boomed proudly, "the great master painter, Rogier van der Weyden."

*Isabella*

"How could you, Philip? You knew Lily came here to escape her situation. How could you choose this man, of all the many artists in the Low Countries, to paint my portrait?" Isabella paced the length of the duke's solar, her footsteps stomping the stone pavers harder with every step. She stopped suddenly, facing her husband. "Rogier did not know she was here. 'Twas the way she wanted it."

Philip sat in his high-backed chair, leaning his raw-boned chin on one hand. "She was in Tournai, was she not? When you told me she was involved with the Master of Tournai, I did not realize 'twas this man... Rogier van der Weyden. Is the Tournai master not called Rogier de la Pasture?"

Isabella crossed her arms and glared at the duke. "Aye, he is. 'Tis to obscure to those in the Tournai workshop that he is the same man, but one living a very different life than the one he leaves behind in Brussels. Lily knew nothing of Rogier's family. Nothing of his wife, nor of his children." She sighed and pinched the bridge of her nose. "I had hoped to keep her innocent of this knowledge. Her guilt overwhelms her enough."

*You, of all people, of all men, should have realized what Rogier was doing...*

Philip lifted one shoulder. "I did not know. Honestly, Isabella, I somehow thought when regarding Lijsbet's situation, we were discussing a different man entirely." He sat up abruptly and poured them both some wine. "No matter. The artist is here now, and here he will stay until he has completed your portrait." He raised glittering eyes to hers. "Until he has immortalized my dear duchess in pigments, for all eternity."

*Lijsbet*

Feigning sudden illness, Lijsbet made her excuses and quit the great hall abruptly after Rogier's arrival. She could feel his eyes upon her, but she kept hers averted. She had been discovered. She had hoped to start her life over here, dedicated to her work and serving the duke and duchess, never having to look back.

But her past had followed her. He stood before her, and would reside under the same roof for the foreseeable future.

As she bolted the door to her quarters, Lijsbet leaned back against it and covered her face with her hands. Rogier had not wanted her to go. He had been less attentive of late, true. They had spent fewer and fewer nights together near the end. She had even asked him once, "Do you want me to leave?" His answer was no. He cared deeply for her, he told her, and wished their relationship to remain as it had been.

Rogier's long trips were, he had said, for business. He had several other workshops in the Low Countries, and often traveled to them to work with other artists, such as Robert Campin, the Master of Flemalle, and with Jan van Eyck. She did not mind his frequent absences, but after nearly eight years, Lijsbet wanted something more from the artist. She obviously could not give him sons—not that he wanted any—but she would like to have been bound to the artist, and not just as his mistress. She had wanted to become the wife of Rogier de la Pasture.

So why did the duke introduce him as Rogier van der Weyden? She had heard this name and the tales of a great but elusive artist. But 'twas not him in the great hall. 'Twas Rogier de la Pasture, the Master of Tournai. 'Twas *her* Rogier.

Why he went by two different names, Lijsbet did not understand. Something deep in the pit of her stomach told her she was better off without such knowledge.

Confused, terrified, and weary beyond imagination, Lijsbet removed her travel-soiled gown and refreshed herself with lavender scented water from the basin. As she drew the light linen nightrail over her head, thoughts of Davion drifted into her mind. How complicated her life was about to become. Surely, Rogier would approach her, ask her about her disappearance. He may not want their relationship to continue, but still...

To have one's former lover under the same roof as their present one promised high tension. If not more serious trouble.

*Davion*

Davion wandered the streets of Leuven like a lost sheep in the hours after the carriage left. 'Twas a dreary day, the skies gray and heavy with threat of rain. At least he did not have to stay to the shaded side of the street to avoid the sun.

The day matched the feeling in the earl's heart. Like the sky, his sun was gone.

Three times he wandered toward Dr. Vanderhoff's residence, but thought better of bothering his son too many times. He would wait, he decided, until the evening meal was nigh. Surely, by then, the doctor would have returned home.

A light mist had begun to fall from the clouds when Davion rapped the knocker on Dr. Vanderhoff's door. There was only a moment's hesitation before it swung open. The doctor himself was on the other side.

"Lord Price," he said, "do come in. I called for you at Groot Beginjnhof earlier this afternoon, but they said you were out."

*So he must have the answers I am waiting for.*

The servant brought a tray with pitchers of ale and a loaf of coarse brown bread to the meeting room where Davion had visited with the doctor before.

"We were preparing for the evening meal," he said, "but I fear there is not enough to share. We have plenty of bread to sustain us. Please, help yourself."

Davion studied the round man who filled out the chair opposite him and thought, *Nay, there probably is not much left at table when you are through.*

"I have no appetite, Dr. Vanderhoff, but for the news you have received from England."

The doctor grunted and reached for the loaf, tearing it into two. "The response arrived. I now have details of the event your family suffered." He took a large bite of the bread, closed his eyes and moaned in pleasure. "My apologies. I am famished."

Davion wrung his hands in his lap. "What did you discover, Doctor?"

Vanderhoff laid down the piece of bread he had been devouring and brushed the crumbs off the front of his tunic. "I will tell you, Lord Price. But remember what happened when we first began discussing your family. 'Twas apparent the memory was too much for you to bear. I do not want you to experience another episode, mayhap fall again."

Vanderhoff turned and motioned toward a long, padded bench along the wall. "I would feel better if you were seated there, my lord. 'Tis safer."

Grumbling with impatience, Davion moved to the seat indicated. He sat back, placing his hands flat on the cushion, one on each side of him. "I am steadier now, Dr. Vanderhoff. I am stronger. Lil... Lady Lambert has been very kind to me. She has helped me with my confidence. I do not believe I shall fall victim to another spell."

The first half of the brown bread was gone, and the doctor had started on the other half. He turned his chair to face Davion. Washing down his bread with a gulp of the ale, he leveled his gaze on the earl.

"When you became ill, we were speaking of your sister. Diana. You did not seem to remember her."

At the sound of her name, Davion felt a whoosh of air leave his lungs. *Sister. Diana.* He shook his head as if to scare off a fly.

"You are mistaken, Doctor. I have no sister. I am an only child."

But even as the words left his lips, Davion knew, somehow, they were a lie. A high-pitched ringing began in his ears, making him dizzy. The fading light falling through the window highlighted particles of dust in the air. In the earl's vision, they grew in size and began to pulsate, balls of ethereal light. He sucked in air and curled his fingers into fists beside him, fighting the sensations.

Nay, this would not take him down again.

"I am afraid, my lord, 'tis you who are mistaken. I have your family records here before me." Vanderhoff patted a stack of papers on the table, one Davion had not noticed before. Crumbs littered the top leaf, and the doctor swept them off. Then he tapped a finger on the stack. "Not only did you have a sister, but you and she shared a birth date." The doctor leaned forward and spoke softly. "Diana Price, my lord, was not only your sister, but also your twin."

# Chapter Twenty-One

*Lijsbet*

Her night was fitful, with sleep elusive. A myriad of thoughts and emotions tumbled through her brain as if thrown about by the wind. A storm had, in fact, blown in during the night. Lijsbet could hear the howling wind and the thunder even through the thick castle walls. At one point, rain pelting on the lancet windows in her chamber sounded like a deluge of tiny arrows. Pulling the woolen blanket closer around her, she lay there in the dark, her mind as tumultuous as the storm.

She was not surprised when a soft knock sounded on her door. Her handmaiden had arrived early this morn. Lijsbet looked forward to seeing her again.

Cecile greeted her hurriedly, concern etching lines on her brow.

"My lady, I am pleased you have returned. I must tell you, there is a man who wishes to speak with you, waiting in the great hall. He asked where your chamber was located, but I would not tell him."

Panic made it difficult to breathe. This she knew, surely, was Rogier. How dare he be so bold as to ask to come to her quarters?

Then again, with their history, why would he even hesitate?

Dressing hurriedly in her brown frock, Lijsbet had Cecile fashion her hair into two braids on top of her head, then cover them with a linen kerchief. Covering one's hair sent out a clear message to men: *this woman is off limits.* 'Twas the message Rogier de la Pasture, or whatever name he called himself, needed to receive.

Her love for the man, she realized, mayhap had not been love at all. 'Twas admiration, and awe, and lust. Even if at some point she had given her heart to the Master of Tournai, he had made his intentions clear. Now, she must do the same.

Still, as she stepped from her chamber, panic clutched at her throat with clawed fingers. She would rather not meet with this man alone. If only Isabella would consent to accompany her...

"Cecile," she turned back toward the room, "do you know if the duchess is up and about yet?"

"Aye, my lady. In fact, I passed her on the stairs. I believe she was headed to break her fast."

Whooshing out a sigh of relief, Lijsbet gathered every ounce of her courage and headed for the great hall.

She found the artist sitting on the dais next to the duchess. An honored guest, for such a seating.

Her stomach clutched tighter in her belly. She had not spoken with the duchess since Rogier's arrival last evening. Was she even aware that the Master of Tournai and van der Weyden were, in fact, the same man?

Surely then, Isabella would understand Lijsbet's dilemma. She prayed 'twas so.

The artist sat regally, dressed in the finest silk tunic and wearing his usual adornments. Rogier liked jewelry, and wore several chains and pendants around his neck, and multiple rings on his fingers. Gold and precious gems, of course. Although not a member of the nobility, the artist liked to flaunt his position as an esteemed guild member, along with the wealth earned for producing his art.

Lijsbet recognized the cross-shaped pendant lying against his burgundy tunic. Studded with emeralds and rubies, there was no mistaking the piece. Any hopes Lijsbet had of this man being a double for the man in Tournai, a twin or close cousin, quickly evaporated. Nay, 'twas the same man.

When he looked up and saw her, Rogier leapt to his feet, reaching out one hand toward her.

"My love, my dearest Lijsbet... I had no idea I would find you here. I am surprised and pleased."

Then he hit her with one of his smiles, those warm expressions that lit up his face, making him appear years younger than his nearly fifty years. Tingling began in Lijsbet's chest, spreading to her belly. She had come to know this man well. Very well, over a very long period of her life.

Isabella scrutinized her face. "Lady Lambert, I do not believe you have been introduced to our guest. This is Rogier van der Weyden of the Brussels school. Philip brought him here to create my portrait."

Did she not know? Or was she allowing this deceit to reveal itself on its own?

Lijsbet tipped up her chin. No sense prolonging the inevitable. "I have been introduced, Lady Duchess. At an earlier time. To a man with a different name."

The expression on Rogier's face sobered. "I had no idea I would find you here, Lijsbet." He repeated his words slowly, only now tinged with an ominousness that caused a sheen of sweat to rise on Lijsbet's skin. He paused to clear his throat, waving a hand toward her, beckoning her to join him on the dais. "I am surprised and pleased."

Lijsbet turned her attention to the duchess. "If your grace pleases, I shall break my fast at the lower table. I am, after all, a mere artisan. Not a great master."

Sitting close to Rogier was much too risky. His proximity, his scent, they would all work to break down her defenses. He also would have the opportunity to speak words to her no one else's ears would hear.

The bread tasted like dirt, the cheese like wax. Lijsbet found she could barely swallow the mouthful she had consumed, and lifted the cup of mead to wash it down. Rogier, by contrast, ate and drank freely, enjoying a lively conversation with the duchess. His eyes, however, fell upon her more often than she liked.

"Where is it you will paint my portrait, Master?" Isabella asked, tipping her head. "We have a scriptorium, but I am assuming you might prefer a more secluded setting. My solar, mayhap?"

Rogier rushed to finish chewing his last bite before answering. "If it pleases Your Grace, I would like to tour the castle to determine a suitable location, one with just the right light. Would this be possible?" Almost as an afterthought, he added, "Is there a particular setting you would like to be portrayed in?"

Isabella's laughter tinkled through the hall. "At my age, you will be challenged enough to portray me as more attractive than an old, faded tapestry. A plain setting will do. And I do hope you will be kind with your oils and brush."

The duchess, Lijsbet knew, was several years older than Rogier. Years of dealing with the duke, along with several lost children, had etched lines on her face and turned the hair at her temples a wiry gray. She had her handmaidens remove even more of the hair around her face than was customary. An exaggerated high forehead, fortunately, was the fashion anyway. Her elaborate headdresses obscured the remainder.

Again, Lijsbet finished what food she could force down quickly, then rose to excuse herself.

"I am anxious to return to my work station in the scriptorium, Lady Duchess. Please come by at your convenience. I should love to show you the techniques I learned in Leuven."

'Twas a comfort being back in the scriptorium, even though she hadn't been there very long when she left for Leuven. Brother Johannes was there, toiling away with a candle burning at each upper corner of his station. Lijsbet glanced around, frowning. She had forgotten how dark this place was.

She would have to ask the duke why he chose such a dark chamber for his artists to work. The scriptorium at Groot Beginjnhof, and in Tournai as well, had been held much brighter atmosphere. Then she remembered Lord Price's aversion to sunlight.

Would this resolve with his delusion? Her thoughts drifted to him, the handsome young man with the luminous blue eyes, truly windows to his soul. She wondered how he was faring in Leuven since her departure. Did he miss her?

Did she want that he missed her? Surely not. The man in the great hall was a reminder of just how tangled her life and her heart could become if such an emotional bond continued with the earl.

Hating to admit it, she realized she missed Davion. Very much.

*Davion*

Davion's palm grew damp against the faded tapestry covering the long bench. Fighting the nausea and dizziness overtaking him, he stammered, "There must be some mistake. I am an only child. My father impressed upon me my responsibility to take over the earldom if something should happen to him—"

"Aye, as the only son, this is true. But your sister did exist. Sadly, she died very young." Dr. Vanderhoff, for once, appeared totally focused on Davion, the bread beside him forgotten. He folded his hands between his knees, studying the earl with an intensity that made Davion quiver inside. "Think back, way back, to when you were a very small child. Do you remember nothing? Nothing about a little girl with raven black hair, much like your own?"

He began shaking all over now, and closed his eyes to avoid vomiting. Every instinct warned him not to go there, to that place in his mind that seemed like a deep, dark abyss. Not to even try to remember anything before his seventh birthday, when his father told him a monk would be coming to school him, privately. This news had excited Davion greatly. He had an active, curious mind as a child, and had grown bored with his existence as a pampered, sequestered child.

*Very* sequestered. Looking back, Davion realized he had been spent his younger years mostly alone, in his bedchamber, or in the playroom with his nursemaid—alone. He had not been permitted to play in the courtyard with the other children of the manor. Neither his mother nor his father ever demonstrated affection to him. 'Twas as though the sight of him caused them pain.

'Twas not strange to him at the time. 'Twas all he knew. Now, though, he wondered why. He wondered why he had been treated so delicately, as though...

*As though he were made of glass.*

"Lord Price? Do you remember a little girl?" The doctor's words penetrated the haze shrouding his mind.

He shook his head. "Nay. No little girl. No other children at all. I had no playmates. 'Twas not allowed."

The doctor sighed and his head fell forward. Then he leveled his gaze on the earl. "I cannot help you unless you dredge up these memories on your own, my lord. My telling you will not cure your problem. You must remember." Vanderhoff rose and motioned for Davion to do the same. "I suggest you go away for a while, and think upon this matter. Go to sleep with these thoughts on your mind. Mayhap your dreams will enlighten you. They often do."

*Dreams.* Should Davion tell the doctor about his tortured dreams? Mayhap they held a key.

The doctor, however, was in a hurry to get to his evening meal. "Come, come, Lord Price. The hour grows late. Return to me on the morrow, and we will continue our discussion."

That night, when the earl's exhausted body finally gave in to sleep, the dream did return. This time, 'twas more distinct in detail than he had ever remembered.

'Twas almost as though he had been transported back in time.

Chapter Twenty-Two

Davion recognized the grand entry hall in the palace, the place where he grew up. 'Twas as though he were floating into the scene, a specter transcending time and place. He somehow knew he was no longer there, no longer a child. Yet the details were so clear, so distinct.

The broad, heavy oak entry doors were to his left, complete with their arched, iron-gridded windows high up—too high for a child to peer through. No, looking outside was only possible through the glass on both sides of the doors, although 'twas still a challenge. There was a pattern in the glass, bright colors that allowed in the light, but one could not see through it.

Except in one, small place in the very corner. The glass here was clear. 'Twas just the right height for a child to peek through, using one eye.

"But why do they call it *stained* glass, Mama? 'Tis different colors. Pretty colors. 'Tis not stained like the berry spots on my favorite dress."

The voice shot through him like a blade, sharp and painful. A child's voice. A little girl's voice, sweet and lilting.

His mother's laughter resonated around him then, so real Davion woke with a start, convinced the woman stood over his bed. Sweat soaked his body and the linen sheet in which he was tangled. Moonlight streamed in through the window, casting the small room in a cool, eerie glow. He was on his narrow pallet, the one in his shared quarters of the artists' residence.

His mother was not standing over him. In fact, there was no one else in the room at all. Apparently the other guest had left. The pallet was empty, made up with linens and blanket folded neatly atop.

Slowly, he sat up and rubbed his eyes. The dream had always been the same before. This time, 'twas different. This time, he heard no scream, saw no blood, felt no stab of pain in his heart.

*Diana.* Was that whose voice he had heard?

Davion scrubbed his hands through his hair until his scalp prickled. *Why cannot I remember? Can it be true? Did I, in fact, have a sister?*

*A twin named Diana?*

And if he had, what had happened to her? This question, of all, was the most frightening. A shudder racked his shoulders and Davion shook his head. Denial stepped in to cast its protective cloak around him.

*Nay. The doctor was wrong.* He had researched the wrong family. Price was a common name in England. There were many different ones, distantly related. Surely, Dr. Vanderhoff had retrieved records on a different Davion Price.

He sat on the edge of his bed for a very long time, his face in his hands. He knew not how much time remained until daybreak. Yet he feared surrendering his mind to sleep once again.

Davion feared the dream would reveal more of this memory, the memory of the stained-glass window beside the heavy oak doors. Stained-*glass*. Fragile, delicate, breakable. Just like him.

Lighting a candle, the earl made his way on bare feet out of the bedchamber and down the hallway toward the kitchen. Mayhap 'twas some ale, or some mead to unstick his dry tongue from the roof of his mouth. As he turned the corner in the hall, however, he was surprised and pleased to discover light streaming from the kitchen doorway.

Jehan was already awake, preparing the meal for breaking of the fast. Dawn must be imminent, he thought with relief. 'Twas no need for him to even try to go back to sleep.

He found the house servant kneading bread at the other end of the long work table. The earl's presence startled him. Apparently, few ever awoke this early but Jehan.

"Good morrow, Lord Price. 'Tis not nearly dawn. Is there something I can get for you?" Jehan brushed the flour from his hands and came around the end of the table, then stopped. "My lord, are you well? You are . . . pale. You look as though you have been haunted by a spirit."

*Aye, but I have. Alas, the ghosts who haunt me may have been real.*

Davion rubbed his eyes and yawned, feigning no concern. "Nay, I simply woke with a thirst, Jehan." He pointed to the earthenware pitcher on the sideboard. "May I?"

"Allow me." Jehan produced a cup from the shelf above and filled it, handing it to the earl. "Sit while you drink. I get lonely working here so early, barely past the witching hour." The servant returned to kneading the bread dough. "Did Dr. Vanderhoff find you? He came here yesterday to see you."

Davion sipped the sweet mead and swirled it in his mouth, hoping to flush away the bitterness of the thoughts in his head. "Aye. I met with him last eve, at his residence."

"Master Bouts was seeking you as well." Jehan spoke softly and avoided the earl's gaze.

"Oh? I did not think I had any further business with the master."

Jehan lifted a shoulder. "I know not why he asked for you. He has gone away now, though. The Master said not to expect his return for many moons."

Tension twisted in Davion's chest. "Did he say where he was traveling?"

*Bouts knew the lady left for Coudenburg. He also knew I was remaining in Leuven. Would he have the audacity to follow her to the duke's palace?*

"Nay, my lord. He did not say." Jehan shaped the loaf and laid a linen towel over it, then slid the board on which it lay aside. "I have learned not to question Master Bouts' affairs. He is a very . . . private man."

*A very devious one as well, and one without decent morals. I must finish my business here in Leuven and return to Coudenburg as soon as possible.*

"Is dawn near?" he asked, draining his cup.

Jehan glanced toward the window. "Nay, not for at least an hour, mayhap more. You have time to return to your bed."

*The last place I want to be.*

"Thank you for quenching my thirst, Jehan. I will return later for a hunk of that bread. It looks like 'twill be delicious."

THE SCRIPTORIUM WAS as silent as a tomb and nearly as dark when Lijsbet arrived. Brother Johannes had not yet arrived. Using her candle, Lijsbet lit the torch above her work station, then lit the candles on its surface. Her artist's box had been stored beneath by the court's servants upon her arrival. She lowered to one knee to slide it out.

On the drying table, she laid out the folios she had worked on, or completed in Leuven. Even in the dim light, their brilliance thrilled her. This was what her life's purpose was, always had been, and would continue to be.

Lijsbet lived to create beauty, timeless illuminations that would outlive her and all of future generations by countless decades.

Hers was important work. Creating it brought her joy and fulfillment. 'Twas all she needed in this life.

When she heard footsteps behind her, she assumed 'twas the monk coming in to begin the day's work. Turning, she realized 'twas, instead, the man she least wanted to see. Rogier de la Pasture.

Or van der Weyden. Whatever he was calling himself these days.

"My lord," she said in a loud voice, hoping someone in the hall would hear her, " 'tis not proper for you to visit me here with no one else about. I must ask you to leave. Return, if you must, once the other artisan has arrived."

The artist ignored her and strode across the room. Lijsbet staggered back until she collided with the drying table. Van der Weyden stepped so close, she could feel the heat of his body.

His scent surrounded her as well, that of linseed oil and chalk from the canvasses. She knew this smell. She herself had worn it, many nights, upon leaving the master's chambers.

"Lijsbet, I have been frantic. I returned from my travels to discover you were gone. Why? Why did you leave without notice? Without sharing your plans with me?"

Rogier stepped even closer, and although Lijsbet pulled away, there was nowhere for her to go. Her back was up against the table, and when she attempted to sidestep around him, he caged her with his hands on either side. His breath, even at this early hour, reeked of ale.

She realized by his clumsy movements he was already deep in his cups—or was still, from the night before. 'Twas not unusual for the master. He liked his drink.

" 'Tis over, Rogier. I came here to start my life anew. Without you." She turned her face away, avoiding his sour breath that turned her stomach. "*You*. Who *are* you? You come here introduced as Rogier van der Weyden. I know no such man."

She cringed as he ran his hand up and down her arm. "Ah, but you do know me, Lijsbet, and quite well. Do you not remember our passionate nights together? Do you not recall how I brought you to heights of pleasure you had never known?"

"I do not believe that is any way to speak to a lady, my lord. Nor will I allow it in my house."

'Twas Isabella's voice. She stood in the doorway of the scriptorium, hands on her hips, fire shooting from her eyes. Lijsbet's knees nearly buckled from beneath her with relief. The artist pulled back immediately, folding his hands behind his back as though he'd done nothing improper.

"I was merely trying to get a closer look at the lovely work of your illuminator, Lady Duchess." Strolling casually down the length of the space where Lijsbet's leaves were laid out, the artist feigned interest. "Ah. This one, in particular, I find most fascinating."

Lifting the parchment between two fingers, he waved the leaf in the air toward the duchess. "Have you examined the intricacies of this piece, Lady Isabella? The details are quite . . . unique."

Lijsbet's skin prickled as she realized 'twas the leaf bearing the unusual man-beast she had created in the Groot Beginjnhof scriptorium.

*It started out as a boar, but gained the wings of a dragon and the talons of a hawk somewhere along the way. She was in the process of adding a beard, but not of the kind found on a dragon. A man's beard . . .*

At present, Rogier's face was clean-shaven. But in the earlier years, in the years when he had captured her heart, she had found his hairy chin one of his most alluring features.

Mayhap, she thought now, because it covered most of his face.

"I have not yet had time to peruse Lady Lambert's work. She's only just arrived from Leuven." The duchess scanned the room, confirming Lijsbet was alone. "You should not be here, my lord. Lady Lambert is alone in the scriptorium, and she has come here to work. She is anxious, I am sure, to resume. Please, Master van der Weyden, allow my artisan to do her job." The duchess' arms were now crossed over her chest, her expression severe. 'Twas clear she had no intention of leaving until the artist did the same.

Pursing his lips, the artist kept his hands folded behind his back as he strolled toward the duchess. "My apologies, Your Grace. I did not realize 'twas a protocol here at Coudenburg. In my workshop, the master does not need to make an appointment to see the illuminators' work."

" 'Tis not your workshop," the duchess spat, "nor is Lady Lambert one of your artisans. Kindly, sir, I ask you to take your leave. At once."

Lijsbet was surprised to see this side of the duchess, one she had not seen before. The lady was strong-willed, she knew—how else could one stay married to the likes of Duke Philip? But Isabella was strong in other ways as well. Strong, and wise.

*I should like to be more like Lady Isabella.*

After van der Weyden was gone, the duchess whooshed out a breath. "I am so sorry he accosted you, Lijsbet. I shall have the duke speak with him. He had no right to take such liberties."

Lijsbet, leaning on the table for support, covered her eyes with one hand. "How can this have happened, Lady Duchess? Did the duke not know I was running from this man?"

She felt a warm hand on her shoulder then. Isabella's words were soft in her ear. "The male of our species can be as stupid as a pig sometimes. Nay, he knew not the artist he brought to paint my portrait was the same man known as Rogier de la Pasture in Tournai." She huffed. "How he could not have known is beyond my comprehension."

"Why does the artist go by two names, Lady Duchess? Why?" Lijsbet asked, her voice thick as tears threatened.

Isabella's sigh said more than words. "Join me, Lijsbet. Come to my solar and I will have our morning meal brought there. There is information you need to know."

# Chapter Twenty-Three

Davion knew 'twas early morning, but he did not care if he awakened the doctor. He needed answers, and he needed them now. With Bouts gone, destination undisclosed, the earl's worry for Lily had reached a panic point in his mind. The master may not have told Jehan of his intentions, but in his gut, Davion knew where Bouts was headed.

He must return to Coudenburg and protect Lily from the ill-intended advances of Dieric Bouts. *His* Lily. He swore under his breath, cursing himself for not declaring his feelings for her before she left Leuven.

Again, 'twas the doctor's disheveled son who opened the door. The boy's shoulders drooped when he saw the earl, and he could almost read the annoyance on his face. Proper to a fault, Vanderhoff's son simply greeted the earl with a sleepy smile and ushered him into the front room.

"Father still sleeps," he said. "I shall rouse him."

After what seemed an eternity, Dr. Vanderhoff appeared, his tunic rumpled and a sleep-crease marring his pudgy left cheek. He shuffled to his chair without a word to Davion. Behind him, his son followed with a tray bearing a pitcher, cups, and a platter filled with pastries and wedges of cheese.

"Good morrow, Lord Price. I did not expect you so early. Please join me as I break my fast." Without hesitation, the doctor poured a cup and lifted a large tart to his mouth. He finally met Davion's eyes and spoke, spewing crumbs. "What brings you to call at such an hour? Has there been an event? Did your dreams reveal the root of your delusion?"

Davion sat on the padded bench, where he had been directed to sit before. "Nay, no root cause revealed," he began. "But the dream... a dream I have suffered repeatedly for most of my life returned, different this time."

The doctor stopped chewing and stared at Davion. "Dreams. You mentioned nothing of these on our last visits."

Davion shrugged. "I did not think them of any consequence. They are tortured. Difficult to talk about."

Vanderhoff sat back in his chair, hands folded across his round middle. "Well, you must speak of them now. How can I determine the significance of this new dream if I know nothing of the previous ones?"

As the doctor ate, Davion described his repetitive dream, haltingly. 'Twas, indeed, painful to put into words. When he mentioned blood, and shiny shards of glass, Vanderhoff stopped chewing and met his gaze. "Go on."

"That is all. I always awoke with a terrible ache in my chest, as if an arrow pierced my heart. The sounds of a woman's screams echo in my head long after I awake."

"Hmm. And last night? How was this dream different?"

The earl went on to describe his latest nighttime imagining. " 'Twas much less unpleasant than the old dream. I felt almost a sense of wonder, as if I were reliving part of my life over again. Hovering, like a spirit, in a place and time from long ago." He paused, gazing off into the distance, remembering. "The details were so crisp, so real. I saw the pattern on the glass panels flanking our front door at the manor. They were multi-colored, so brilliant, with a design reminiscent of a flower garden in full bloom." He paused and took a deep breath. " 'Twas lovely, but frustrating because the color blocked my view. Only one tiny place in the corner where the glass was clear."

"Stained glass," the doctor said.

"Aye, that's what the woman said. Aye, I also heard voices. One was my mother's. The other was that of a young girl. A child." He raised his eyes to the doctor. "My *sister*, mayhap?"

"Mayhap," Vanderhoff said, setting down his mug and leaning forward. "But no screaming? Like in the dreams before?"

"Nay. No screaming." Davion shuddered. "I was relieved to have awakened before any screaming commenced."

One of the doctor's bushy eyebrows lifted. "*Before*. How do you know the screaming came after the scene you witnessed ... dreamed of last night?"

"I do not know. I just do."

Vanderhoff drained his mug and reached for another small, meat-filled pie. "I believe you are well on your way, my lord. Mayhap tonight's dreams will bring you the answers you need."

Panic filled his chest and Davion leapt from the seat. "Nay! I cannot wait any longer. I must return to Coudenburg at once."

The doctor leaned back in his chair and sighed. " 'Tis true, if the memory has not surfaced after all these years, 'tis not likely 'twill surface on its own. Any more than it already has."

"Is there no other way you can help me, Doctor?"

Vanderhoff rubbed his chin. "The only way I can hope to help you, my lord, is to reveal to you the facts, the events as they occurred. 'Tis all right here in these records, which I obtained—with your good father's permission—from the church where you were baptized. You, and your sister, Diana."

Davion shook his head to clear it. "You keep saying I had a sister, a twin. Did she die at birth? Why do I not remember her? And why do my parents insist I am an only child?"

" 'Tis probably easier for them to bear the loss if they pretend the tragedy never happened. You do this as well, Lord Price. Though with you, the denial is deep inside your mind. Beyond your control."

Davion stared out the window, silent for a long moment. "Is this why I cannot remember? I have chosen—albeit unconsciously—to pretend it never happened."

"Aye."

"Then you must relate to me the events, Dr. Vanderhoff. Today. You must share with me what you have learned. I will try, very hard, to bring the memories back into my mind. How, though, can this knowledge explain my ridiculous fear? My delusion that I am made of glass?"

The doctor's eyes narrowed, and he pointed a finger at the earl. "Ah, so now you are regarding your fear as *ridiculous*. You are referring to your beliefs as a *delusion*. You are coming to terms with this, my lord. I think, mayhap, you are ready to hear the truth."

Two hours later, dazed and weak in the knees, Davion staggered from the doctor's residence. Vanderhoff urged him to allow his son to accompany him back to the artists' residence, but the earl refused. Although he felt weak in his body, his mind was now clear. He may not be completely cured, but now, at least, he understood why he feared his body would shatter like glass.

Like brilliantly multi-colored stained glass.

He wandered the streets of Leuven aimlessly for several hours, until the sun was high in the sky. 'Twas no longer a concern for him to walk in the sunlight. In fact, he found its warmth reassuring, fortifying.

Davion strolled through the city until he found a stable, the flies and reek of dung drawing him straight to the spot. A man out front was hammering a horseshoe on an anvil, a drowsy horse standing nearby swishing flies with his tail. The earl approached him.

"My good man, does your stable offer horses for hire? I require a mount—a very gentle one, mind—to carry me back to Coudenburg. I can have one of the ostler's men return the beast once I have arrived."

"A gentle one, hey? Aye, I have a sensible mount. He's old, but sturdy and trustworthy. I cannot lend him out, however. To take Markus, ye must buy him."

The last thing the earl had planned on in securing passage back to the duke's castle was the cost of buying a horse. He shuffled his feet, then scratched his neck where a horsefly had just taken a blood meal. "What is Markus' price?"

*Lijsbet*

Lijsbet sat with the duchess in her solar, a table between them holding the makings of a morning meal. Coarse bread, a wedge of cheese, and some small dried fish were arranged artfully on the wooden platter. Isabella poured some sweet pink mead into two pewter goblets.

"You must eat first, Lijsbet. Your body falls away to nothing. Did they not feed you at all at Groot Beginjnhof?" the duchess chided.

"My appetite fails me," she answered quietly.

'Twas true, Lijsbet had become very thin. When she washed her naked body, she noticed hip bones that stuck out like those of an emaciated old horse. Her breasts had shrunken to near nothingness. In truth, if not that she wore a woman's clothing and dressed her long hair, Lijsbet could well pass for a young boy.

Though mayhap not a young one. The soft skin under her arms and inner thighs hung loosely, like a withered old woman. Her cheeks had taken on the hollow appearance of some of the beggars in the city, and the lines around her eyes and mouth deepened. Thinness—and stress, no doubt—had aged her. Rallying herself, she wrapped some cheese and a fish in the bread and began to eat.

Isabella sat in her high-backed chair while Lijsbet ate, staring out the multi-paned windows overlooking the bailey. Her face was drawn down, her mouth curving at the corners. With the morning light on her skin, the duchess looked older even than her years. Lijsbet ate slowly, forcing herself to chew and swallow. 'Twas as though she had forgotten how to enjoy the taste of food.

She did not press the duchess, knowing the woman would tell her whatever 'twas needed told in her own time. Worry simmered in the pit of her belly, making eating all that much more difficult. Questions swirled in her mind. Was she to be cast out from the duke's castle? Would the presence of this artist, bidden by the duke himself, make her own presence forbidden?

Finally, Isabella faced her with glistening eyes. "I cannot tell you how shocked and appalled I was last eve at the duke's arrival. I had no knowledge of where he had gone, but was under the impression he would be away for a long time." She closed her eyes and shook her head. "It happens often enough. But this time, apparently, he was only going as far as the city. To Brussels, to fetch Master van der Weyden."

Lijsbet swallowed a ball of bread in her throat that was threatening to choke her. " 'Tis not the name by which I know this man, Lady Duchess. He is Rogier de la Pasture, Master of Tournai. 'Tis how I have known him since I entered his workshop over five years ago."

The duchess studied her. "The artist, it would appear, does go by both names. I am assuming you have no knowledge, then, of his life in Brussels. As van der Weyden."

Lijsbet shrank in her seat, and could almost feel the weight of a blade hanging above her head. A guillotine.

"Nay." Her words came on a whimper.

Isabella huffed and began rubbing her hands, one over the other. "I had heard rumors, but knew none to be fact. Until I saw your face when the man stepped into the room. Only then did I come to realize the truth."

The duchess began, in as gentle a tone as she could, to reveal the details of the artist's life—the one he lived in Brussels, as van der Weyden. Lijsbet's pain rose in her chest, clamping down her air until she felt faint. Her tears rose and spilled over, running down her cheeks unchecked. A number of times questions rose she wanted to ask, but she could not. Her throat had nearly closed, making speaking impossible.

A wife. Three children, a daughter and two sons. Not only married, but married almost as long as Lijsbet had been alive.

When Isabella finished her tale, she fell silent, her gaze cast down on the floor. A gracious lady, one who was giving Lijsbet time to absorb this information. To accept the horrible, embarrassing truth. Her tears continued to flow, and only once did she hiccup on a sob choked back. When she could finally find the strength to speak, 'twas only one statement—one she knew now had been a terrible lie.

"I knew I played the role of a mistress. But he said we would marry, someday. Someday soon."

# Chapter Twenty-Four

Davion Price had never ridden a horse in his life. He was not afraid of the beasts, but had taken care never to stray close enough to one that he might be knocked into by their massive, lumbering bodies. Sitting atop one had always been out of the question. Today, however, was the day for him to overcome this fear.

He was not, by any means, cured of his illness. Warnings still flashed in his mind with every movement. But now, somehow just knowing why these fears existed helped him to get past them. Besides, at the moment, he had no choice. The court carriage was gone, and 'twould take too much time to send a missive to ask for another. He must return to Coudenburg immediately. Today.

The only way he could make the trip quickly was on horseback.

Davion exchanged most of the few coins he had left in his pocket for the ownership of said beast. The ostler dropped the coins in his apron and disappeared inside the stable. A few moments later he returned tethered to an animal so large, the earl's mouth dropped open. Tall and massively broad, the palfrey's thick, shaggy coat was jet black. His head was, Davion estimated, at least as large as his own torso. The beast tipped his head and studied the earl with a large, black eye, like a hawk eyes a rodent upon which is about to pounce.

"Will ye be needing a saddle too, my lord? I can sell ye this one. 'Tis old, but 'twill get ye both to Coudenburg."

Grumbling, Davion fished out the last of his coins and dropped them into the ostler's grimy hand. In exchange, he was handed a strap of leather which was wrapped about the palfrey's head.

A few days ago, the earl feared the jostling he would suffer from a rough carriage ride. Now, he owned a horse. One he must ride, all the way back to Coudenburg.

Davion reached out to touch the horse's muzzle, stroking a velvety spot between flaring nostrils, two gaping holes as big around as his fist. How could an animal this large and powerful feel so soft to the touch? The beast—Markus—reached toward the earl and sniffed at his hair. Then he snorted, spraying him with horse snot.

Wincing, Davion swept the visible drops off the sleeve of his tunic as he asked, "How does one get on top of such a large mount?"

The ostler chuckled, revealing a single, yellow tooth on his lower jaw. "There's a block right over there."

Davion led the giant animal over to a thick section of tree trunk standing near the corner of the building. It took him several tries—he was still trying to move as carefully as he could—but shortly he found himself on top of Markus. The horse was wide, and the insides of Davion's thighs strained as he wrapped his legs around his barrel. Then he sat up tall and kept his eyes straight ahead, trained between the two fuzzy, black points that were Markus' ears.

"How do I make him go?" he asked.

The ostler stuck a piece of straw in his mouth and grinned his toothless smile. "Ye really have never ridden a horse before, have ye?"

"Nay. Tell me. How does one drive the beast?" His voice quivered, and heat flooded his face.

"Ye kick his ribs to make him go, and pull on the reins to make him stop. Easy as can be." The ostler ran his hand along the horse's neck, murmuring, "I'll miss ye, old boy. But this young man will take good care of ye. Ye do the same for him, now, hear?" He then took a step toward the rear of the palfrey and smacked him on the rump.

Davion jolted, fearing the worst. Hanging on desperately to the front of the saddle with both hands, he was relieved when Markus, who snorted again in protest, took his time taking the first plodding step.

As they departed, the earl asked the ostler for the quickest way back to Coudenburg. It was a straight ride, he told him, out of town and on the dirt road heading west.

"Keep following the sun," the ostler called to him. "If Markus is not too lazy today, ye should arrive before sundown."

*Follow the sun.* Davion squinted in the brightness of the yellow globe above his head. But no longer did he cringe.

They were off. The earl tried to relax and allow his hips to move with the rolling of the horse's back, and made a point not to look down. A fall from this height would surely reduce him to the tiniest splinters of glass.

Would it not?

Markus continued to move forward, but at his own chosen pace—slow. This was fine with Davion. Plodding along with heavy steps, they clopped their way along the cobbled streets to the edge of town. The ostler had been a good, honest man, Davion thought. The palfrey was, indeed, as gentle and safe as he had said.

Reminiscent of a snail. A very large, hairy snail.

As he rode and further relaxed, Davion's mind replayed the tale Dr. Vanderhoff shared with him of his family's loss. Of the death of his sister, Diana. His twin. Search his memory as he tried, he could conjure no recollection of the girl, or the horrific event that had taken her life. She had been, the doctor told him, only five years old when she died.

Davion had no memories of his childhood at that age—nor any memories earlier than that. They had all, the doctor explained to him, been blocked out, locked behind a heavy door through which the earl could not pass. 'Twas his mind's way of protecting itself, Dr. Vanderhoff had said.

Such tragedies could, and did, cause permanent damage to a child's mind. Davion wondered if the memories would ever return. Mayhap in a dream. But now that he knew what had happened, he prayed they would not replay in a nightmare. He did not want to have to relive those hellish days ever again.

Thinking ahead toward Coudenburg, the earl dreaded what he might find there. He was certain Master Bouts had gone after Lily. He did not believe the lady would indulge the artist, but he could not be certain. After all, she had no ties to Davion, even though they had become lovers. She did not know of his feelings for her.

Even if she did, would she return those feelings? The earl did not know. He simply knew the urgency which drove him onward, mile after mile, into the afternoon sun.

He hoped he would arrive in time.

*Lijsbet*

Instead of returning to the scriptorium after their talk, Isabella advised Lijsbet to take the remainder of the day for rest.

"You have had a tumultuous couple of moons," the duchess said, "and now have much to think about and absorb. To accept. 'Tis no hurry for any of the work you are doing in the workshop to be finished. Take some time for yourself, Lijsbet, and search for your peace."

That peace, Lijsbet knew, may be beyond the realm of her reality. She returned to her chamber, but after an attempt to return to sleep failed, she rose and made her way down to the kitchen. A cup of mead, mayhap a chat with the cooks and servants, would cleanse her mind.

Cleansing her soul, she knew, was not possible. She would have to settle for a cleansing of her mind.

The cook at Coudenburg, a stout woman whose breadth surpassed her height, was named Charlaine. From farther south in the Burgundian duchy, the woman spoke with a decidedly French accent. Her imposing form belied the soft, girl-like features of her round face, rosy from the heat of the kitchen. Her clear blue eyes twinkled when she saw Lijsbet, even though they had never actually spoken.

"Welcome, my lady fair. Welcome to my cuisine équipée—my workshop to perform my artistic endeavor." She winked. "My art is not as enduring as yours, nor as holy. But as I am sure you will agree, 'tis a very necessary art for any man, woman, or *enfant.*"

Lijsbet relaxed and slid onto the bench lining the long work table. "Your meals do tempt even those with no appetite. Like me." She smiled weakly. "I was wondering if you could direct me to the gardens. 'Tis a lovely day, and I am in need of some solitude."

The cook tipped her head. "You are sad, my lady. 'Tis true, some time alone in the gardens will raise your spirits. 'Tis no charm more powerful than that of nature. But first," Charlaine wiped her hands on her apron and bustled to the black iron pot steaming over the fire in the hearth, "I shall tempt you with something very special. To sweeten your soul from the inside out."

With that, the cook produced a pewter plate from the shelf above the hearth. From under a linen covering a mound of what Lijsbet assumed was rising bread, Charlaine produced a small golden cake about the size of her fist. She ladled something out of the steaming pot and poured it over the cake, then set the plate down before her.

"Canelé," she proclaimed proudly. " 'Tis one of Duke Philip's favorite treats. The hot honey soaks into the cake to create," she paused to kiss her fingertips and hold them in the air, "a masterpiece."

Lijsbet could not disagree. The aroma of warm honey enveloped her, and before she realized what she was doing, she had consumed three of the delicacies. When Charlaine went to retrieve a fourth, Lijsbet held up a hand and protested.

"Nay, my lady. I have eaten to excess already." She pressed a hand to her middle. "I must say, 'tis a treat for the gods."

Another kitchen maid, younger and taller than Charlaine, came in the back door carrying a basket overflowing with leafy greens. Lijsbet remembered seeing her chatting in the bailey with the ostler's wife, Eva, while two young girls scampered about around them. The woman smiled shyly at her.

"Ah, Nettie. I am glad you have returned. Can you please show Lady Lambert to the gardens? You can go through the kitchen yard. Show her the wonderful herbs we grow here at Coudenburg."

Lijsbet followed Nettie out the door and into a well-organized arrangement of square plots, marked off by stones. Each plot boasted several varieties of herbs, some of which Lijsbet actually recognized.

"Your lavender grows so tall!" she said, admiring the fragrant blooms that stood hip high.

Nettie smiled. "We use lavender for many things. All of our soaps are scented with the herb, and Charlaine has even shown us how to use the dried flowers to season various dishes." She ran her fingertips along the purple heads, causing bees to rise in a buzzing cloud. "Helps with the honey harvest as well." She wove through the planting beds toward an iron gate constructed of fancy scrollwork. "The flower gardens are through there, my lady. There's a turfed bench at the far end, from where you can see the goings-on in the bailey."

*A turfed bench.* The words caused memories to pop into Lijsbet's mind, and her cheeks warmed. "Many thanks, Nettie. I can find my own way from here."

Lijsbet found the turfed bench and settled there for the remainder of the morning hours. From here, 'twas true, the bailey was in full view. Only a slatted wooden fence separated the garden from the main courtyard, where she saw children playing, women carrying baskets to and fro, and the smithy shoeing a horse. This turfed bench was not as secluded as the one at Groot Beginjnhof. Her secret unions with the earl would never be possible here.

Davion's image flashed into her mind, clear and vibrant. His glossy black hair, his luminescent blue eyes. His scent, musky and intimately masculine. Those lips that tasted as forbidden as any sin she had ever committed. Closing her eyes, she allowed herself to drift back, back into his embrace.

The warmth in her chest quickly turned from pleasing to pain. Her heart, beating faster now, felt raw and battered. It ached too—for the man: his company, his conversation, his gentle smile that hid nothing.

He hid nothing.

This, Lijsbet realized, is what endeared Lord Price to her heart. 'Twas his innocence, his inability to conceal his emotions. His honesty.

Fear had ruled the man's life since he was a child, almost to the point of paralysis. Yet Lord Earl Price was, in reality, one of the strongest men she had ever met. He had no fear of revealing his flaws, his shortcomings.

A man who is not afraid for the world to see his weaknesses is a strong man, indeed.

Davion was a young, strong man, one who deserved much more than a worn-out mistress who could not bear him any children. An Englishman who would, no matter what he claimed, eventually seek his place and his earldom in his own country. There, he would find a woman deserving of his love and of the title of countess.

Turning him away would be painful, for both of them, she knew. But 'twas a necessary action. 'Twas the only way.

The view of the bailey blurred behind unbidden tears, and Lijsbet wiped them angrily away. She had vowed never to open her heart to any man, ever again. Her affair with the Master of Tournai was reason enough for her to pledge herself to a life alone. This new information about the man scored the injury deeper still, a hot blade to an open wound.

Even though she had only spent a fortnight at the beguinage, she found it odd not to hear the tolling of the prayer bells. She had come to structure her day by them. A pang of homesickness ached in her chest. Was she missing the beguines? Or their way of life? She had, at Groot Beginjnhof, for the first time in her life, felt as though she were part of a family.

Mayhap the beguinage was where she truly belonged. She would discuss this with the duchess. She knew Isabella would not want to see her leave Coudenburg. But she also would completely understand Lijsbet's motivations.

She was too scarred by sin to enter a convent, but the beguinage may welcome her. They had accepted Sister Fenna, who was their mistress, even after she had found herself in a position so much like Lijsbet. Mayhap, by joining the sisters at Groot Beginjnhof, Lijsbet could work toward earning forgiveness for her sinful past.

Rising from her seat as the afternoon sun began to sink in the sky to the west, Lijsbet felt a new sense of purpose. She finally had a direction. On the morrow, she would ask for audience with the duchess once again. She would ask her to write to Sister Fenna and ask if Lijsbet would be accepted as an apprentice at Groot Beginjnhof.

# Chapter Twenty-Five

*Davion*

The journey from Coudenburg to Leuven had seemed much, much shorter a distance when riding in a carriage. The earl had been told the trip on horseback took less time. Of course, riding astride a speedy charger, and balancing atop the likes of plodding Markus were two entirely different modes of transportation.

Markus took his time. Davion, although fearful the jostling might cause him injury, was mad with frustration at the slow pace the horse maintained. It seemed, however, that no matter what he did, he could not convince the horse to move any faster.

*Dieric Bouts could be wooing the lady at this very moment. My Lily. I must get there as quickly as possible.*

The earl mustered his courage and set his jaw. They had emerged from a forested area and around the bend, he saw a long, flat section of road. Davion gathered up the reins and sucked in a deep breath. Then, remembering the ostler's words, he prepared to take action.

*Ye kick his ribs to make him go, and pull on the reins to make him stop. Easy as can be.*

*Aye,* he thought, *if your body is made of flesh and bone, and not fragile glass, 'twill be easy as can be.*

But this couldn't be true. If 'twas, he would be dead by now. The fall and bump of his head on the stone hearth were proof. Nay, his body must be sturdier than he thought.

Davion closed his eyes and lifted both feet away from Markus' sides as far as he could. Then, with all his might, he kicked him.

*No sound of tinkling glass,* was his first thought. His next was, *God's bones. What have I done?*

Markus lurched forward, throwing Davion back in the saddle so he hit his arse on the back of the leather covered seat—hard. Grappling to hold onto the front of the contraption, his balance wavered dangerously, and he felt himself sliding to one side. At the last moment, his fingers caught a tuft of the palfrey's thick mane. The earl twisted his fingers into the rough hair and hung on desperately.

As if his life depended on it, because, he was sure, it did.

This was not, he realized, the bouncy, two-beat gait he'd seen men riding. Markus apparently had no middle gear. He went from plodding walk to thundering gallop.

The wind in his face took Davion's breath away, but cooled the sweat on his brow. After a short while, he figured out the rhythm of this gait. 'Twas a rolling motion, like a child's rocking horse.

*Rocking horse.* An image flashed through his mind of a carved, wooden horse on curved tracks. A toy. One he didn't want to share.

*Nay, Papa. 'Tis my turn now. Make Diana get off the horsey. 'Tis my turn!*

He shook his head, willing the images away. His mind refolded around the memory, but his body remembered the rocking sensations. Davion found if he relaxed into the saddle, the gait 'twas not so uncomfortable. 'Twas almost enjoyable. Exhilarating. And they were covering far more distance, far faster, than they were before.

A kind of euphoric bliss soon replaced his fear, and Davion felt his heart grow wings. He was riding a horse! He was galloping a horse—astride. And he had not shattered, nor splintered, nor sensed nary a crack form in any of his body parts.

His arse was the only area of concern, but 'twas too late to worry about that now.

The long, flat section of road was coming to an end, and quickly. Up ahead was another wooded area, where the path narrowed and disappeared into the dense forest around a sharp bend. Hang on as he might, Davion was not sure he could stay atop the galloping Markus for that abrupt a move.

*Ye kick his ribs to make him go, and pull on the reins to make him stop. Easy as can be.*

'Twas time to pull on the reins, which Davion did.

The ostler was right. Markus stopped. The earl did not.

For the briefest of heartbeats, the earl found himself airborne, tumbling over the massive head of his mount and flipping once before coming down on the road, hard. He landed on his arse, the reins still clutched in his hand. He was afraid to move, afraid to breathe. Davion sat there, certain that at any moment, he would shatter into tiny shards of glass in the dirt.

But nothing happened. He looked up at Markus, who stood over him, eyes at half-mast.

Davion looked down at his body, his legs, feet, and arms. All was intact, and he felt no pain anywhere. Except, of course, for his arse, which was sore to begin with from simply riding the horse at the walk. He slid one hand under his backside. 'Twas sore, but he felt no sharp edges. Nothing appeared to be broken.

Markus snorted, startling him so badly that Davion yelped. A shower of horse snot settled over him, and his lip curled as he slowly climbed to his feet. He soon realized, however, he now had yet another problem to solve.

The horse was gentle, but truly a giant. The stirrup at Markus' side hung roughly level with Davion's armpits. 'Twas physically impossible for him to raise his foot that high to re-mount the horse. He glanced around for a rock or a fallen log he could climb up on to allow him back into the saddle.

Nothing in plain view. Mayhap once they entered the forest, there would be a large stone or fallen log.

They walked only a few yards into the woods before he found what he needed. With a shout of joy, Davion dragged the giant palfrey toward a downed tree someone had rolled off onto the side of the road. 'Twas plenty big enough. Within moments, the earl was astride again. Although he maintained the slower pace until they came out into open fields once again, they were making progress.

The earl was careful, this time, to acknowledge Markus' three distinct gates: slow plodding, thundering gallop, and catapulting stop. He made his requests from thence onward with legs and rein very, very carefully.

Although the sun was setting faster than Davion would have liked, he felt sure they must be approaching Coudenburg. He cared not if he had to ride the whole night through. He must make it to the duke's castle in time to prevent Master Dieric Bouts from stealing away his beloved Lily.

Night had draped the countryside in near blackness by the time Davion saw a glow on the horizon. Since the sun had set, he had not had a guide to insure his journey remained west. There had been several forks in the road, and he was forced to guess which way would lead him toward Coudenburg. He knew the castle lay only a few miles east of Brussels—a city large enough for its torchlights to color the night sky. Saying a silent prayer he had nearly arrived at his destination, Davion was sorely tempted to kick Markus up into faster gait.

But darkness, ruts, and rocks in the dirt road made this too risky a move. He took a deep breath and forced himself to be patient with the palfrey's slow but unfailing footsteps. Surely, if 'twas not Brussels or Coudenburg Castle itself, at least 'twould be a village where he might discover how much farther he had to travel.

It seemed like hours after the night sky had revealed its hundreds of pinpricks of light, and Davion had all but dozed off atop Markus. The echo of a horn blowing jostled him to alertness. Against the glow beyond it, the earl could make out the massive shape of the castle, the ramparts dotted with flaming torches. 'Twas the duke's palace, and one of the sentries must have seen him, and sent up the alarm.

He was nearly there, close enough to Lily he could almost smell her. Grinning at his foolishness, Davion ran a hand over his face, which was gritty from the journey.

Soon, he would be with her. Soon, Lily would be in his arms. He hoped.

*Lijsbet*

She had retired early, having little appetite for the evening meal and feeling restless about her decision. Lijsbet spoke with Isabella briefly at table and made an appointment to speak with her the next morning. Her choice was made. Still, she wanted to sleep on the decision before asking the duchess to write to Groot Beginjnhof.

Sleep, however, remained elusive. After lying awake for several hours, Lijsbet poured some water into a cup and perched on the sill of one of the lancet windows in her chamber. From here, as from the duchess' solar, the portcullis was visible.

Lijsbet could not help but feel a sense of awe as her eyes took in the view. The bailey was empty and silent, lit by flickering torchlight. The only activity came from the guards who milled around the portcullis, talking and laughing. Torches lined the ramparts as well, where the shadows of sentries punctuated the sputtering flames. A peacefulness settled over her like a comforting blanket.

She would miss this place, her haven for far too short a period of time. Barely months had passed since she arrived, exhausted from her two-day journey from Tournai. The duchess had sent a horse and a chaperone to bring her back to Coudenburg. In the chill of pre-dawn, Lijsbet had watched the soldier tie her small bag of belongings to his saddle before they headed out of the city. Lijsbet had never looked back until now.

Nay, not now, but two nights ago when her past caught up with her here, at the duke's palace. How different her life might be if she'd never known of Rogier's other life. 'Twould not have cleansed the guilt of her being his mistress. But the wrongdoing would not be nearly as damning.

She was about to return to her bed when she heard the voices, no longer laughing now. A shout went up, followed by the blast of a horn. The alarm. Lijsbet made out the shouted words: "Rider approaching!"

Standing close to the window, Lijsbet waited until the squeal of the portcullis being raised. A visitor at such a late hour? A lone rider atop a massive horse clopped through the entry. Lijsbet couldn't make out much in the dim light, but it not appear the man was wearing armor. The guards lowered the gate behind him.

'Twas apparently a visitor the duke had either been expecting, or didn't mind receiving in the middle of the night.

Crawling back upon her bed, Lijsbet curled on her side and closed her eyes. She sighed, relief flooding her now that her new path was decided. A twinge nicked her heart when the thought of Davion drifted across her mind. She wondered if her farewell to him would happen here before she left, or if the earl would still be in Leuven when she returned to Groot Beginjnhof.

'Twould be farewell, forever.

The knocking on her door jarred Lijsbet just as sleep was about to claim her.

# Chapter Twenty-Six

*Lijsbet*

She was afraid to answer the door. It was Rogier, she was certain. He had discovered the location of her chamber. He would be coming to try to re-claim her. Convince her he loved her, no matter what anyone had said about him. He may even try his most convincing "we will marry soon" fantasy.

Lies, lies, lies. The very thought of his face caused her stomach to twist.

Mayhap, if she lay here long enough, he would give up and go away. Surely he would not dare make enough noise to alert anyone. 'Twas her belief. But the third time the pounding recommenced, 'twas accompanied by a voice. A man's voice, and not that of Rogier.

"Lady Lambert. Please, come to the door. A visitor is here to see you. The duchess granted permission for you to meet with him in the great hall."

*Him.* Who could that possibly be? Rogier was already sleeping within the castle, so he would not be considered a new visitor.

As she pulled her brown frock over her head and twisted her long hair into a messy braid, Lijsbet remembered the lone rider coming in through the portcullis. A visitor, at this hour?

Realization came as a bucket of water in the face. 'Twas Davion. He had returned.

But astride? Nay, it could not possibly be the earl.

A blast of warm, stale air blasted Lijsbet in the face as she descended the stairs. The great hall seemed cavernous, empty, lit only by two torches set alongside the door leading into the kitchen. There was a man there, waiting. It took her only a moment to realize who 'twas.

The earl stepped forward anxiously when she entered the room. Lijsbet could not help the tumble of her heart. He looked bedraggled, exhausted, but still exceedingly handsome. Even in the dim light, his eyes shone as blue as a summer sky.

She must be careful. Her emotions were unstable, a wound to her heart bleeding and sore. Part of her wanted to run to him, wrap herself around him and never let go. Another part knew 'twas the worst possible move she could make.

As she crossed the room, she approached as to keep the long table between them. Even though she knew what she must do, Lijsbet was not sure she could say the words while he held her against him.

*Davion*

Davion was not about to allow a plank of wood to stand between him and Lily. Not now, not after what he had been through in getting here. Not without knowing whether or not she came to him from a bed where she slept alone, or from one shared with the artist, Master Dieric Bouts. A wave of nausea washed over him at the thought.

With haste, he limped his way to the end of the table and skirted it before Lily had a chance to change course. His backside throbbed like he had been dragged behind a carriage all the way from Leuven, but nothing had broken that he could detect. The only thing perilous, at the moment, was his heart.

Whether made of glass or no, if Lily bore the scent of another on her lovely skin, Davion's heart, he knew, would shatter. 'Twould be the end of him.

As he wrapped his arms around her, he felt the tension. She was warm but not soft. Tension kept her slim, statuesque frame stiff, unwielding. She did not draw away from his embrace, but she did not return it either.

"Lily... Lily, oh praise the saints, I have come home to you. I only hope I have arrived in time."

She did not soften. But as he buried his face against her neck, Davion smelled only her—the lavender in her hair, from her bathwater, mingling hot with the enticing scent of the woman herself. He breathed her in, and a sigh of relief escaped. She had been sleeping alone, he was certain of it.

"In time for what?" she asked in a small voice.

He drew back and held her shoulders. "I knew he had come after you. I only hoped I would arrive before he broke down your defenses. Before he convinced you to—"

Her eyes flashed fire, and she stumbled back a step. "Nay," she snapped, "Do you think me a complete fool? Not him, not ever again!" Her voice was strung high with fury, and again, relief surged in his chest. For a moment, but her words did not slip past him.

*Not ever again.* What did she mean, not *again*? Had Lily history with Dieric Bouts he was not aware of?

"Again?" he asked, tipping his head. He searched her eyes, which looked glassy and a little wild with the torchlight flickering in them. In their luminescent gold. Flame-colored eyes—'twas what drew him to her from the very first day.

In those eyes, however, he did not see reflected back what he held in his own heart. *Love.* 'Twas no sign of love here. Only surprise and anger. Anger? Why would she be angry with him?

"Davion, I am relieved you have come back, and you appear safe." Her tone was cold, clipped. "But 'tis late, and I am drowsy from sleep. We have much to discuss. I will meet with you on the morrow to discuss my future." Bobbing a quick curtsy—she had never done *that* before—Lily wheeled and strode from the room with such swiftness, he wondered if her feet ever touched the floor.

The earl stood there for long moments, exhausted, bruised, and confused. To discuss *her future*. Not *their* future.

The crackling he heard—was it from his heart shattering? Or merely the fat sputtering from the torch behind him?

Wincing with every step paining him, he made his way to the stairs to find his bedchamber.

*Lijsbet*

How could Davion have known Rogier was coming to Coudenburg? He was one of the artists' confidantes, true, but Davion had never mentioned knowing Rogier de la Pasture. Or van der Weyden. Or whatever he called himself.

The truth came upon her like a wave crashing on the shore.

*The earl had known.*

Davion had known more about her and her situation in Tournai than even she had herself. He knew the artist had deceived her, in the most sacrilegious sense of the word. The earl understood that Lily had been the mistress of a married man, a father.

He had never let on. He had never said a word.

To possess such knowledge, and to not share it with her, caused ire to rise into her throat. Anger foamed so hot and spicy, she was certain she would either explode or melt like a candle into a sticky heap.

She could not go to sleep. Not now. Not until she had answers to some very perplexing questions. Perched on her windowsill all the rest of the night through, Lijsbet waited for the sunrise. The whole while, she practiced in her head the ranting she intended for the prestigious Earl Davion Price—glass man or no.

The *English* earl. Aye, the man *was* made of glass. Now, Lijsbet could see right through him.

*Davion*

When Davion awoke, 'twas already well past sunrise. Exhaustion, he knew, had taken him down hard. As he struggled to sit up on his pallet, he was grateful no dreams had haunted him. He realized, however, that he ached from head to toe. More in some places in between.

The most painful throb was inside of him, where his heart should be. He wasn't sure yet how 'twould all play out with Lily, but judging by her greeting last night, his future looked bleak.

At least, his future with Lily.

Slowly, carefully, he changed into clean braies and tunic. The water in the basin was cool and clean, smelling like the lavender he associated with the woman he loved. Another pang of pain shot through him.

All of this time he had feared his body shattering, literally, into pieces. Davion had no idea the breaking of one's heart could hurt far worse.

When he arrived at the great hall, 'twas empty save for a servant sweeping out the rushes. Turning on his heel, he headed down the hall toward the scriptorium. There, he hoped to find Lijsbet.

Or so he believed. When he entered the dimly lit room, the only occupant was Brother Johannes, toiling away by the light of two candles on his work table. Davion frowned. He did not remember this room being so infernally dark.

He strode over to the wall where he knew windows hid behind heavy draperies. With both hands, he grabbed the heavy cloth and yanked them apart. Sunlight flooded the room. Brother Johannes shrieked and nearly fell off his stool.

"Lord Price," he stammered, squinting in the sudden brightness, "I did not hear you come in."

Davion squinched his eyes as well. *Sunshine.* 'Twould take some getting used to, for certain.

"Where is Lady Lambert? Is she not working this morning?"

The monk shook his head. "Nay, she has left to meet with the duchess. I do not know when she intends to return."

The earl pressed his lips together. He scanned the scriptorium as if seeing it for the first time. In truth, he *was* seeing parts of the room for the first time—in full daylight. Some cobwebs swaying lazily from the tops of the dusty draperies caught his eye.

"I will ask the servants to dust in here more thoroughly," he said, motioning toward the wispy strands. " 'Tis not good to have dirt and grime floating down to settle on our parchment, is it?"

The monk's eyes widened, and then he broke out in a smile that transformed his face from a serious man of God to a brown-robed imp. Davion looked at Johannes—really looked at him—for the first time. He realized the man was not old and dowdy, as he had thought on first meeting. He was a young man, barely beyond boyhood. Mayhap not even as old as the earl himself.

" 'Twill be wondrous to work by the light of the sun," the monk murmured, staring at Davion in amazement. " 'Tis good to have you home, Lord Price."

The earl made his way along the halls until he encountered a group of servants bustling from in from the laundress with armfuls of clean linens.

"My good ladies. Who shall I speak to about cleaning duty in the scriptorium?" he asked.

The young women looked at each other, then shrugged. "We do not know, Lord Price. We shall ask the house matron. Is there a problem?" the tallest one asked.

Davion tipped up his chin and folded his arms across his chest. "Only one of my own doing. 'Twas so dark in there, a proper cleaning was not possible. Please, will you ask the scriptorium be more thoroughly dusted?"

They nodded, but before allowing them to scurry past him, he asked, "Where might I find the duchess' solar? I am in need of speaking with her."

The earl knew he was breaching protocol, seeking audience with the duchess without an appointment. But following the maids' direction, he climbed the stairs and headed for the chamber they had described. Before he reached the door, however, the duke, Philip himself stepped out into the hall ahead of him.

*Was Lily meeting with both the duke and the duchess?*

"Davion, so good to have you home. I heard you arrived late last night. Quite the palfrey brought you here, I heard." Philip's tone was chiding. "I thought you did not ride astride?"

The earl squared his shoulders. "I have overcome a good deal of my idiosyncrasies since I left Coudenburg. Tell me, is the duchess' chamber in this hallway?"

Philip draped an arm over Davion's shoulders, making him wince only briefly. "Nay, 'tis down the north hall. This is the west wing. Besides, I believe she is occupied at present. Come. Let us sit in my solar and share a cup. I would like to hear all about your adventure in Leuven."

*Lijsbet*

"I cannot believe Lord Price had any knowledge of this," the duchess said, staring at Lijsbet in shock. "He is a good man. An honest man."

Lijsbet folded her arms tightly around her and paced the room. "I believed so as well. But it seems in sharing my affections, I have chosen poorly. Again." Her throat was tight, but she refused to cry.

*No more displays of feminine weakness. Never again.*

Isabella pinched the bridge of her nose. "I cannot believe how out of hand this situation has spun. I thought, in bringing you here, I was protecting you." She met Lijsbet's eyes with tears swimming in hers. "Instead, I have dragged you onto the fire itself."

Lijsbet waved a hand in the air. "You are not to blame for any of this, Lady Duchess. I am the one at fault here. My weakness, my foolishness has led me astray one too many times. Which is why I have come to ask from you a favor."

"Whatever I can do to help your life resume some sense of stability, Lady Lambert?"

"I wish to join Groot Beginjnhof in Leuven. If you would, your grace, I ask that you write to Sister Fenna, the mistress there, and ask if I might be admitted as a novice."

# Chapter Twenty-Seven

Davion

"So the good Dr. Vanderhoff has cured you, then!" The duke's voice echoed in his sparsely furnished solar. Truly a man's room, Davion thought. A man who does not spend much time at home.

The earl lifted a shoulder. "Not completely. But whatever relief I have gained, 'twas not without another's help. I have your illuminator, Lady Lambert, to thank as well."

One of Philip's dark eyebrows lifted. "Lady Lambert, you say? I was under the impression you two did not like each other very much. At first meeting, it seemed."

"Nay, we did not. But behind the considerable barriers she has constructed to protect her softer side, I have discovered she is a gracious and caring woman. Dr. Vanderhoff enlightened me as to the cause of my delirium. But 'twas Lily... Lijsbet who helped me to overcome a great deal of my fears."

Philip sat back and crossed his long legs at the knee, balancing a pewter goblet atop. "I will admit, I do not know the lady all that well. She came to us by invitation, through the duchess. I was very pleased to add her talents to our new library." He paused to sip his wine, thoughtfully. "It seems you are not the only man who finds the lady to be, let us say, gracious and caring."

Davion bristled. "As I am coming to realize. Unfortunately, 'tis not these attributes men first notice. I am aware of her previous involvement, and this concerns me not. 'Tis the new threat that worries. Tell me, your grace, when did the master arrive?"

Philip blinked, staring at the earl, confused. "You say her previous involvement concerns you not, yet..." He shook his head. "Of what new threat do you speak?"

The earl clenched his fists. "When did Master Bouts arrive, your grace? And for what business has he come to Coudenburg? Unless he has some business here at all, I believe he has come to pursue Lady Lambert."

Philip shook his head again and set down his goblet. "I am confused, Davion. Is it Dieric Bouts of which you speak? I have not seen Master Bouts for nigh on a year or more. Not since the last time I was in Leuven."

Davion stared at Philip, blinking. "He is not here?"

"Not to my knowledge. Of course, I only returned home a day or so ago. I brought Master van der Weyden with me, to paint Isabella's portrait. I also brought another of my relations."

"But Lily... Lijsbet told me last night when I arrived that the master was here. I assumed 'twas Master Bouts—"

"The only painter I know who has come to Coudenburg of late is Master van der Weyden." Philip shrugged and filled his cup. He took a deep draw on the wine. "Or Master of Tournai. Whatever he is calling himself these days."

It took Davion long moments to absorb this perplexing information. "Is it not the Master of Tournai with whom Lily had been associating?"

"Aye, he goes by that name, in Tournai. Apparently, the painter calls himself van der Weyden in Brussels. I had no knowledge of this, nor did the duchess. Only when he arrived did we discover the truth." Philip pursed his lips. "Lijsbet, apparently, recognized van der Weyden as the Tournai master. She was not happy I had brought him here." He cleared his throat. "Neither was the duchess."

"But why? Why the deception? Why two names in two different cities?"

Philip blew out a breath and slammed his cup down on the table. "Apparently to convince those who did not know him well—such as those in Tournai—he was not attached. A single man. Which he is not, by far."

A sinking in the pit of Davion's stomach made the room spin around him. "Wha-what do you mean? The artist is married?"

"Not only married, but has been for many years. Long enough to produce four children—legitimate offspring who are only a few years younger than Lijsbet herself." Philip frowned and turned to gaze out the window. "Rogier may be a talented artist, but as a man, his reputation is less than savory."

The earl left the duke's solar with his head spinning. Part of him was relieved that Dieric Bouts had, apparently, not followed Lily to Coudenburg. One threat, at least, did not exist. Even Rogier's presence here was not truly a threat, as now the secret of his double life had been revealed. Surely, Lily would want to have nothing to do with the man with this new knowledge.

No wonder she had been so adamant last night, saying, "Not him. Never again."

Suddenly Davion's heart felt light and free. Mayhap he could now proceed with his plan to confess to Lily his true feelings. Mayhap now, the two of them had a chance at a life together.

*Lijsbet*

Isabella stared at Lijsbet in shock. "Surely, you cannot be sure of this decision. 'Tis a drastic one, to be certain."

Lijsbet stood tall and straight, hands fisted at her sides. "I am certain, Lady Duchess. I have lived a life of sin beyond even my own imagining. My soul is destined for hell, even if I transform my ways at this late stage in life. Pledging my life to God is my only chance for redemption. A vow of chastity is my only hope to redeem my soul. Here, 'twill not be possible." She motioned to the room around her. "Lord Price has returned, and I must tell you he is quite taken with me. I was taken with him as well, but we both know this liaison is a candle in a windstorm. 'Twill not last long, and then," Lijsbet dropped to her knees before the duchess, "then I will be as before, only more tarnished by carnal sin." With clasped hands, she begged. "Please, Isabella. Help me to absolve my soul."

The duchess stroked her hand down Lijsbet's cheek. "You do not believe the earl's feelings for you are true?"

As she squeezed her eyes shut, a tear rolled down Lijsbet's cheek. "Nay. He is young and inexperienced. I was his first. We both know how this can color a young man's emotions." A laugh choked out on a sob. "Or a woman's. 'Twas how Rogier trapped my heart, all those years ago."

She felt the duchess' eyes on her. "There is no more to your relationship with the earl than lust? You are certain of this?"

Lijsbet's mind whirred back into the past, into those first few days together with Davion. Something about his frankness, and his gentle nature even though he was a noble—these traits appealed to her. She enjoyed his sense of humor. Something about the man made her heart beat out of control, and a tempest form in her middle.

At first, all she had wanted to do was help him. She found it a simple task to encourage him through his fears, some of them. She had brought him to understand his glass delusion existed only in his mind. There was immense satisfaction from knowing she had helped one suffering.

Somewhere along the way, her heart had snuck past her defenses. But was it love? Or simply lust?

For the earl, she was certain, her help conjured feelings of gratitude. Not love.

She shook her head. "He may be appreciative of my helping him to overcome his fears. But a relationship based on indebtedness is not one I desire. Love cannot exist and flourish if the earl feels beholden to me."

"Do you love him?" Isabella's words were barely above a whisper.

Sitting back on her heels, Lijsbet covered her face with her hands. "I do not know. How can I profess to love a man when what I understood as love for all those years was a lie? I do not know the true meaning of love."

Isabella placed her hand on Lijsbet's shoulder. "Mayhap you should give it time. In time, the truth between you and the earl may come to light."

Abruptly, Lijsbet sprang to her feet. "I cannot risk my heart again. So what if love does flourish in my heart for Lord Price, and then he decides to return to his homeland? I do not wish to live in England, if even he decided to take me with him. I am not an English countess. 'Tis enemy territory, truly. Nay, my life is here, in Burgundy." She gazed at the duchess with pleading eyes. "In Leuven. My future, the only one safe for me to pursue, is at Groot Beginjnhof in Leuven."

As she emerged into the long hallway, Lijsbet saw a man approaching from the far end. She could not tell who the man was, although if either Lord Price or Rogier, the confrontation would not be easy. One she was not yet ready to face. She froze, knowing this passage dead-ended in an elaborate stained-glass window behind her, down the far end. There was no other way out.

The figure halted as she did, standing stock still for long moments. She watched as he swayed, reaching out to steady himself against the wall. 'Twas probably Rogier, already in his cups, as he was most often this early in the day. Holding her breath, she waited.

Her fingers went to her lips when his knees buckled from beneath him. The man collapsed in a motionless heap on the floor.

Rushing to his side, she found 'twas Davion. He lay in an awkward position, with one arm twisted in an unnatural angle behind his head. Frantic, she called out for help.

"Guards! Duchess! Assistance, please! The earl has fallen."

Within moments, the hallway was swarming with activity. Two guards came running from the flanking passageways. Isabella appeared from behind Lijsbet, crouching to place a hand on the earl's brow, and then upon his chest.

"Bring him to my solar at once," she ordered, adding, "and take care with his arm. It appears there may be some damage there."

Lijsbet stood in the open doorway of the duchess' solar, measuring each breath as the healer, a stout woman by the name Gillette, examined the earl. He still lie motionless, even after the jostling he'd received being carried by two clumsy guards. When the healer waved a tincture of sharp herbs under his nose, he did not stir. His skin was pale and glistening with sweat.

He appeared, to anyone's eye, to be dead. Or dying, surely.

But of what? What could have happened between last night, when Lijsbet spoke with him in the great hall while he held her against him, and now? He had ridden—astride—she was told, a giant palfrey all the way from Leuven. Could this be an after effect of that journey? Internal injuries, mayhap.

Yet he had appeared whole and undamaged when she saw him last eve. The earl, regardless of his delusion, was surely not made of glass. Mayhap the stress of the trip had taxed him more than he realized.

"I cannot identify a cause for this man's distress, your grace," Gillette proclaimed. "He is not fevered. His sweat though his skin as cold as death. His heart beats steady and true, yet he will not awaken."

"What about his arm?" Lijsbet asked. "It twisted when he fell."

The healer moved Davion's arm about, flexing at the elbow and rotating his shoulder. The earl remained lifeless. "No bones seem broken, my lady. He may be sore and bruised when he wakes, but—"

"How can we get him to wake?" the duchess snapped.

Gillette pressed her lips into a grim line. "I have tried the pungent herbs. 'Twill usually bring one around, but he seems to be in a very deep sleep. A torpor, mayhap." The old woman turned toward Lijsbet. "When he fell, did he hit his head?"

"Nay. He simply crumpled to the floor." Her voice cracked as tears threatened.

The healer straightened slowly and rose to her feet. As she picked up her basket of supplies, she said, "If he does not wake by morn, ye should send for the barber-surgeon in Brussels. He may know what to do."

After Gillette left the solar, Lijsbet went to Isabella. "Lady Duchess, I should like to stay with Davion... Lord Price, to watch him. Can this be arranged? My handmaiden can remain as well, for propriety's sake."

Isabella gazed down upon the prone young man, then back at Lijsbet. "I don't think there is any worry of impropriety in this case, Lijsbet. You can remain here with the earl, in my solar. My handmaidens are in the room across the hall. If you have need of anything, just call for the guard outside the door."

# Chapter Twenty-Eight

*Davion*

Davion drifted into a world that seemed to transcend space and time. He was floating, as before, in the house in which he grew up, in London. Other people, servants, even his parents passed through this room, but did not appear to see him. He called out to them once, but they did not acknowledge his presence.

Part of him felt comforted at being in this familiar place. Another part was squirming, frantically crawling away with eyes averted. There was something here he did not want to see. Did not want to remember. Did not want to experience again.

The stone stairs seemed huge, as they had when he was a child. Overhead in the entry hall, a many-candled chandelier bathed the space in brightness. But the fixture 'twas not the only light source. There were windows as well.

They were playing. He and another child, a girl, playing, in their favorite place in the hall. Tucked into the curve of the stairwell. Hidden from all who might pass casually. Invisible, only if they remained very, very quiet.

"I am going to retrieve my dolly," the girl said, hopping to her feet.

"Nay," Davion said, fisting the cloth of her dress in his hand, "they will see you. They will follow and discover our secret hiding place." He whispered, or thought he had. Yet his words boomed and echoed inside his head.

"They won't see me," she shot back, cocking her hip. She smacked his hand. "Let me free. 'Twill only take a second."

"Nay," Davion pleaded, feeling as though a dark cloud was looming ever closer and closer. "Do not go. 'Tis not safe. Stay here with me, *Diana*."

He heard rumbling, like thunder. Yet the sun shone. Pouring in bright colors through the window. Then the crash. The stained glass exploded, sending sharp splinters to shower everywhere.

Mostly outside, on the steps. Splintered glass, and blood, and—

His mind raced ahead to a room he begged not to enter. A holy room. A chapel.

Sunlight streamed in through the single window spanning nearly the entire wall of the room. Colors bathed the space, brilliant and glowing, in a pattern that made one dizzy. He felt dizzy already, heart racing, fear prickling his skin. The room smelled of candle wax and death.

In a box lined with shiny fabric lay his sister. *Diana*. A mere child, now shrunken even smaller than her five years.

*"Maman, why is Diana here? Why does she not awaken?"*

*His mother clutched him to her side so firmly, it hurt. She ran her hand down over his head, and he could feel how it shook. Through a sob, she replied.*

*"Your sister will not awaken. Never again. She has gone to live with the angels."*

*Never again. Gone. Angels.*

*Davion approached the box, standing on tiptoe so he could peer inside. 'Twas Diana, but it did not look like her. Not really. Dark lashes fanned sunken cheeks, one of them darkened to the color of a crushed grape.*

*A rainbow of patterned color fell over her face, and danced on the cloth covering every other inch of her body. The light was alive, but she was lying so still. A strong, pungent smell in the air stung his eyes.*

*But she cannot be gone. Look at the lovely colors on her skin. She is glowing. She is beautiful. She must be alive! Yet when his small hand touched his sister's cheek, Davion felt its cold, hard surface.*

*Like glass. Colorful and glowing, but cold and hard.*

Hurtling toward consciousness as the speed of one drowning seeks the surface, Davion sucked in a panicked breath and sat up. Dazed and confused, he knew not where he was. His heart hammered inside his chest, a pulsing in his ears so loud he heard nothing else.

'Twas a woman sitting beside him. He knew her, or thought he knew her. But confusion and panic clouded his brain. What was her name?

"Davion. 'Tis all right. 'Tis me. Lijsbet," the woman said, laying both hands upon his chest. She was pushing him to lie back down. But he did not want to lie back down.

If he did, he would drown. Not by water, but in emotion stirred by horrific dreams. Terrifying images. Heart wrenching memories. Dr. Vanderhoff said 'twould complete his cure, but Davion was not sure he could withstand the stress of such turmoil.

"Davion, what happened? Another dizzy spell? Like the one at Dr. Vanderhoff's office?"

His gaze drifted around the room as he struggled to gain his bearings. "Where am I?"

"In Isabella's solar. I had just left here when I saw you coming down the hall. Then suddenly, you collapsed. You called out once, a few moments ago." She brushed the back of her hand down his cheek. Her touch was the balm he so desperately needed. Needed to make him whole. But when he reached up to take her hand in his, she shrank away.

"What caused your spell? I know you traveled a long distance on horseback," she went on. "Astride. How did you manage that? And bravo to you for your courage!"

Warmth spiraled up through his body, and he felt his face flush. " 'Twas a challenge, and frightening. But I did not break apart, Lily. Mayhap I am not made out of glass after all."

She was smiling at him, but 'twas a sad smile. "Nay. You are not made of glass. I wish I knew whatever made you believe this. You have not remembered the details of your sister's passing?"

Like flashes of lightning, images stuttered through his brain. Playing with a little girl on the rocking horse. Hiding in the curve of the staircase. Sunshine through the window, dappling in many colors on the floor, on the stone risers. On the ghostly pale face of a little girl—"

He met Lijsbet's eyes. "Stained glass. Is there a stained-glass window in this hallway?"

"Aye. 'Tis truly beautiful."

Davion ran both hands through his hair. "Sunlight has been a source of fear for me, all of my life. But light passing through stained-glass..." He shuddered. " 'Tis almost more than I can bear."

The door swung open then, and Isabella whisked into the room, her voluminous skirts swirling about her. "He has awakened. Saints be praised."

She sat on the arm of the bench Davion reclined upon. "You had us all quite concerned. And perplexed. Are you better now?"

He bobbed his head, but never took his eyes off Lijsbet. "I will be even better after I have some time alone with Lady Lambert. We have, as she herself has mentioned, much to discuss."

Lijsbet swung her head away from the earl and rose, wringing her hands. "I am not quite ready to speak with you, Lord Price."

*Lord Price? After what they had shared, why this sudden return to formality?*

Davion scrambled to sit up, thinking better of the move when the room began to spin once more. He held a hand to his temple.

Isabella called for her maids. "Ladies, please. Bring Lord Price some sustenance, some food and drink." She patted Davion's shoulder. "I suggest you remain here until your spell has completely resolved, and you have regained your strength. Later, you and Lady Lambert can take a stroll to discuss matters." She made a shooing motion toward Lijsbet. "Off with you, now. Allow Lord Price to regain his wits more fully."

After she had gone, Isabella and Davion were left alone, waiting for the return of her handmaidens.

"I know you wish to speak with the lady, my lord. But first, you and I must have a discussion. I fear the news you will be receiving from Lady Lambert will not be favorable to you."

Davion swung his gaze toward the duchess. "How so? What news does she hold? Surely, she does not intend to return to the master's side. Not after what she now knows about him." He shook his head and stared at the floor. "The swine."

"A swine he is, and truly. I shudder to think I shall be sitting for him to paint me over the next few weeks." She drew breath and let out a heavy sigh. "The man may be a genius with quill and pigment, but after this discovery, he has lost my respect forevermore."

"What news, then? I must tell you, Lady Duchess, your illuminator has captured my heart. I believe I am in love with her. I wish to make her my wife." He paused, his heart clenching at the grim expression on Isabella's face. "You do not approve of such a match? I realize our relationship as overseer and artisan must change, but—"

"I do not believe she will have you, Davion."

His heart seized. "But, why not? Is it because I am English? Or too young, mayhap."

Isabella was shaking her head sadly. " 'Tis nothing of your doing. The lady has suffered a terrible blow. To her pride, to her conscience. You see, she takes upon herself the blame for not only her own sins, but those of the master. Even though she had no way of knowing the truth about him."

Davion blinked fast, scrambling to find the right words in his still fuzzy brain. "But I am aware of all the lady's *sins*, as you call them. I judge her not. In fact, I love her more because she is a woman who does as she pleases, no matter what society dictates." He reached out to grasp both of Isabella's hands in his own. "I am far from perfect myself, your grace. My hope and prayer is Lily will find me good enough for her."

He watched as the duchess' shoulders drooped in defeat. Her voice was thick when she spoke again. "She wishes to take a vow of chastity, Lord Price. To live a life dedicated to God to atone for her sins. To her mind, 'tis the only way to save her soul."

"Nay, nay, this cannot be true. I have come for the lady, to fall at her feet and offer my heart to her. She cannot be serious in this decision."

"Ah, but she is. She has asked that I write to Sister Fenna at Groot Beginjnhof. Lijsbet wishes to enter the beguinage."

*Lijsbet*

Lijsbet did not return to the scriptorium. A mixture of confused emotions bubbled in her chest like a foaming cauldron on the fire. Resolution of her future path had brought her peace. Anticipation at the thought of returning to the beguine sisters was exciting, and made her smile.

Explaining this all to a lovesick young earl would be difficult. She must not mistake his adoration of her, though understandable, for something more enduring. Still, the task weighed heavy upon her heart.

She wandered through the great hall and out into the bailey, which was bustling with activity. The duke's royal guard, whose encampment flanked the bailey on the east side, were busy with their knightly tasks of polishing armor and sharpening blades. The blacksmith was molding a length of red-hot iron around the end of his anvil, his hammer sending sharp clangs to echo against the stone curtain walls. A group of the duchess' women, carrying baskets of linen from the laundress' shop, chattered like bickering sparrows.

This was life in a medieval village. Normal, everyday life, one from which she had been shielded for most of her days. Lijsbet grew up, literally, on the floor of a tapestry mill. While her mother spent her days at the loom, she untangled threads and swept the floor of the detritus of tapestry weaving. She grew to hate the art, *this* art, yet found herself driven by creativity as well. And she loved those rare commodities, codices. Books. Someday, Lijsbet dreamed of applying her talents to the production of one of those wonderful books.

She was overjoyed beyond measure when, somehow, after a group of artists passed through their town on their way to Tournai, her mother had secured her an apprenticeship in an artists' workshop. Miniaturists, they had been called. Illuminators. She had been relieved to discover the small artists' commune was made up entirely of women.

Who, she wondered, had sponsored such a place? And who received the payment, as well as artistic credit, for the magnificent codices created there? Lijsbet shuddered now to think what price her mother had paid to be granted such an apprenticeship for a girl with no father, a bastard daughter of a weaver.

She had been fourteen when she entered the women's' workshop of Robert Campin, a great master of Flemish painting. He was an old man even when she first arrived, nearing sixty winters. She had been drawn to him as a father figure, since she had known none of her own. He introduced her to Margaret, the grand mistress of the women's studio, younger sister of Jan van Eyck. She had taken Lijsbet under her wing and taught her everything she knew about the art of manuscript illumination.

Lijsbet sat for Master Campin once, as he desired to create a portrait of a young woman. He draped her in a white linen headdress and painted her as she had dreamed she could be: an innocent, beautiful maiden. She had just turned seventeen.

If only the fates had laid a different path for her than the one she traveled.

Rogier de la Pasture, master of his own workshop in Tournai, saw the painting several years later. He wanted to meet the beautiful innocent in Campin's *Portrait of a Woman*. Campin brought Rogier to the women's workshop. 'Twas where Lijsbet met the man. After a few years of gaining her trust, and endearing himself to her, 'twas where he seduced her.

'Twas the beginning of her life of carnal sin.

Deep in thought, Lijsbet wandered aimlessly until she found herself at the stables. She was curious about this beast that had brought the earl from Leuven to Coudenburg. Mayhap, if there was need for the palfrey's return, she would offer to ride him back when she left for Groot Beginjnhof.

"Good morrow," the ostler greeted her. He was busily scrubbing the dusty coat of a chunky, grey charger with a handful of coarse straw. "How may I help you today, milady?"

Lijsbet curtsied, feeling awkward around this man whom she had never formally met. Yet she knew who he was, and had seen how easily he conversed with not only the duke and duchess, but also with Admiral La Laing, an influential member of Philip's Order of the Golden Fleece. The ostler, she was told, had been with the duke and duchess a very long time.

Like one of the family.

"I am Lady Lambert, illuminator for the duke's library," she began. *At present*, she thought. "I understand a great palfrey brought the English earl from Leuven last night. May I see him?" Worrying her hands, one over the other, she added, "I may be traveling back to Leuven in the near future. Mayhap I can return the beast to his home."

The ostler laid down his bunch of straw and bowed before her. "I am Mathieu de Flambre. I shall be pleased to have you meet Sir Markus. But I must warn you, he is no small creature."

Mathieu disappeared within the stable. Moments later, Lijsbet heard what she thought might be thunder rumbling. The storm must be close, for the very ground shook with it. Scanning the horizon, she knitted her eyebrows. Not a cloud to be seen.

'Twas not thunder. 'Twas the giant feet of Sir Markus making his way down the stable aisle and out into the noonday sun.

Lijsbet staggered back a step and covered her open mouth with one hand. "Oh, my Lord and all the saints above," she whispered. "*This* is the steed on whom Davion travelled?"

"Aye, and to be sure it is true. A remarkable beast, this palfrey. Palfrey *now*, but a charger in his younger days, I venture. A horse like this is well-equipped to carry the most massive warrior, in full armor."

*There is no way I can ride this animal. How on earth did Lord Price accomplish the feat?*

"He's quite docile now, in his senior years." Mathieu reached up to stroke the horse's giant head with one hand. His coat was so black, it shone blue in the sunlight. The only white on his body was a small star between his huge, dark eyes.

Stepping closer, tentatively, Lijsbet reached out to stroke the horse's soft muzzle. She saw the grey flecks then, generously threading his jaw and the top of his head. Aye, he was aged. A stab of pity pinged her heart. How hard a life had this beast lived?

"I cannot believe—" she began.

"Neither can we," Mathieu replied. "Lord Price not only rode the horse all the way from Leuven, but he bought him. The earl owns this gentle giant."

Lijsbet was at a loss for words. What kind of courage must it have taken for Davion, so fearful his body would shatter, to climb aboard a beast of this size and strength? And how determined he must have been to return, to *purchase* the animal. He had been determined to return... to her?

Another twinge of guilt, like an invisible arrow, stung her.

"He is impressive, to be sure." Were her words describing Markus? Or Lord Price?

Both, mayhap.

"He is gentle as a lamb. Would you like to ride him? I had just saddled him. I am taking my wife and daughter for a ride through the fields. 'Tis a lovely day. I am certain the earl will not mind." He patted the black horse's massive shoulder. "Markus is in need of a leisurely stroll to stretch his muscles after his long journey."

# Twenty-Nine

*Lijsbet*

Lijsbet had never ridden a horse in her life. She wasn't afraid of them. Not really. But this one... he was so *huge.*

Before she could think up an excuse, Mathieu's wife, Eva and their young daughter appeared from within the stables. Each led a palfrey. A normal-sized palfrey. Animals suited for their dainty feminine riders.

"Are you ready to go, Mathieu?" Eva was a softly rounded woman with the pink cheeks of a cherub. A loosely fitting kirtle clung to her slightly rounded belly. Another child on the way, Lijsbet thought. How lucky is she?

Their daughter was the image of her mother, only with long, wavy brown hair just like her father. Eva came around the front of the horse and noticed Lijsbet. She curtsied. "My apologies, my lady. I did not realize my husband was occupied."

"This is Lady Lambert, our new illuminator, Eva," Mathieu said. "I was just asking if the lady might want to join us for our ride this afternoon."

The child, a wiry girl of about seven or eight years old, rolled her eyes and climbed up on her own horse, a bright red palfrey. "Can we go *now*?" she whined.

"Meadows!"

Lijsbet feared the sharp look from her mother would knock the child to the ground. The girl shrank in her saddle and lowered her eyes. "Sorry, Maman."

"My apologies for our daughter. She can be, well... she has just seen her eighth winter."

Lijsbet smiled and shook her head. "No offense taken."

Eva stepped back and studied Markus with wide eyes. "Is this your horse, Lady Lambert?"

"Nay, nay. I guess this is the beast who brought Lord Price home from Leuven," Lijsbet sputtered, taking a step backward. "I need to be going, so I won't be able to join you on your ride. But many thanks for the invitation." She nodded to the ostler and his wife. "Mathieu. Eva."

"You must join us sometime, my lady. The fields are glorious this time of year. The air is fresh and clean, scented heavy with wildflowers."

"I shall. I promise. Go now. Enjoy your ride."

Mathieu patted Markus' neck. "Well then, Sir Markus, I guess you will be carrying my sorry arse around for the next hour." Tall as he was, the ostler easily lifted a foot into the stirrup and swung a leg over.

"Mathieu!" Eva hissed.

"Ah, beg pardon, Lady Lambert. *Backside.* Markus will be toting about my sorry backside this day."

As they rode off beneath the raised portcullis, chatting and laughing, Lijsbet watched with a squeezing in her heart. *A family.* The ostler had a lovely family—a wife, daughter, and another child soon to be. How lucky a man was he? As she listened to their animated conversation fade into the distance, Lijsbet wondered: are all families like this one?

*Was Rogier's family in Brussels like this? While all the time he came back to me in Tournai to share my bed, hiding the truth and making empty promises?*

Lijsbet suddenly felt ill. She blotted the sweat beading at her temples with the handkerchief she kept tucked in her sleeve and turned toward the entrance to the gardens.

*Davion*

Davion searched what felt like the entire castle, though in truth such a task would take days. But after the library, the scriptorium, her bedchamber, and the great hall, the earl did not know where else to look. He must find Lijsbet. He must convince her not to take a vow of chastity and pledge herself to a life in Groot Beginjnhof.

He only hoped he was not too late.

As he stepped out onto the steps of the keep, he caught sight of a woman slipping through the slatted wooden gate into the garden. He couldn't be sure 'twas her, since he had not seen her face. Just a plain wool frock, the same as any handmaid would wear.

The same as Lily wore every day to work in the scriptorium. With hurried steps, he followed.

Unlatching the garden gate, Davion stepped from hard, packed dirt onto a path fashioned of tiny pebbles. A hush settled over him as the dense growth all around him muffled the activity in the bailey.

'Twas cooler here, with branches thick with greenery arching to form a leafy tunnel. The air even smelled green. The path, straight for only a few feet ahead, turned and disappeared around the massive base of an old oak tree. He stood, listening, but heard no footsteps.

He had only taken three or four steps when he spotted an alcove off to his left. There, shrouded by a thicket of dense vines, was a turfed bench. Perched atop, her knees pulled up to her chest, sat his Lily.

She did not see him at first, and he did not want to startle her. With her chin on her knees, her body wound tight around itself, she looked like a lost child. When she sniffled and then hiccupped, he realized she was weeping.

"Why, my lady fair? Why weep thee with such heart-wrenching sadness?"

She turned toward him. Her smile was sad and slow in coming.

"I find myself lost, once again. Too many times in one life," she said.

"But why, my love? I have come home to you a whole man. Dr. Vanderhoff is not the one who healed me, 'twas you." He sat beside her, their bodies touching. "For that, you own my life. My heart you own for another reason entirely."

As if touched by a scorching pot, Lijsbet unwound her arms and leapt to her feet. She kept her back toward Davion. "I am truly happy you have been healed. Your gratitude touches me, Lord Price. But I fear I can never accept your heart."

He stood and moved behind her, placing a hand on each of her shoulders. "But I wish to give it to you, Lily. How can I convince you—"

"You cannot. I will be leaving soon, returning to Leuven. As soon as granted by Sister Fenna, I will be joining the beguinage, my lord." She faced him, taking a step back. The sudden distance between them felt to Davion like an icy cavern. "I am taking an oath of chastity, Lord Price. Until now, I have lived the life of a sinner. From henceforward, my existence belongs to God."

Davion refused to accept her words. In one swift movement, he had her in his arms, their bodies pressed close. At first, she resisted his kiss, but then her body went soft against him.

A gentle dance, he held her closer, slanting his head and taking her mouth without mercy.

The moment shattered too soon. With both hands on his chest, she pushed him away. Davion stumbled back, still reaching for her when she wheeled on one heel and strode away. As she disappeared around the bend in the path, he heard her say, "Never. Not ever again."

He sat on the turfed bench for a long time, his head in his hands. How could he convince her his feelings were true? There was, it seemed, so little time.

"Lord Price?"

The voice startled him. Davion looked up to see one of the duke's guards standing just outside the alcove.

"My lord, the duke and duchess ask for your presence in the duchess' solar."

Davion asked, this time, for the guard to accompany him. Coudenburg was a huge castle, and he had gotten lost last time he was headed to the duchess' solar. He did not want to lose his way again.

When he entered Isabella's solar, he was amazed at how different a place 'twas than that of the duke. Lavishly decorated with lots of color and gold accents, 'twas clearly a lady's room. A woman who spent a great deal of her time at home, one she loved.

He vaguely remembered the high-backed bench where he had awoken from his latest spell. Hopefully, his last. 'Twas the day *he had remembered*.

Today the bench was occupied by a young woman, one he had not yet met. Isabella and Philip sat in the two chairs in front of the windows. The duke rose when Davion entered the room.

"Davion, I told you earlier I had brought a relative with me from Brussels." Philip motioned toward the girl on the bench who sat forward on its edge, her hands folded in her lap. "Lord Price, this is Margery Fiennes." He paused and cleared his throat. "Margery Fiennes of Burgundy. She is my daughter."

The girl did not raise her eyes as she stood, ducking her head as she curtsied. "Hail, my lord."

*Hail.* This was an English greeting, one he had not heard since leaving his home country. He stepped forward and took her proffered hand.

"Hail, Lady Margery. From England, then?" He tipped his head, still holding her hand.

"Aye, my lord. Born in Kent. My mother is Alice, Baroness Saye and Sele. His Grace, Duke Philip tells me you are from London."

Her voice was light and sweet, like the trilling of a wood thrush in spring. Like a girl very much younger than her years.

*Like Diana.*

"Margery has come to us for sanctuary," Philip said. "Apparently, the political tensions in England are escalating."

"Additionally," Isabella said, "we wanted Margery to come home to Burgundy since she is coming of age." Davion met the duchess' gaze. "Margery celebrates her sixteenth winter soon. The duchess did not wink, but she may as well have. Her unspoken message was clear.

*Lijsbet has shunned you. This girl is not only your equal in rank, but is young and virginal.*

*So young,* Davion thought.

Although the body of the girl belied her age. Curvaceous to the point of plump, Margery's gown failed to conceal generous breasts, accentuated by the tiny span of her waist. High cheekbones defined her noble lineage. Her round, expressive eyes matched the green of a pine forest. Pink, bow-shaped lips curved upwards as she studied him.

Davion dropped her hand, mayhap too abruptly. She was an alluring young woman, true, with her soft curves and wavy, golden brown hair. But so young. More a child, to his mind, than a woman.

Especially now, after he had known the allure of a mature, sensuous woman.

"I am honored, Lady Fiennes." The earl could not hide the stiffness in his tone.

"Pray thee, you may address me as Lady Margery," the girl's lilting voice tinkled in the air. "Lady Duchess tells me you studied art at University."

Davion nodded, taking a step backward. "Aye, I did. I am the duke's overseer, for the library and the scriptorium. With the duke's permission, Lady Margery, I should like you to visit our facilities. We have a very talented illuminator—"

"At least, for now," Isabella cut in. "But she is scheduled to depart very soon. Margery, you should go meet Lady Lambert before she takes her leave."

Her words punched him in the chest. For a moment, Davion could not draw breath.

*So it is true, then. And the duchess obviously approves.*

"This evening," the duke interrupted his thoughts, "we will host a grand banquet to welcome Lady Fiennes home, as well as Master van der Weyden as our guest. He will begin production of Lady Isabella's portrait on the morrow."

*Lijsbet*

Lijsbet had pleaded with the duchess for permission to take her meals in private until her departure. Isabella would not concede.

"You may be dedicating your life to God, but today you are still one of us, Lady Lambert. Your presence at table will be expected, as is any other member or guest of the court."

She had heard of the other guest of the court, a young woman who arrived with Rogier. Had she been one of his lovers as well? Nay, she thought not. Another daughter of the duke, the chattering maids confirmed. They bragged about her youth and her beauty.

As well as her royal roots. Lady Margery Fiennes was also the daughter of a baroness. An English baroness.

Lijsbet was surprised at the number of people in the great hall. Additional long tables had been brought in to accommodate a much larger group than was usual. Scanning the crowd, she realized these were not just members of the court, but included many villagers as well.

A celebration, she thought. To welcome Rogier? Or this young bastard baroness?

She was sitting at the high table between Isabella and Admiral La Laing. An esteemed position, to be sure. On the other side, Rogier sat beside the duke, with Davion on his right.

*A regal group,* Lijsbet thought. *One above me.*

She took a seat at the very end of the last table near the kitchen door.

"She's a comely one now, isn't she?" The whispered voice of the cook, Charlaine, rasped into her ear. "Bet the duke had forgotten all about her mother. Didn't even know she existed until now."

"Why is she here?" Lijsbet asked, immediately knowing her question was mute.

"We are offering her sanctuary. Uprisings in England. Not a safe place to be, 'specially for a maiden." Charlaine squeezed Lijsbet's shoulder. "One who is about to become a young woman."

Beautiful, she was. Cherubic of feature, her figure was everything Lijsbet's had never been—soft, curvaceous, buxom. Even at her young age, the girl looked ripe for plucking, like a late summer peach. Surely she would find a suitable match here at Coudenburg.

*... a suitable match here at Coudenburg.*

Dread flooded Lijsbet's chest when she realized exactly what would happen here at court once she rode off toward Leuven. Toward her future. Toward her life of chastity.

The thought pierced her heart, the mental image of Davion, young and strong and virile, his body intertwined with this lushly rounded woman.

*He can do this now, without fear of 'breaking.' I taught him well. For another.*

*For a beautiful, virginal English baroness. How fitting.*

# Chapter Thirty

*Lijsbet*

Lijsbet knew not how long 'twould take for the duchess' message to reach Sister Fenna and an answer received. Isabella assured her the missive had been written, and a rider assigned to dispatch it. Now all she could do was wait.

All the more difficult a task this would be for Lijsbet, living under the same roof as former lovers—two of them. Rogier knew better than to approach her in any public space, but Lijsbet remained wary whenever she ventured out into the castle or bailey alone. He would corner her, she knew. Excuses, more empty promises, surely. She caught him staring at her numerous times during the evening meal. She cursed herself for not choosing a seat placing her back to him.

Also in full view of her present seat was Davion, who appeared nonplussed by her rejection in the garden. She was not surprised. The earl was young, and now free from the chains of his illness, much less reserved. He chatted amicably with his tablemate—Rogier, a man for whom he once vowed hatred. Two of them, side by side. A sad irony.

The contrast was vivid. Rogier was clearly showing his age, growing wide in the middle and hair thinning atop. Lijsbet could never remember seeing him this way—through unfiltered eyes.

Davion, dashing as ever, oozed nobility. His hands, unmarred by manual labor, were smooth and graceful as he gestured, capturing the attention of his audience.

One of whom, she noticed, was the English baroness, who leaned forward over her trencher to see him past the duke and duchess, her bosom nearly obscuring the plate before her.

Lijsbet sighed. She had never wished for curves such as these. Never really thought to have much use for them, since she was barren. The mounds surely attracted the eyes of men, however. When they spoke to the baroness, they addressed the cleavage spilling from her gown, not her eyes.

Again, she could barely eat enough to feed a bird. After pushing her meat and pottage around on her plate for what seemed an eternity, Lijsbet waited until she thought all interested parties were occupied. Then she rose, planning to slip out through the kitchen.

"Lady Lambert, why do you take your leave so soon? The duke has hired entertainment for the night. You must remain." Lijsbet flinched, as the duchess' tone left no room for interpretation.

Indeed, entertainment ensued. A small group of musicians set up down the end of the great hall, and commenced playing even before the sweetmeats were brought out. The wine and ale served with dinner was replaced by pitchers of bold, dark ale. Lijsbet clutched her cup, reserving what mead remained. She could not bear the heavy, yeasty brew, especially on a stomach mostly empty.

In what appeared a synchronized movement, the servants began moving aside long tables to clear a spot for dancing. The rushes were swept away, and the musicians' song increased in both volume and pace.

*Dancing.* The very last thing Lijsbet wanted to do was dance. She did not believe she could, with a heart as heavy as hers. But why heavy? She was headed for a life of her choosing, was she not? Should not she be as filled with joy as all the other revelers this eve?

She watched as Davion rose, his gaze set upon the young girl beside the duchess. He was going to ask her to dance. *Not until I dance with him first,* she thought. *After all, I was the first to teach him to dance—the dance.*

Hurrying along the front of the dais until she stood at his place, Lijsbet waved a hand to catch his attention.

"Lord Price. I realize 'tis breach of protocol, but may I ask you to dance?"
*Isabella*

Isabella's eyes rounded, and she flashed a worried glance at the duke. Philip was oblivious, already well into his cups, deep in conversation with Admiral La Laing. Davion, initially as surprised as she, closed his eyes and nodded. Then he headed down the dais to join Lijsbet.

*Always a gentleman*, Isabella thought. *Such a well-bred, nicely mannered young noble. I am so glad he has overcome his affliction.*

*'Tis good fortune Lady Lambert has decided on a beguinage. The earl shall make a fine husband for Philip's English daughter.*

The duchess watched them make their way through the crowd to the area cleared for dancing. Taking her hands stiffly at first, the earl attempted to keep distance between their bodies. Lijsbet, however, stepped in close until their faces nearly touched.

Isabella sighed. She knew well that Lady Lambert knew not what she wanted out of life. Not really. She had been betrayed, and had wasted most of her life in the arms of a man who would never be hers. The illuminator had every reason to be cautious about opening her heart again.

She was also right in her assessment of the English earl. He was much too young to hold interest in her for very long. 'Twas possible now, but Lijsbet would age, seemingly much faster than the earl. Before he saw his thirtieth year, the lady would be middle-aged.

And barren. Surely, no matter what the earl said now, he would want sons. A legacy for his family. Although 'twas possible for Lijsbet to bear a child at her age—nearing thirty—'twas unlikely, as well as risky. The duchess herself bore three children past the age of thirty, but only two survived. She was truly blessed by God her third-born, Charles, still lived.

They danced several songs, holding a quiet conversation between them the entire time. Lijsbet smiled and laughed more than Isabella had ever seen. She did not think the woman possessed the ability for happiness. But it seemed Earl Price brought this to her. Isabella watched with pity, knowing the liaison between the earl and the illuminator was not only short-lived, but 'twas, truly, already over.

Lijsbet had simply not accepted fate's path as of yet.

*Lijsbet*

"Will you stay in Burgundy, now that there is upheaval in England? Does your father not require your support?"

Davion laughed. "My father has not required anything from me since I was born. Except an heir, mayhap." He searched Lijsbet's eyes. "If I never bear an heir to the earldom, 'twill die with me. Matters not."

Lijsbet averted her gaze. "Oh, come now. You are young and strong. You are healed and whole now. I am sure there will be countless young ladies vying for your hand. For the title of countess."

"I want none other, Lily. The woman I want is in my arms, right now. Why can you not believe this?"

Lijsbet buried her face against Davion's shoulder, holding back quick tears. " 'Tis not to be, Davion. I will cherish the memory of our time together for the rest of my days."

Their dance had brought them near to the front doors of the great hall, which were opened to allow fresh air into the steamy space. One moment, they were dancing. The next, the earl had closed a hand around her wrist and whisked her out the door.

"Walk with me, Lily. In the gardens."

The long rays of evening sun were still filtering through the branches of the fruit trees in the garden. A sweetness scented the air from the many blossoms, some of which were already carpeting the paths with spent petals. The quiet here was deafening. There was no sound to distract Lijsbet from the thoughts spinning in her mind. But her busy mind, she realized, was her least complaint.

*It will be like this at the beguinage*, she thought. *Quiet and lonely, with nothing to lay balm to the ache in my heart.*

"Why Lily? Why such a sudden and drastic change of heart?" Davion turned to face her, clasping both hands on her shoulders. They were so close she could feel the heat from his body, inhale the male scent of him. These, she knew, were dangerous elements, but nothing to compare with his gaze, his eyes seeming to probe the very depths of her soul.

"Nay, Davion. This conversation has no validity. The decision has been made."

"But why?" he probed. "With the affection between us growing ever stronger, why would you deny our connection? I, for one, believe it to be sacred."

"Ha. Sacred. I do not deserve anything considered sacred." Lijsbet pushed away from him and turned, crossing her arms over her chest. "Surely, you must see, Davion, that my actions up to this point in my life have tarnished not only my reputation, but my soul. I must make reparations now or spend eternity in hell." Her tears came then, mercilessly paralyzing her. The tightness in her throat kept her from saying anything more for several moments.

Several long, silent moments. His silence spoke volumes to her. He offered no further argument or cajoling. He must, when not blinded by physical desire or some silly notion of love, realize the truth.

Her heart seized in her chest when she looked back over her shoulder. The earl was gone.

# Chapter Thirty-One

*Davion*

The next morning, Davion returned to the scriptorium on a mission. Surely, Brother Johannes could enlighten him on how to approach Lily's notion that her soul would burn in hell if she did not do penance by joining the beguines. He was a learned monk, after all. Monks were, other than royalty who received education, the only ones in society who were literate. He must have some advice to give.

Shouldn't he?

Unfortunately, his arrival in the scriptorium was fraught with complications. Brother Johannes was busy in the binding room, stacking dried prayer book leaves into order. He needed to speak with him in private, not a possibility with Lily at her workstation in the same room. He would ask the monk to join him in one of the smaller rooms where new projects awaited.

Not only had the duke brought van der Weyden and Margery with him from Brussels, but also some additional artwork for the library. Two paintings and three manuscripts were stacked on a small table there for examination, cataloguing, and listing for restoration if need be. While he waited, he hummed as he turned the pages of one of the manuscripts, taking note of what needed to be done to restore it to new condition. The colors were faded, worn away in spots. Surely, Lily had the talent to breathe new life into the old codex.

She certainly had breathed new life into him. He glanced into the scriptorium, no longer a place as dark as a dungeon. Sunlight streamed in through the windows, bathing the entire room in a golden light. From where he sat, he could see her, bending close to her work table, quill in hand.

A servant appeared in the doorway. "My lord, you have a visitor. Lady Margery has come to tour the library. She told me you invited her."

Davion muttered an oath. He had extended the invitation to be kind, never believing the girl would have any interest in actually seeing a place filled with old books. Apparently, this Lady Margery was one with a curious mind. He wondered absently if she could read, then quickly reminded himself: *she is a noble. Of course, they would have taught her to read.*

She stood in the entryway to the scriptorium, her hair flowing in burnished waves nearly to her waist. The gown she wore today did not contain her generous curves any better than the one she wore the night before. Its forest green color accentuated the color of her eyes, which lit up when she saw him.

"Good morrow, Lord Price. I hope 'tis all right for me to visit... you did say I should come see the library." She curtsied as she approached. "I do love to read, my lord."

He kissed her hand, then tucked it into the crook of his elbow as he led her through the scriptorium toward the library. Brother Johannes glanced over his shoulder, scanning her form with raised brows. Lily did not appear to know she was even there.

"We still have much to do to get the library up to the standards Duke Philip insists upon. Many of the codices are faded or damaged. Between our scribe, Brother Johannes, and our illuminator, Lady Lambert, the task shall be achieved to the highest standards."

Margery paused at Lily's workstation, peering tentatively over her shoulder. "How beautiful! Such brilliant colors and intricate borders. I should love to have such a fine prayer book."

Davion tilted his head. "Your... family has not provided you with one? I shall speak to the duke on the matter. Of course, these are not translated into English—"

"No need," Margery replied, tipping up her chin. "I read Latin fluently."

*Lijsbet*

Lijsbet's skin prickled as Margery stood so close she could feel the woman's breath on her skin. She even smelled different. Rich, privileged. No doubt of her nobility, since her skin was perfumed with fragrances out of reach for a simple artisan.

For Lijsbet, lavender from the garden would have to do.

As further insult, she did not acknowledge Lijsbet's presence, simply gazed at the folio on which she worked. 'Twas as if she were not even there. Just a work horse, doing its job.

Ire flared in her chest. She could sense how impressed the earl was with the girl. After all, few women were ever taught to read, let alone learn Latin. Most who owned their own Books of Hours memorized the Latin verses, repeating them at the designated hours, yet knew not what the words said.

Latin, French, English, and Dutch. Lijsbet had been fortunate, indeed, to have learned all of these in the performance her work. Her skills with language arts, however, had not ever been of interest to her overseer.

She sniffed and bent closer to the folio as the two continued on into the library. In many households, women were not allowed into the library. Since Margery indicated she loved to read, *and* was the duke's daughter, Lijsbet guessed she would have free access.

*The ideal countess. She will make the English earl a perfect wife.*

Trying as she might to fix her concentration on her work, the illuminator could not help but hear the animated conversation echoing from within the library walls. The girl's laughter tinkled often, followed by Davion's. They were getting to know each other, very well. Apparently, they had much in common.

"Your degree is in art, you say. Please enlighten me, Lord Price. I always wanted to study at University. But of course, for a woman..." Margery spoke animatedly, her free hand fluttering, as they reentered the scriptorium.

"Another point I shall take up with the duke," the earl assured her. "You are his daughter, are you not? You have the right to pursue an education if you wish."

"Why, thank you, Lord Price. That is most kind." She was already hooked onto Davion's arm, but now leaned even closer to him. Then, from clear across the room, Lijsbet heard the audible rumble. Margery pressed a hand to her belly. "Is the noon meal imminent? I'm afraid my hunger torments me."

"Of course, my lady. Allow me."

*It must take copious amounts of nutrition to keep that figure so lush.*

They passed through the scriptorium on their way to the great hall, their chatter fading as they traveled down the corridor. Tears blurred Lijsbet's vision. Unable to focus on her work any longer, she covered her pigments and left to get some air.

The bailey was quiet, as everyone had gone inside to dine. The only activity she could see from the keep's steps was the ostler, Mathieu, busily sweeping out the aisleway of the stable. A cloud of dust hung about him like a mantle. She headed in his direction.

Matheiu, she knew, would be the first to know when Lijsbet was cleared to leave for Leuven. He would be arranging for the mount and chaperone.

He looked up as she approached, leaning his broom up against the barn door. He swept dirt off his hands and smiled.

"Good morrow, Lady Lijsbet. Finished with the noon meal already?"

She flattened her lips. "Nay. Not a hunger for it today." *Or any day of late.* "Tell me, Mathieu. Any word of an escort arranged for me to return to Leuven as of yet?"

The ostler scratched his head, then used both hands to rebind his long hair at the base of his neck. "Not yet. I was not aware you were returning so quickly, Lady Lambert. Another apprenticeship?"

Lijsbet folded her arms and looked away. "Nay. I will be staying longer this time." *Mayhap forever.*

Mathieu froze and studied her with concern. "You do not plan on leaving us here at Coudenburg, do you, my lady?"

"Aye. Plans for my future have changed."

The ostler's eyebrow rose. "I happened into Lord Price in Leuven last month. I was under the impression…" He broke off. "Never mind, my lady. 'Tis none of my affair."

At that moment, at the mention of the earl's name, Lijsbet lost the battle against her tumultuous emotions. To her utter embarrassment, she burst into tears.

Mathieu, obviously discomforted by the outburst, stood awkwardly for a moment. Then he laid an arm over Lijsbet's shoulders. "Come, my lady. Eva is in our apartment. I am certain she has a cup of mead to settle you." He patted her gently as he led her through the stable. "My wife is a very good listener. Mayhap 'twill help to share your distress with another woman."

Moments later, Lijsbet found herself sitting in the tiny apartment at the back of the stables. Mathieu's wife, Eva, bustled about in the kitchen area, pouring a cup of drink and arranging some small cakes on a wooden platter. She brought them to the table, handed Lijsbet a clean linen cloth, and sat across from her.

"Drink, Lady Lambert. Try to eat something. You are so thin, I fear I may disappear before my eyes."

The tears had continued unabated, and 'twas long moments before Lijsbet could open her throat to speak. "I thank you for your kindness, Eva. But this is none of your concern... what I mean to say, 'tis nothing you should worry yourself over."

Eva leaned forward and laid a hand over Lijsbet's.

"It may help to talk about it. I have not a wagging tongue, my lady. Your words stay safe with me."

She knew not why, but the floodgates broke open. Lijsbet, who forever had been the one to hold her emotions in check, began to spill the tale—haltingly, punctuated by hiccups, nose blowing, and an occasional sip from the cup. Eva sat silently, an expression of true concern on her face. She was, as others had said about her, a kind and caring woman.

"So you see," Lijsbet said, "I have no reason to be distraught. My future is decided, and 'tis a path I must follow. My sadness has no basis. That is why I am so confused."

Eva sat back and rested her hand across her rounded belly. "I would say, with all due respect, Lady Lambert, that your decision has come from your head, and not your heart."

Lijsbet blinked. Aye, 'twas the problem. But to follow her heart surely led down another path of misery and disappointment. The earl was young, and an English noble. Surely, he would be returning to his homeland to seek a suitable countess for his wife.

Plus, there was the question of her eternal soul. Every day, bent over the prayer books, Lijsbet was reminded of the fate of a sinner. Fear of eternal damnation, burning in hell, loomed ominously over her.

Was there no other way?

"From what Mathieu shared with me, I know Lord Price is very fond of you. I believe in his discussion with my husband, he spoke of love."

"Love. I heard the word so many times over the past eight years, and I thought I understood its meaning. Alas, I do not. I have no earthly idea."

Eva tipped her head. " 'Tis unfortunate, the heartache you have suffered. 'Tis true, you did not deserve what you endured. But mayhap with the earl, your future can change." She paused, weighing her next question. "What is it you truly want for your life, Lady Lambert? Do you want to dedicate your life to God? 'Tis a noble quest, but..."

Meadows, Eva's daughter, burst through the door, then froze when she saw Lijsbet. "So sorry, Maman. I did not know you had a visitor."

"What is it, Meadows? Do you have need of something?"

The girl, twisting her fingers before her, murmured, "Aye. A wee drink. 'Tis a warm day."

Eva rose and poured water from a large pitcher into a small wooden cup. "Here you go, my love." She brushed the girl's hair back from a sweaty brow. "Don't stay out too long in the sun, Meadows. You are right. 'Tis a hot day. I do not want you to become ill."

After the girl left, Eva returned to the table. "My apologies, my lady. Motherhood is a full-time job. Mathieu swears caring for horses takes more time, but I beg to differ." She smiled and patted her belly. "And 'tis about to become even more challenging."

To Lijsbet's dismay, her tears began anew. She had never been around children much. As an only child—an only, bastard child—her early years had been robbed from her. She always assumed that bearing children was not for her. She was convinced she would not make a very good mother. Her own maman set a very poor example. It seemed the fates agreed with her, since her many years sharing Rogier's bed produced no pregnancies.

Now, she suddenly yearned for a family—a real family, like that of Mathieu and Eva. Sadly, she knew 'twas not to be. She was barren. Even a loving partnership, a marriage, was out of reach. 'Twas not to be with Lord Price, for certain. He would tire quickly of an older widow with such a plain physique, not rounded with womanly curves as was Margery. A commoner. Lijsbet knew in her heart she was not suitable to be the wife of an earl.

Even an English one.

Eva broke into her tortured thoughts. "Lady Lambert, I know you wish to join Groot Beginjnhof. This may be your true calling. Just be sure before you commit your life to one of chastity and prayer. It's not a convent. I know there are no vows, but you do not want to discover you've made the wrong choice and then leave the beguinage. 'Twould only seem like another failure to you."

"I am lost, truly. Torn. If I stay here, 'twill be torture to watch Lord Price pursue another. Yet mayhap, if I stay, in time, I may meet another. One not interested in heirs. One not swayed by my past." Lijsbet sighed and wiped her eyes.

Eva pushed the plate of cakes toward her. "No matter what you decide, you must eat. You are withering away to a wisp of a woman." She patted her own thighs. "Most men prefer lying on a feather bed to a bundle of sticks." Her sympathetic smile made Lijsbet's throat close again.

"I will try," she sputtered, lifting a cake. "What you say about what men prefer, I know it to be true. Lord Price is no exception."

# Chapter Thirty-Two

*Davion*

Davion noticed the duchess' pleased expression when he entered the great hall with Margery on his arm. She even cast a slight bow of her head his way. He already knew Isabella was favoring a liaison between him and the English lass.

'Twas no doubt, she was delightful. Humming with youthful energy, Margery possessed a keen intellect. She was curious about everything. And, ironically, her interests lie in the same area as Davion's. Art, art history, artists and their techniques.

He would take her under his wing, he thought. Teach her whatever she wanted to learn. Mayhap Lily would spend some time with her as well, teaching her the finer points of manuscript illumination.

'Twas no more talented miniaturist to ask than his Lily.

He noticed her silence in the scriptorium this morning, and assumed she was afraid to display too much emotion while at her work table. In front of Brother Johannes. Nay, 'twould not do at all.

Davion must be very careful about his pursuit of Lily in public places here at Coudenburg. He must retain a respectful, overseer-to-artisan relationship for others' eyes. But he must speak to Brother Johannes. He must find a way to convince Lily that committing ot a life in the beguinage was not necessary for her to cleanse her soul.

'Twasn't, was it?

Davion's plans for the future were, for the first time in his life, crystal clear. Once he convinced Lily to abandon the idea of the beguinage, he would move forward with purpose. He would make appointment to speak with the duke concerning a marriage proposal. Philip, after all, had to consent to the betrothal of any of his daughters. Once, of course, Lily had given him her heart.

"Come. Join me on the dais," Isabella called to Davion and Margery. "The duke is busy with other matters today. Master van der Weyden prepares a studio in which I must pose." She held up both hands and glanced about the high table. "Seems I may be sentenced to eating alone."

"Does the master begin today?" Davion asked.

"Aye. An assignment I do not look forward to. Sitting perfectly still for hours on end, well," she laughed and threw her napkin down on her lap, "such patience, 'tis not in my personality."

The noon meal was appetizing as always. Sliced roast boar from the previous night's meal, freshly roasted vegetables from the court's gardens, coarse bread and churned butter. Davion handed the platter of meat to Margery.

"After you, my lady."

The girl chattered endlessly throughout the meal. Davion knew he was only a few years older than she, but mercy, he did not remember ever having so much energy to burn. Of course, his situation had been different. He had lived through a family's worst nightmare before he had cut all his adult teeth. He had lived with an armor of fear restricting his every movement.

Margery heaped food upon her trencher, and after respectfully waiting for him to take the first bite, began eating.

*Well-trained in the noble's ways. Impressive for one so young. And so beautiful.*

What little Davion had learned about noble women told him they were mostly spoiled, willful, and selfish. 'Twas one of the reasons why he had maintained a solitary path, immersing himself in his other passion—art.

The earl had not been aware then, but he would discover another passion. Another love. For Lily.

He paused, his eating knife halfway to his mouth, when he realized Margery had stopped her chatter. She was staring at him, quizzically. What had he done—or *not* done—now?

"Is something amiss, Lady Margery?"

She smiled with a mischievous twinkle in her eyes. Bending close to his ear, she whispered, "I... I would not mind sharing the meal from your trencher, my lord." She blinked rapidly.

*Hmm.* Sharing food from a single trencher was something done by couples, either those married or about to be. Was she suggesting—"

Margery covered her face with her hand. "How forward of me. My apologies, Lord Price. 'Twas completely improper of me."

Davion drew her hand down from her face, admiring the cherubic beauty beneath. She was as perfect as any portrait painted of a young woman in her innocence. Soulful expression, blushed cheeks, a plump lower lip. Her green eyes danced over his face expectedly.

Youth and innocence appealed to most men his age, of this he was aware. Yet for him, he found no interest in pursuing a relationship with this young woman. He had he realized with a start, already given his heart away.

An image of Lily drifted into his mind, and he glanced around the hall. She was not there.

The earl cleared his throat and shifted in his seat. "Enjoy your meal, Lady Margery. I must speak with the duchess."

Davion skirted behind Margery and Isabella's chair to sit beside the duchess.

"Your Grace, pardon the interruption, but have you seen Lil... Lady Lambert this morn? She was in the scriptorium all morning, but she has not arrived for the noon meal yet."

Isabella laid her knife down on the plate with a sharp click. Turning to face the earl, she lowered her voice. "You have been informed of Lady Lambert's plans, my lord. I must ask you respect that decision, and move on."

Davion shook his head, desperate to disclaim Isabella's words.

*Nay! She is not bound for Groot Beginjnhof. This cannot be true.*

Inappropriate words to share with the duchess. He struggled with an alternate plan.

"I worry for Lady Lambert. She eats almost nothing. Her body, 'tis down to skin and bone." He quickly added, "From what can be seen through the shapeless frock she wears."

Isabella's eyebrow rose. Her features softened, and she patted the back of his hand. "I understand your concern for your most talented illuminator. She will be sorely missed here at court. But I suggest you direct your affections to another, Lord Price." She nodded toward Margery, almost imperceptibly. "Philip has another daughter who may better suit. For you, for your family. For your future."

Davion spent the rest of his meal dodging the flirtations from Margery. She was lovely, true. Intelligent and bred of nobility. Blatantly feminine. Young enough to bear him many sons.

He shook the thought away. Children? After suffering the loss of a child, a sibling, resulting in mental scars he may never completely overcome, Davion was quite sure the role of father did not suit him. Birth was always, sooner or later, followed by death. Loss of a child, he had been told, was the worst pain a parent could imagine.

'Twas bad enough losing a sibling.

Nay. Even if she would make a fine countess, Davion knew he must take care not to mislead the girl. Margery's curves was too lush to deny. Children would come and with them, the perpetual fear of losing them.

Was this part of his attraction to Lily? Knowing she was barren? Safe?

Aye, mayhap. But there was much, much more to his attraction to the lithe artisan. More than desire, there was respect. Respect for her artistic flair. Respect for the lady's wisdom. Respect for her patience with him. She had seen Davion at his worst and helped him overcome.

Were these feelings love, truly? In a flash of insight, all became clear to him. He was in love with Lijsbet. He must tell her quickly, before an alternate path took her away from him.

*Lijsbet*

When Lijsbet left the ostler's quarters, she felt worse instead of better. The sweet cake she had washed down with weak mead roiled in her stomach. Delay, she knew, would lead her down a path she did not want to take. Davion would come for her again. Her defenses were not strong when it came to the earl. He had touched a place in her heart she had not known existed before even with the master. The only way she could keep her soul safe was to avoid him, even as he insisted on pursuing her.

Or mayhap he would not. Mayhap he had become more interested in the charms of the lovely English maiden. That, she realized, would hurt much worse.

Nay. She could not wait for a letter from Sister Fenna. The beguinage, she was quite sure, would accept her. Her brief time at Groot Beginjnhof taught her an important lesson. She had a family there, albeit of a different nature—a sisterhood. Lijsbet went to her quarters to begin packing what little she would take with her to Leuven. Then, she would approach the duchess and ask for a mount and an escort.

She must leave Coudenburg, today. To delay could mean disaster.

Lijsbet stopped in the stable on her way out, seeking Mathieu. She found him checking the shoes of one of the Royal Guard's destriers.

"Mathieu, if the duchess grants permission, I would like to leave today. For Leuven. Is there any chance someone would be available to chaperone me? I would also need a mount."

The ostler gently set the horse's massive hoof down on the straw and looked up. "Today? Is there an urgent matter you must attend to in Leuven, my lady? 'Tis a full day's ride. 'Twould be better to leave early morn."

Lijsbet sighed. She knew the ostler was right. One more night, she would need to stay hidden. For one more night, she must avoid the earl's enticing attention. She was not quite sure if her heart and soul could be contained.

"On the morrow, then. I will speak with the duchess. She will send word if she approves."

*Eva*

"I cannot believe she is making this decision so abruptly. 'Tis the wrong one, I am certain. For both of them."

Eva lay next to Mathieu in the dark, the light of an almost-full moon bathing them both in icy light. 'Twas a warm night, and Mathieu had propped the window open wide with a chunk of firewood. Only the faintest rustling of the linen curtains told of a breeze, but 'twas no cooler than the air they breathed.

"I agree. Although the earl does seem quite taken with the new daughter. The English one."

Eva growled in her throat. "Poor timing, that. For Lijsbet, for sure." She shifted to lay on her side, facing her husband. "She is in love with him, Mathieu. I am quite certain of it."

Mathieu stroked her cheek. "Aye, but the lady has many fears. One is for her soul, a valid worry."

Eva slapped him on the shoulder playfully. "We both know that the true test of faith is in the living. Surely, good people do not go to hell."

He caught her hand and pressed a kiss into her palm. "Aye, I hope so as well. If not, we shall both go to hell. At least we will be together."

Eva wrapped her hands around his neck and snuggled in close. "The only true hell I can imagine is one without you." She sighed. "Lady Lambert risks living a similar hell, I fear, at Groot Beginjnhof. If she does love the earl, truly, she will awake one day in the not-too-distant future and realize her mistake. By then, 'twill be too late."

*Lijsbet*

He came to her quarters that night, as she had feared. Lijsbet prayed he would not. As she lay there, hearing the soft knocks continuing, repeatedly, in brief bursts, she squeezed her eyes shut against the tears.

Surely she could remain strong enough, brave enough to see him one more time. She knew she should not leave Coudenburg tomorrow, in the dark of pre-dawn, without at least saying goodbye. Lijsbet rose and went to the door.

Chapter Thirty-Three

When the door swung open, Lijsbet nearly swallowed her tongue.

'Twas not Lord Price. 'Twas Rogier de la Pasture. Or van der Weyden. Or whatever his name truly was.

Her attempt to slam the door in his face was derailed by his boot in the jamb.

"Pray thee, Lijsbet. Allow me a few, brief moments. I wish to explain—"

"No explanations will change the matter," she rasped, trying to keep her voice quiet enough so her maid would not awaken. "There is nothing more to be said between us, Rogier. The truth says it all."

"But I do love you. Truly. I know I deceived you, but I intended to marry you, once the children were grown and no longer a burden. My youngest is twelve, and will enter an apprenticeship very soon. Then we will be free—"

*Free. Free for what?*

"You will still be married, Rogier. I doubt the pope will grant an annulment for a man who is the father of four."

*Four babes.* Not one or two. Aye, it must be Lijsbet's barrenness preventing her from conceiving a child with the artist. He is obviously fruitful.

All this conversation through a crack in the door a hand's breadth wide. "Can I please come in, Lijsbet? I promise, I will not approach you in any manner not of your liking."

Sighing, still hoping not to attract the attention of her maid or the guards, she stepped back and allowed him through. He pushed the door closed behind him with a click. Then he held out his arms.

But Lijsbet was shaking her head as she backed away. "Nay. Never again."

"But Lijsbet, there is hope for an annulment. I have spoken with the priest at Saint Nicholas in Brussels. There are grounds." He paused, his face taking on a puzzling expression. He mumbled the next words. "I have suffered, you see, an impairment."

*Impairment?* "How so? And how would that affect the status of your marriage?"

Rogier stepped closer to her and grasped her shoulders. "An injury, soon after my youngest son's birth. I developed a sore from too much time in the saddle." He paused to grimace and swipe his hand down his face. " 'Tis embarrassing to discuss, Lijsbet. But the result is this: I can no longer father children. My wife is still young. She wants more children. I cannot provide them. The priest in Brussels claims 'tis basis for the marriage to be dissolved."

Lijsbet could not believe the words she was hearing. Even if they were true, how could she be expected to forgive Rogier's lies? His double life?

She fisted her hands at her sides and spoke through clenched teeth. "You will take your hands off of me, Master van der Weyden. Or de la Pasture. Who are you really, anyway? It comes clear to me now I never knew you. Not at all. I shared my life with a stranger for nigh on eight years. I wasted my life—"

A knock sounded on the door. "Lily? Lily, are you well? I can hear voices. Please, let me in."

'Twas Davion. *God's bones, life is about to get interesting now.*

The look on the earl's face when she pulled open the door, even in the dim light, spoke volumes. Emotions flashed across his face, one after the other—shock, suspicion, then anger.

"What goes here?" he barked. "Lily, did you let this scoundrel in? Or did he force his way?"

Davion stepped toward Rogier, fisted hands raised. Lijsbet stepped between them.

"Nay, I allowed his entry. But now 'tis time for him to go. I am not interested in more of his lies." She motioned toward the open door. "Good eve, Master... artist."

"Nay. I have business with your overseer, Lijsbet. Mayhap he is more than your overseer." He turned to the earl. "Do you often check in with your artisans in the middle of the night?"

"What I do, and what the lady does, are none of your affair, sir. Now, as the lady requested, you need to leave." Lijsbet had never seen this side of the earl before. She had seen his anger, but this bordered on rage.

*Fighting over me? A used-up spinster? A barren one?*

Rogier, even at his more advanced age, was an imposing figure. Taller, broader, and heavier by much than the earl, she feared for Davion's safety if the confrontation came to blows. She must stop this now. She called for the guard.

But in the few moments elapsing between her cry and the guard bursting into the room, Rogier managed to get out these words:

"My dear Lord Price. I sincerely hope you do not have romantic fantasies involving our dear Lijsbet. She is acceptable, but not exceptional. With one's eyes closed or in the dark, you must always remind yourself she is a woman. Her body is thin, sharp, and angulated. Feminine curves are nonexistent." He leered at Lijsbet. "I have taken pity on her all these years. What a waste of eight years of my life."

A sword through her heart could not have been any more damning.

She did not return to her bed after the guard escorted both Rogier and Davion from her chamber. Yet another embarrassing, damning moment. Lijsbet was certain that before dawn, rumors would be buzzing throughout the castle.

*Lady Lambert had not one, but two men in her bedchamber!*

As the moon began to sink over the horizon and dawn's glow threatened, Lijsbet gathered her satchel of clothes and her box of quills and pigments. Then she crept down the stairs and out the front door of the keep.

Isabella had approved her leaving. There had been none other to escort her, though, except the ostler himself. She found Mathieu waiting for her with three mounts: a palfrey for her, his own destrier, and a pack horse for her belongings. The squealing of the portcullis rising punctuated the ending of Lijsbet's life at Coudenburg.

By days' end, she would be a novice at Groot Beginjnhof. She was not sure, as her horse plodded along beside Mathieu, if the emptiness in her gut was from a sense of loss, or a sense of foreboding.

Or simply hunger.

*Davion*

Davion did not sleep well at all. After the guard escorted him to his own chamber, the earl paced its length, slamming a fist into his palm and muttering obscenities. How absurd to be removed—nearly by force—from a lady's bedchamber? How utterly embarrassing. His anger needed a target. Davion blamed Lijsbet.

She had invited the blasphemous Rogier into her chamber—willingly. Was it for the same reason he had come to her? Nay, it had sounded as though they were arguing, from what he could hear through the heavy oak door.

Then why allow him entry at all?

His love for the woman was strong, but Davion began to feel the edges around the feeling begin to crack. Mayhap she was not all she appeared to be. Mayhap what he felt for her was not true love.

Besides, she certainly did not appear to return those feelings. She had remained reserved, sharing superficial sentiments, but never anything from within her heart. Her family background was a mystery to him, other than knowing she was a bastard daughter of the duke. Her history, for the past eight years, was not one any woman would be proud of.

*... you must always remind yourself you are lying with a woman. Her body is thin, sharp, and angulated. Womanly curves are nonexistent.*

The man spoke truth, but Davion had not noticed these traits as deficiencies before. In fact, he had been pleased with her firm, lithe figure.

Of course, he had never known another. Were his feelings toward Lily premature? And because they were so new to him, mayhap exaggerated?

At dawn, he heard the squeal of the portcullis going up. He could not see the gate from his window, but caught sight of a trio of horses making their way across the meadow. They were headed east, toward the sunrise. Who would be leaving so early?

Mayhap the scene in Lily's bedchamber last night convinced the painter to take his leave from the palace. If 'twas the case, Isabella's portrait would not be painted. Neither duke nor duchess would be pleased.

His answer came at table for breaking of the fast. Rogier was there, sitting next to Philip on the dais. Lily was nowhere in sight.

Without taking a seat, Davion backed out of the room before he was noticed and made his way to her chamber. He knocked on the door, surprised when it swung open easily. 'Twas not latched, merely ajar. Her maid was stripping linens off the bed.

"Cecile, where is Lady Lambert? Has she gone to the scriptorium already?"

The maid stood up and stared at him. "Nay, my lord. The lady has gone. Left early this morn with the ostler to chaperone."

In his heart, he already knew the answer, but he asked anyway. "Where has she gone?"

"Why, to Groot Beginjnhof in Leuven, my lord. The lady is pledging her life to God." She crossed herself. "An honorable vow, that. I hope she will find peace and happiness there."

Davion returned to the great hall in a daze. He could not believe Lily had left, and without bidding him farewell. A hard woman, she must be. Unfeeling. Incapable of the kind of emotions he had felt for her.

He hadn't been seated long enough to fill his cup when a high-pitched squeal startled him. From across the room, he watched Margery hop to her feet and scurry around the end of the long table. Perching beside him on the bench seat, she laid her head on his shoulder and crooned, "I was looking for you, Lord Price. Good morrow. So happy to see you this morn."

Her body was soft and warm beside him. She smelled exotic, scented with spices from the east. Spices not readily available to those who were not nobility.

'Twas then he realized what he found so appealing about Margery. The girl smelled faintly familiar. These were the perfumes used by his mother, and his sister. By Diana. Even at the tender age of five, his mama had already begun teaching the girl the ways of an aristocratic woman.

'Twas a nice smell. Nice memories. He smiled down at the girl and said, "You look lovely this morn, Lady Margery."

# Chapter Thirty-Four

*Lijsbet*

They had ridden in silence as the sun rose lazily in the eastern sky, soon to be shrouded by clouds.

"Looks like we may encounter some stormy weather, my lady. I hope you brought a cape," Mathieu warned.

"My cloak is hooded," she snapped back. "But have no fear. I will not melt."

Mathieu turned to study her with squinted eyes. "Why so glum, Lady Lambert? I was told this relocation was your own choice, not one put upon you."

Lijsbet cast her gaze straight ahead, avoiding his. " 'Twas. 'Tis where I belong. 'Tis my only option, however. Even a voluntary decision, when one has no choice, becomes oppressive."

Mathieu's voice grew soft. "Eva believes otherwise. She believes you have feelings for the earl. She believes—"

"I care not what your lovely wife believes, ostler. She had different opportunities when she was a maid. She was lucky to find you and to claim your love, before her life became a soiled folly. Like mine."

"You judge yourself too harshly, my lady."

Lijsbet's chuckle was not a happy one. "Not nearly as harsh as I will be judged for eternity."

They did not encounter rain. The summer storm clouds threatened in the distance, but always skirted their path. Rumbles of thunder and an occasional flash of lightning provided an entertaining backdrop as they traveled. The journey, it seemed to Lijsbet, took much less time than her first trip to Leuven.

In the carriage. With Lord Price. With Davion.

*Nay. That was before. This is now.*

As they clopped up the cobbled street to the front door of Groot Beginjnhof, Lijsbet had a sudden flash of unease. What if Sister Fenna refused her? What if a missive, right now, was on its way back to Coudenburg, denying her entry to the beguinage?

Too late to reconsider now. If she was turned away, there was always the artists' residence. Not her most attractive choice, by any means. But if she had no other place to live, she would make do.

Her fears were unbased. Sister Fenna herself greeted her on the steps with a hug and a cry of pleasure.

"We have missed you, Lijsbet! I was just about to send a reply to the duchess' letter."

"No need now. I could not wait. I hope 'tis all right."

Fenna cupped her cheek in one hand. " 'Tis more than all right. 'Tis splendid, indeed." She stepped back and waved her in. Mathieu followed, laden with Lijsbet's belongings.

Having secured lodging in a local tavern, Mathieu bid the sisters farewell on the steps of the beguinage as the moon rose above the tops of the buildings. He took Lijsbet's hands in his own.

"I hope you will be happy here, Lady Lambert. 'Tis obvious you feel at home in the company of these wonderful ladies." Mathieu kissed the back of both her hands, then pressed his cheek against hers. "I wish you happiness. I wish you peace."

Then he was gone.

Lijsbet stood alone in the hallway, listening to the murmur of the sisters in the chapel across the hall. They were reciting the hours of compline, the prayers before retiring. She had inscribed these prayers dozens of times, in multiple languages. She had created fanciful borders around these lines of dedication almost all of her life. Yet she had never once recited them herself.

'Twas about time she learned how. Pulling the hood on her traveling cloak over her head, she crept into the chapel. The glow of torchlight against the stained-glass window caused a flare in her own chest. Swallowing hard, Lijsbet slid into the pew at the rear of the chapel and knelt, bowing her head.

Her new life. Would it be enough? She had no right to question. It must be.

The days turned into a fortnight. Fortnights ran together into a month. Before Lijsbet could believe how much time had passed, the leaves on the trees had begun to color as brightly as her pigment palette. A burst of glory before the world withered, turning gray and cold.

At times, she felt as though her heart was following suit.

Something else, however, was happening to her body. The food here at Groot Beginjnhof was to blame, she was certain. Rikita's cooking, including her decadent sweet French pastries, was a balm to her shrunken appetite. Lijsbet's hipbones no longer poked so painfully into the thin pallet on which she slept. Her cheeks were not as hollow as before. Even her breasts—Rogier had called them *nonexistent*—had begun to fill out, round and firm.

Quite firm. Almost painfully so. There was also the matter of her monthly, which had ceased completely from the day she'd arrived at Groot Beginjnhof. Lijsbet assumed 'twas God's way of affirming her decision.

One chilly evening, when the sisters had wandered through the vineyard to clip back wayward vines, Sister Wilhelmina was working beside Lijsbet. *Sister* Lijsbet. She would retain her given name until such time as her apprenticeship as a novice had been completed. Then, like with nuns, Lijsbet would choose another name to signify her rebirth as God's child.

"You are looking well, Lijsbet," Wilhelmina said, smiling over at her. "There is color in your cheeks now, and they are not nearly as sunken as when you arrived."

"Sister Rikita is a marvelous cook. And her pastries! They will be the death of me."

Three months had passed since Lijsbet's arrival at the beguinage when the sickness began. She awoke most mornings with a sour taste in her mouth and her stomach roiling. Several times she even retched before consuming a single sip of ale. The other sisters who shared her dortor were concerned.

"Mayhap we should call for a healer, Sister Lijsbet. You risk losing all the weight you've gained since you arrived," Wilhelmina said after offering Lijsbet a cool, wet cloth for her head. "I will alert the mistress."

Later that morning, Lijsbet met with Sister Fenna in her quarters. Lijsbet was surprised at the look of concern in the mistress' eyes. This was not a sickness of concern, she was certain. A change of humors with the season, 'twas all.

"When did your last monthly come to pass?" 'Twas the first question Fenna asked her, without preamble.

Lijsbet blinked. "I . . . I do not believe one has come since I arrived, Mistress. I believed 'twas God's way of indoctrinating me—"

"Do not be a fool, Lijsbet." Fenna's tone was firm, but kind. "You have put on weight. Have you noticed any other changes in your body?"

Lijsbet laid her hands over her breasts—gently. They were larger, firm, and sore of late. "Aye, Mistress. My breasts are tender . . ." Her eyes grew wide with sudden realization. "It cannot be. I am barren."

"Nay, my lady. You are not barren. You are with child." Fenna rose and folded Lijsbet into her embrace. "Lord Price's child, I assume?"

"It . . . it could be none other," Lijsbet stuttered.

She remained that way for long moments, wrapped in the arms of a woman who had become like a mother to her. A young mother, but still, a matronly influence. Stunned, and unsure of how she felt about this new revelation, she was at a loss for words.

Fenna pushed her back and met her gaze. "Lijsbet, I am happy for you. But we cannot allow you to birth and raise a child here at Groot Beginjnhof. We are simply not that kind of beguinage."

Panic clogged Lijsbet's throat. "But where will I go? What shall I do?"

With two fingers, Fenna lifted Lijsbet's chin. "You must tell the babe's father of his existence. 'Tis only fair and right for him to know. 'Twill be up to him as to what happens next. I will send a letter to the duchess."

AT THE DUCHESS' URGING, Davion began a tentative courting of Margery Fiennes. Her body was tempting, and the earl fought his own body's reaction to her every time they spent time together. But 'twas lust alone. Of that he was certain. Before much time at all had passed, he realized that conversation with the girl was limited, almost painful. Although they had much in common, 'twas on the surface alone. Facts on a list. Nothing deeper than superficial.

He wanted her, he would not deny this. Since his sexual awakening with Lijsbet, his body wanted desperately to make up for the years he had lost.

After an evening in the gardens or wandering the autumnal woods with Margery, Davion returned to his bedchamber frustrated to the point of pain. He took himself in hand more than once to relieve his need.

Always, his imagination conjured Lijsbet by his side. Beneath him. Atop him.

He refused to use the English lass this way. To do so would be not only sinful, but deceitful as well. Try as he did, he could not feel anything more for the girl other than lust, and mayhap a sort of camaraderie one develops with a sibling. He kissed her once. 'Twas a disaster. He may as well have kissed one of the marble pillars supporting the palace balustrade.

Margery was cute and sweet, and filled with childish chatter and notions. She was not a woman. Not one for whose maturity he had the patience to wait.

He missed Lijsbet, horribly. Finally, after nearly three months of misery, he asked to speak with the duchess. Her portrait, he had heard, was nearing completion. Davion breathed a sigh of relief to know the artist, Lijsbet's former lover, would be gone from their midst soon. After her afternoon sitting, Isabella consented to meet with him in her solar.

"How is the portrait progressing?" he asked, wanting to know how much time he had left before bidding Master van der Weyden farewell.

Isabella sighed. She looked tired, with dark circles under her eyes. Her skin was sallow, since instead of wandering the gardens, as was her wont, she had been cooped up in a studio most every day.

"The master will not allow us to see it until it is complete," she said. "Hopefully, very soon."

"I look forward to the day I can view his handiwork."

"Now Philip wants his portrait painted as well. So it seems Master van der Weyden will become a more permanent fixture here at court. At least for the coming months."

Davion stifled a groan. Not his concern, however. And not the reason he asked to speak with the duchess.

"Your Grace, any word from Lady Lambert? From Leuven?"

The duchess shook her head, but studied him with curious eyes. "We have no reason to believe all is not well at Groot Beginjnhof, Lord Price." She paused, then added, "Are you enjoying the company of the English countess? She certainly seems taken with you. You are all she talks about."

Davion swiped a hand down his face and rose to pace the room. "I am sorry, Lady Duchess. Margery is sweet and lovely. But she is a child yet."

"She is maturing every day. One day very soon—"

"I cannot help seeing her as a sister, Duchess. I am fond of her. I do not love her, and refuse to lead her on." He shoved his hands into the pockets of his braies. "I am in love with another. I am afraid when Lady Lambert left for the beguinage, she took with her my heart."

Isabella's mouth flattened. "That is most unfortunate, Lord Price. It appears you have given your heart to one who does not want it."

Davion huffed and raked a hand through his hair. "I know 'tis how it appeared, when she left. How she left. But I am unconvinced. I must try, one more time. I must do what I can to convince her my feelings are true."

Isabella crossed her arms and glared at him. "Do what you must, my lord. But promise me this. When you return to Coudenburg, alone and with your pride damaged anew, promise me you will try to find comfort in the arms of the young woman who is so desperately enamored with you."

"I will, I promise. When may I go?"

Isabella called for the guard. "I will send word to Mathieu at once. He will accompany you. I wish for you to get this last formality over with as soon as possible."

THE MISSIVE ARRIVED the same day as Davion rode out with Mathieu. When Isabella saw 'twas from Sister Fenna, her heart seized. Fumbling to open the letter, she dropped it twice.

*Your Most Gracious Lady Duchess,*

*I write to you with disturbing news. It seems, although we welcomed Lijsbet Lambert into our sisterhood with open arms, she did not arrive alone. She is with child, Your Grace. As you may be aware, Groot Beginjnhof is not the kind of sanctuary for women with children. Mayhap there is another. I will do some research on the matter.*

*However, I informed Lijsbet she must notify the father of the child of its existence. She claims that man is Lord Davion Price. If you will please pass this information on to the earl, I would be most appreciative. He shall be the one, ultimately, to decide the lady's future.*

*Respectfully, we await news from Coudenburg.*

*Sister Fenna, Mistress*

*Groot Beginjnhof*

Isabella dropped back in her seat, shocked. Lijsbet was so certain she was barren. Apparently, 'twas not the case. Worse yet, at this very moment, Lord Price was hurtling toward a future for which he possessed not all the facts. He would arrive at the beguinage, ignorant of Lijsbet's condition.

Would this new development change her mind about marrying the earl? A marriage under obligation, for either party, seldom comes to good end. A child certainly added a sense of duty to their union.

How 'twould all would play out, the duchess had no idea.

# Chapter Thirty-Five

*Davion*

With Mathieu leading the way and determining the pace, he and Davion made it to Leuven by mid-afternoon. The ostler knew the roads well. Knew where they could let the horses run, and where they were wiser remaining at the walk. One thing was for certain: Markus' gallop ate up the miles, and fast. There were several times he had surged so far ahead of Mathieu on his own charger, he'd had to slow Markus and wait for them to catch up.

"You bought yourself quite a horse there, Lord Price. He may be old, but he's still as fast as the wind."

Davion grinned and reached down to pat the horse's sweaty neck. "He taught me how to ride. For that I will always be grateful."

*Lijsbet taught me the ways of love. For that, I will be eternally grateful.*

The bells for the hour of None were tolling as they made their way down the cobblestone street to the beguinage entry. Mathieu glanced at Davion.

"We may as well find a place for a cold drink, mayhap a meal. No one will answer the door until the prayer hour is over."

Davion paused. "I believe Lijsbet will answer. She will probably be at work in the scriptorium. She—"

"She has joined the sisters, Lord Price. My bet is she has also adopted their ways. 'Tis what would be expected."

With a sinking in his gut, Davion agreed. There was a tavern, he remembered, not far down the street from the artists' residence. They tied their horses out front and made their way inside.

The interior of the Café Beige was dark and smoky, like most Davion had visited. Not that he was a regular visitor. Only when his colleagues at University had insisted he accompany them for a mug of ale did he occasionally consent.

They sat at a small, square table near the window, where they had a clear view of the street. Leuven was quiet this day, with few people about. Two tankards of ale arrived, but Davion was so wound with anticipation, he hadn't even taken a sip. He glanced up a few moments later to see Mathieu staring at him with a quirk on his lips.

"Not thirsty?" he asked.

Davion blew out a breath. "Aye, I am. Anxious, though. Trying to rehearse in my head what I plan to say to Lily to convince her I am true." He drank from his cup, then leveled his gaze on Mathieu. "How was it with you and Eva, Mathieu? Did you have to work very hard to win the lady's heart?"

Mathieu sputtered on a mouthful of ale and came up laughing. "Very hard? Aye. I accomplished the impossible, I'd say, when I finally won Eva's heart."

"How so?"

"Eva came to Coudenburg with the fantasies of a young girl swimming in her head. She was convinced the only man who would win her heart was a gallant knight." Mathieu raked back the loose hair at his temples. "I had my work set for me, winning Lady Eva's heart. 'Twasn't easy, but as you can see, I overcame." Mathieu lifted his mug as if to toast.

Davion gazed off out the window. "My problem is a bit different, it seems. The lady has some scars the eye cannot see. She's been taken advantage of, and lied to. I don't believe she trusts any man at all. May never again."

"You are quite taken with Lady Lambert, are you not?" Mathieu asked, his voice filled with sympathy.

"Aye. She has captured my heart. Everything about her. Her maturity, her pride, her intelligence, her talent." The earl sighed. "She's older than me, true. But 'tis not a cause for concern. I was not in search of a woman to bear me sons." He paused, peering into his mug as though the answers lie there. "In truth, I never thought to marry at all. Until Lily."

"She's still young enough to bear you heirs," Mathieu said. "Isabella was in her thirties before her firstborn arrived."

*Nay, she is barren, and for that I am glad. No worry of unplanned offspring.*

Davion waved a hand in the air. "I am not cut out to be a father, ostler. I admire you, with your lovely family. But the role, 'tis not for me. All I want is companionship, affection, and love. From Lily. I sincerely hope I can convince her I am worth the risk."

An hour later, they returned to the beguinage on foot, having settled the horses in the local stable for the night. Mathieu accompanied the earl until they emerged from the alleyway, then he stopped.

"I believe you can handle this from here, Lord Price." He saluted him with two fingers to his brow. "Best of luck, I wish thee well. I will be at the room we rented in town if you have need of me."

Davion rapped the knocker and waited, shifting his weight from one foot to the other. He had no idea how she would react to his arrival. He had no idea what he would say, what he would do to persuade her—

"Lord Price. This is a surprise." Sister Fenna herself answered the door, and Davion could not tell if her shocked expression was a good or bad greeting. "You have come... quickly."

"Aye, Mathieu accompanied me. He knew the roads much better than I did. The trip was much less arduous." Somewhere in the back of Davion's mind, a question mark wavered. Odd, her reaction. The mistress acted as if she were expecting him. And how would she know how long the trip took him the last time?

Sister Fenna stepped back and invited him in. "We have just finished the prayer hour. I am not certain if Sister Lijsbet has gone back to work for a time, or if she is resting in her solar. She gets very tired of late."

Davion flinched at the title "Sister Lijsbet." Was he already too late? Had she already been indoctrinated into this sisterhood?

Then the rest of Fenna's words came through. "Tired. Is she ill?" Panic roiled in his gut.

But the mistress was shaking her head with a sly smile. "Nay, she is actually feeling quite well. She looks better too. Wait until you see her." Fenna took his arm and leaned in to murmur, "She's absolutely glowing."

Davion's heart turned to cold stone and dropped into his stomach. So, she was truly happy. The woman really was set on a life of chastity. Life here at Groot Beginjnhof was good for her.

He had made this trip for nothing.

Moments later, Davion waited for Lily in the small room where he had met with her before. Wringing his hands, he paced the length of the chamber with his mind whirring. Mayhap he should not even attempt to coax her away from the beguinage. If this was where she truly belonged, what right had he?

*A visit.* He thought fast and decided he would spin a story around the reason for him being here. Mathieu had to come to Leuven to look at more horses. He asked Davion to ride along. As long as they were here, the earl thought 'twould be rude if he didn't stop to visit her.

The door swung open and there she stood, looking more beautiful to the earl's eyes than ever before. She still wore the shapeless brown frock, yet her cheeks looked fuller, pinker. There was, as Sister Fenna had said, a glow about her.

"Good evening, Lord Price. I did not expect you so soon." Her blink was in slow motion, and she gazed at him from under her lashes.

" 'Tis what the mistress said. I did not realize I was expected at all," Davion said, feeling as though he had missed part of a very important conversation. "You had to know I would come after you, Lily." He paused, staring at the floor between them. "When you left Coudenburg, my lady, you did not leave alone."

Lily kept her chin down, an expression more demure than he had ever seen her. "I know that now. Now the question is, what shall be done for the matter?"

The earl searched her eyes and tilted his head. "Should be done for what matter? I am in love with you, Lily. I want you to become my wife. I have not yet asked the duke's permission, but I doubt he will have any issue with the arrangement."

He watched a tear track silently down Lily's cheek. Yet she continued to stand there, hands folded before her, head down. If she wanted him, would this news not make her happy? Were these tears of happiness or regret?

Wanting nothing more than to sweep her into his arms, Davion took a step toward her. With two fingers, he lifted her chin.

"Will you have me as your husband, Lady Lijsbet Lambert? You have to admit, Countess Lijsbet Price is much easier to pronounce." She did not return his smile. What was wrong here? "You have not committed to the beguinage yet, have you, my lady?"

"Nay. I was waiting for you to determine my fate."

Davion blinked, becoming more confused by the minute. "Why me? You told me your mind was made up. You said you had no choice but to dedicate your life to God. To save your soul."

Her golden eyes, shining with tears, searched his face. " 'Tis no longer me alone I need to worry about."

*'Tis a very strange way to say I love you.*

Davion shook his head, trying to clear his thoughts. Mayhap this was all a dream. Mayhap he'd never left Coudenburg at all. Mayhap he would awaken, any moment, in his own chamber.

He took a step back, lost for the moment.

*Wine. There is wine.*

He set about pouring wine out of the pitcher on the sideboard into two goblets. Handing one to her, he said, " 'Tis odd you have had such a drastic change of heart, Lily. Has something happened? Are you not happy here at Groot Beginjnhof?"

Lily's eyes rounded and her lips parted. "Did Isabella not receive the letter Fenna sent?"

He shrugged. "I know of no missive."

" 'Tis not why you come for me?" Disbelief tarnished her words.

"I am here because I have been dying inside slowly, every day, for almost three months since you left. I decided I must try, one more time. One more time to win your heart."

"So you do not know, then?" Lily squealed, and her cup clattered to the table. Wine spread in a bloody pool on the wooden top.

Davion was too intent on her words to notice. "You speak in riddles, Lily. I do not know... what?"

In the next breath she was on him, her arms winding around his neck. She pressed kisses everywhere—on his lips, his cheeks, his forehead, both eyes. Then she buried her face in his neck, and although garbled through a sob, he made out her words.

"You do not know, and still, you want me."

He smoothed a hand down her head, wanting more than anything to pull free the pins holding her long, dark braids and run his fingers through the silky strands. Taking one of her hands, he pressed it to his chest.

"You feel that? 'Tis a heart, beating. Beating for you. I once thought 'twas made of glass—all of me, glass. Now, the only part I fear for still is the heart beating below your fingers. 'Tis still made of glass, Lily. Will you hold it in your hands and cherish it? Or turn away and cause it to shatter into a million shards?"

She drew back and took his hand, placing it on her rounded belly.

*A belly she did not have before.*

"Do you feel that, Davion? Under that mound lies another beating heart. One you and I made together." She held his gaze, whispering, "Will you hold it in your hands and cherish it? Or turn away, leaving us to make our way alone in this world?"

Realization dawned slowly on Davion. *Another heart, beating. One you and I made together.* God's teeth, was Lily pregnant?

"How can this be? You told me you were barren."

"I believed I was. Apparently, the problem 'twas not with me, but with him." She caressed his cheek. "Your seed took root, and is growing fine."

# Chapter Thirty-Six

*Lijsbet*

" 'Tis wondrous." Sister Fenna hugged Lijsbet when she related the news.

"The earl had no knowledge of the babe," she said, "and he came anyway. He came for *me*. Because he loves *me*. Not because he feels obligated to make me an honest woman." She barked out a wry laugh. "Not that the feat is even possible."

Fenna huffed, then wiped a tear from her eye. "I could not be happier for you, Lijsbet. You are blessed indeed. I was not so lucky." She hugged her again. "How did he react when you told him? Is he elated?"

Lijsbet raised an eyebrow. "I believe 'twas quite a shock. He never expected this, as we both thought I was barren. He looked very tired, though. Riding astride is new, and hard on him. He held me tenderly for a very long time, but then asked if I would mind if he returned in the morn." Lijsbet scratched her scalp between her braids. "He looked a little pale, actually. I hope he is not ill."

*Davion*

"I don't know what to do, Mathieu. How to feel. What to say." Davion paced the small room he and Mathieu had rented for the night. He halted abruptly and shot the ostler a look. "Saints be praised, I feared I would faint away again. I do that much too easily. 'Tis not manly. I must learn how to overcome this weakness."

Mathieu lay sprawled on his pallet, one foot balanced atop his bent knee. A piece of straw he'd plucked at the stable stuck out of his mouth, and he chewed thoughtfully. He was grinning at the earl.

"Aye. Fainting 'tis no way to impress your woman. Nor to show your young son how manly you are."

Davion felt all the blood drain out of his head, and sparkles littered the edge of his vision. "Stop it, Mathieu. You only make this worse."

"Or daughter," the ostler added, smirking.

Davion dropped down on his pallet hard, wincing only momentarily. That fear was dissipating, and quickly. Now there was another fear looming over him. He brought his hand to his forehead. "Stop this, ostler. Please. I told you, I am not father material. After what I have been through, I will never let the chit out of my sight. The poor child will spend its life wrapped in soft blankets to keep it safe from harm."

Mathieu sat up, leaning his elbows on his knees. "I am truly happy for you, Lord Price. For both of you. Children are a worry, to be sure. But they are a joy beyond measure. More than makes up for the fretting they cause."

"She thought 'twas why I came for her," Davion muttered. "The mistress sent a letter. It must have arrived after we left."

"All the better, my lord. Now she knows you came for her, and her alone. With no tether of responsibility. Lady Lambert must be the happiest lady in the entire dukedom right now. Or I should say, Countess Price."

# Epilogue

*Davion*

"Why are men not allowed in the birthing chamber?"

Davion was not happy. Lily's pains had started suddenly, in the middle of the night, a fortnight before expected. He'd awoken to a pallet soaked with, he was told, the "water" the babe lived within.

Lived in. Were they like fish, needing water to survive? What causes them to suddenly, upon their birth, be able to breathe air? This water had been gone now for nearly twelve hours. Does the child live still?

The healer, Gillette, had asked to meet with the earl shortly after Lily's labor began. Leaning close, with a very serious expression, she had whispered the words, as though afraid saying them out loud would make them come true.

"Your lady, my lord, she is... nearing thirty winters. The older a woman becomes, the more difficult 'tis for them to survive a birthing." She winced and looked away. "She is small, as well. Very narrow through the hips—"

"Gillette!" Lady Isabella crossed the room with stomping strides. "Do not plant fear in the earl's mind for his lady, nor his babe's well-being. Lijsbet is very strong. If I could perform the feat past the age of thirty—three times!—Lijsbet will have no problem at all."

Yet as the hours ticked by, Davion's worry escalated out of control. He could hear voices behind that infernal door, the one keeping him out of the room where his woman and his child—truly, his entire world—lay. Occasionally the voices became frantic. More than once, a moan, even a scream reached his ears.

*What have I done to my beloved Lily? Will I be the cause of her death?*

A dark thought consumed him. *What if the child is made of glass?*

Before darkness fell, out of his mind with worry, the earl had nearly paced the floorboards thin. Isabella laid a hand on his shoulder.

"My lord, why don't you go to my chapel? Spend some quiet moments with your maker. Pray."

The earl made his way to a room just down the hall from the one where Lijsbet lay. He had never been very religious. Truth be told, aside from the day Father Michael married them—with Brother Johannes as witness—he had not been in a church or a chapel since... another day, long ago.

The day he wondered why color danced over the body of his sister, Diana, yet within her, life's dance was over.

He had never visited this chapel. 'Twas the duchess' private place of worship. But she had encouraged him to spend a few moments talking with his God. When he opened the door, he sucked in a sharp breath.

A huge, round intricately designed stained-glass window took up one entire wall of the tiny room. It held a kneeling block and podium, but the room was otherwise empty save for a giant crucifix upon the wall. The long rays of evening sun fell through the colorful glass panel, spraying color everywhere. The floor, the kneeler, the podium, even the cross on the wall danced with vibrant hues. *Alive.* Everything in this room appeared to be alive.

Even the effigy of a dead man, crucified.

Davion lowered himself to his knees and made the sign of the cross. It had been so long since he had made the motion, he wasn't sure he had done it correctly. God would simply have to understand.

"I have done nothing in my life to deserve your mercy, Lord. Still, I am asking. For most of my life I turned my face away from you, since you signified all I had lost. I will never understand why you took my sister from me, but 'tis not my place to question the Maker." His voice grew thick and his vision blurred. "I am asking now, Lord. Pray thee, deliver my Lily and our child to safety. I beg thee."

A soft knock at the door caused the earl to jump so, he nearly fell off the kneeler. 'Twas Isabella. She motioned for him to follow her. She was crying.

*Not a good omen.*

He was afraid to enter the room. Afraid of what he might see. The earl feared whatever 'twas would transform him, once more, into a pillar of glass.

What he saw, instead, turned him into a platter of jiggling jelly.

Lily sat propped up, surrounded by more pillows than he thought the castle held. Her hair, covering over her shoulders in a chestnut waterfall, framed a face far too pale. Gaunt, even.

Except for the smile. The earl had enjoyed many of his lady's smiles over the past year. He had never seen her smile quite like this.

"Come, Earl Price. Come meet your heir. The littlest Lord in the house."

The earl rushed to her side and sat on the bed. A blanket-wrapped bundle nestled against Lily's chest, tiny cooing noises coming from within.

"May I see him?"

"Of course. You may hold him."

Before Davion had a chance to refuse, Lily had laid the warm, squirming package into his arms. He lifted the edge of the blanket and peered down at his son.

Pouty lips worked as the baby slept. His skin was porcelain velvet. His eyes, tightly closed, were fringed with feathery lashes. And his hair! Wispy, dark curls formed a cap around a head so round, so perfect, the babe almost didn't seem real.

Mayhap 'twas not real. Mayhap he was made of... The earl touched the babe's cheek, tentatively. 'Twas soft. Warm, not cold. Flesh, not glass.

"What shall we name him?" he asked, his voice thick.

Lily took a deep breath. "Eva tells me," she began, "the ostler's wife tells me he allowed her to name their child."

"So be it," he answered at once. "You carried him within your body for many months. You have suffered immeasurable pain to bring him into this world. You gave him life. 'Tis your right to name the lad."

"I did it not alone, dear Davion. We gave him life, together." Lily cupped his cheek in her hand. "His name shall be Hunter. Earl Hunter Davion Price."

The earl tilted his head. "Hunter? A family name?"

"Nay. Think, Davion. The Roman goddess of the hunt. Her name was Diana."

He jolted at the mention of his sister's name, then closed his eyes against the pain. Swallowing, he agreed.

"Aye. My parents named her so. Our lands, in England, are my father's pride. We boast the finest hunting grounds on the continent."

Lijsbet went on. "There can be no more fitting name for our son, then, than Hunter."

Happiness filled him to overflowing. The earl did not realize his tears spilled over until one splattered upon the babe's nose, causing him to wrinkle his face and bellow. Quickly, he handed the child back to Lily.

"I think I broke him," he sputtered.

Lily smiled and shook her head. "Nay, Glass Man. You did not break the child. You baptized him with your love."

The earl rocked back as if struck. "Glass Man? Why do you call me this?" He could not help but feel a prick to his pride. "Do you still see me as weak? Delicate? I am cured of the delusion, Lily."

"You," Lily touched the end of his nose, "are one of the strongest men I know. Strong enough to face your fears and overcome them. Strong enough to chase after the woman you love, even when she rides away to join a beguinage. Strong enough to step into a role for which you were not prepared."

Embarrassed, the earl studied his fingers, then reached to intertwine them with hers. The question, though, still burned. "Then why call me *Glass Man*?"

"Because in my eyes, Earl Price, you *are* made of glass. You may be able to hide your true self and your generous heart from the world. You cannot hide them from me. I see right through you. As if you *are* made of glass."

Leaning forward, Lily kissed him, then locked her golden eyes on his. "I shall cherish and treasure you and our son, always. Like precious, priceless stained glass."

# Afterword

Truth can be, quite often, stranger than fiction. Many elements of this story, however, are based on historical fact. The author has made liberal use of creative license to develop the characters beyond what the scarce historical accounts hold. The following, though, are absolutely true:

- As bizarre as it may sound, glass delusion, the mental illness afflicting the hero, *did exist*. The condition is described in more detail in the beginning of this book.

- The artist Dieric Bouts did live and work in Leuven, and may have studied under Rogier van der Weyden. Details of the man's personality are strictly creations of the author's imagination.

- Contrary to popular belief, not all medieval scribes and illuminators were monks. There were a number of talented female artists, one being the sister of the renowned painter Jan van Eyck. Her work, however, along with the creations of many other female artisans, was attributed to male artists, or buried in obscurity under the ruse of "unknown."

- Illuminators did, in many cases, add their own unique artistic flair to their creations. Bizarre creatures now called "grotesques" appear in many prayer books—gargoyle-like creatures at odds with the holy words and images on the page. Their presence can be interpreted as spiritual warnings, or bouts of artistic playfulness—or opinion. 'Tis up to the viewer to decide.

- The artist Rogier van der Weyden did, in or about 1450, paint the portrait of Duchess Isabella at the duke's court in Brussels. Philip also had his own portrait rendered during this visit.

- Sketchy historical records exist concerning the artist or artists, Rogier de la Pasture and Rogier van der Weyden. There are few facts of which we can be certain. We do know that Rogier de la Pasture was born in Tournai, establishing himself as a painter there. In 1426 (Lijsbet would have been eight years old at the time), the artist married a Brussels shoemaker's daughter and settled in that city under the name of Rogier van der Weyden. They raised four children.

- Few works of art can be attributed undisputedly to van der Weyden, nor to de la Pasture. It was actually believed these were two different men for over 500 years. It was not until 1953 that art historian Edwin Panofsky established in his *Early Netherlandish Painting*: there was *only one painter with two names.*

We do know Rogier van der Weyden is credited with the duke and duchess' portraits. No disrespect is intended to the memory of the artist: the details of his personal life are purely fabrications of the author's imagination.

- Robert Campin, now called the Master of Flemalle, taught Rogier van der Weyden. His workshop in Tournai is where the young Lijsbet first apprenticed. This is one of his works: https://commons.wikimedia.org/wiki/
File:Robert_Campin_012.jpg

This, in the author's imagination, was the young Lijsbet.

*"A Woman" by Robert Campin*
*Original Oil Painting resides in London, National Gallery*

## About the Author

GEMMA ST. CLAIRE IS in love with medieval history. She's always been mysteriously drawn to Flanders, what is present-day France, Belgium, and the Netherlands, even though she has no family roots in the region. If she ever gets to go back in time, 15$^{th}$ C. Flanders is where she'd want to be.

In this life, Gemma resides in Florida with her very own HEA husband (she's an expert a happily ever after). Her other loves are reading, gardening, and spoiling her grandchildren. Gemma earned her MFA in creative writing from Lesley University in Cambridge, MA, and she now teaches writing at Florida's state college. She also writes award-winning supernatural suspense and women's fiction as "Claire Gem."

Gemma cherishes her readers and loves to hear from them! Sign up for her newsletter at www.gemmastclaire.com[1].

---

1.    http://www.gemmastclaire.com/

# About the Author

Gemma St. Claire is in love with history and loves stories set in historical times. She writes sweet historical romance that is swoon worthy, yet packed with authentic details from the period where the story is set--so detailed, you will feel as though her books are time machines, and not just romance novels. Gemma lives in Florida, USA with her very own HEA husband. She loves to hear from her readers, so please feel free to reach out!

Read more at https://www.gemmastclaire.com.

www.ingramcontent.com/pod-product-compliance
Lightning Source LLC
Chambersburg PA
CBHW030134180626
46812CB00002B/689